A SALT SPLASHED CRADLE

Chris Longmuir

B&J

Published by Barker & Jansen

Cover design by Cathy Helms www.avalongraphics.org

ISBN: 978-0-9574153-1-7

This book is dedicated to all those brave men and women
who make their living from the sea.

PART ONE

1830

1

1830

Belle's teeth clamped down on the thick wad of cloth each time the pain rippled through her. She could taste the mustiness of it, a dry, acrid staleness that caught in the back of her throat. Spitting it out when the pain receded, she wondered how many other women had bitten down on that same piece of cloth.

The sun, struggling to pierce the green glass of the small window, giving an unearthly greenish glow to everything within, suddenly burst through the opening door with an unwelcome warmth which merged with the sweat on Belle's body. She turned her head and, narrowing her eyes against the glare, looked at the woman stooping to enter the small room. Their eyes met momentarily, and Belle knew that Annie was only there because it was her duty to be present at the birth of her first grandchild.

Belle turned her face to the wall, but no matter how much she tried she could not find a comfortable position on the straw filled mattress. Her dark curls tangled damply round her neck and she did not feel pretty, but no longer had the strength to care.

The pain started again. At first it had only been twinges but now the pain deepened and came in waves, closer and closer together. Tears coursed down Belle's cheeks as she twisted her head from side to side, sobbing and moaning. 'Damn! Damn! Damn!' she muttered. 'Damn you, Jimmie Watt!' Clamping her teeth firmly on the rag, she thought angrily, if it hadn't been for you I wouldn't be lying here now, with only your sour faced mother and some damned witch of a midwife for company.

The pain ripped through her, a rending, splitting pain

which threatened to disembowel her. She tried to scream but gagged on the cloth in her mouth. Struggling to dislodge it she finally shrieked and shrieked, while strong hands held her thrashing legs and caught the baby who had struggled so fiercely to be born. Belle, aware of a feeling of release now lay panting and sweating in the enclosed space of the box bed, barely aware of her mother-in-law's silent disapproval.

'It's a fine wee lass,' the midwife busied herself with a pair of scissors, manoeuvring adroitly in the confined space, her rubber apron crackling and smelling fishy in the heat. Belle felt sure it was the same apron she used to gut fish, and she recalled with a shudder the black under the woman's finger nails.

'A first bairn is always the worst,' the midwife's tone was kindly, 'are you not going to look at her then?' She thrust the baby at Belle who instinctively held out her arms. The baby, still covered with birth fluids, puckered her lips and made a mewling sound.

Belle had never actually held a baby before and she had never seen one with such a head of black hair, so long that it reached her tiny shoulders. 'I'll call her Sarah,' she announced.

The tall, well-built woman sitting on the ingle stool at the fireside removed the clay pipe from her mouth and spat in the fire. As the droplets bubbled and sizzled on the coal, she turned slowly and deliberately to stare at Belle. 'Sarah? What kind of daft name's that?' she demanded. 'It's not a fisher name, that's for sure.'

Belle cringed. The feeling of worthlessness, instilled in her by her minister uncle, crept through her making her feel stupid. She looked at the baby and then at Annie. Meeting the contempt in Annie's eyes she stiffened with defiance and said, 'She's my baby and I'll call her what I like.' Belle's arms tightened round Sarah, the only real possession she'd ever had that was all her own.

'Ach, Annie Watt, what does it matter what the lassie calls her bairn.' The midwife thrust a parcel of bloody papers and straw on to the fire.

'We'll see about that when my Jimmie comes home,' Annie muttered. 'He'll have something to say.'

'He's not your Jimmie any more, he's mine,' Belle retorted, scowling at her mother-in-law.

'Hmph,' Annie snorted, turning back to the fire, 'that's what comes of marrying a townie. He should have stuck to his own kind,' and with that final remark she clamped her teeth round her clay pipe, a sure indication that as far as she was concerned the discussion was over.

Belle flopped back on the bed exhausted, unsure whether the wetness on her cheeks was from sweat or tears. Jimmie should have been here with her, but he'd gone out with his father's boat, chasing the herring shoals. The fish were more important to him than something so commonplace as the birth of a child.

Belle looked at the wrinkled, black haired baby, but her feeling of joy had been ruined by the attitude of her mother-in-law, and she suddenly felt too tired to care.

'Don't be such a misery Annie,' the midwife said. She laid a basin in front of the fire and reached for the heavy black kettle simmering on the hob. 'She's just a wee lass, and I mind fine when you had Jeannie, you made a bit of a fuss too as I recall.'

'I don't recall that at all,' Annie's voice was dangerously quiet, 'and I don't see how you can remember. That was all of seven years ago.'

Turning her face to the wall, and grasping the baby close to her body, Belle covered her head with the rough grey blanket. She could not bear listening to the two older women because she knew that neither accepted her as one of their own. To them she would always be an outsider. The incomer, who was not welcome in the fishing community of Craigden. She wished again that her Jimmie was with her to shield her from their contempt.

Belle never noticed the blanket being pulled back, nor was she aware of Sarah being lifted from her arms when she descended into a restless sleep.

2

The mud slithered through Jeannie's toes. She tentatively dug deeper and wriggled them in an effort to detect stones and the precious mussels that clung to their surface. Ma always managed to fill her creel with mussels, so Jeannie knew she wouldn't be pleased with today's harvest which barely covered the bottom of her murlin basket.

'There'll be no mussels today,' Jeannie had heard her ma say that morning. Jeannie knew she should not have come to the back-sands on her own. But she also knew that Da couldn't fish tomorrow if there were no mussels to bait the lines, and Ma had been so busy she had not even noticed Jeannie leave.

Solemnly she studied the bottom of the basket hoping the mussels would magically increase, but nothing magic ever happened to Jeannie, and the weight of her responsibilities pressed down on her young shoulders. The other bairns didn't seem to be worrying, but it did not matter so much to them, because they knew there would be mussels in plenty to bait their father's lines. There would be few mussels for her da's lines because her ma was at home waiting for the birthing of Belle's bairn.

Jeannie knew that if she could get further out on to the back-sands where the mussel beds were thick, she would have filled her basket. She looked with envy at the women already turning to wade back to the shore, and knew by the angle of their shoulders that they had managed to fill their creels.

The first of the women passed her singing out as she went, 'Back to the shore you, young uns. Tide's coming in.'

Jeannie dug her toes stubbornly into the mud. There must be some more mussels somewhere. But if there were, the women would not have had to wade so far out into the tidal waters of the basin. Her eyes stung but she refused to cry. Jeannie had not cried since she was five, and now she was a grown up seven it wouldn't do to let anyone see tears.

Davie appeared at her side with a splash, 'Come on, Jeannie, tide's coming in fast, and Ma would give me what for if I took you home drowned.'

'You might have helped me with the mussels,' Jeannie glared at her older brother.

'Menfolk don't gather mussels,' Davie stretched his twelve years old body as tall as it would go. He smirked down at his sister. 'That's women's work.'

The two children glared at each other, Jeannie, small and thin for her age, and Davie, already showing signs of becoming a tall man. Jeannie was the first to turn her eyes away. She did not like to fight with her brother and did not like it when Davie's eyes lost their usual laughter.

'Anyways, you could have helped, just this once,' she muttered, turning to wade to the shore. Staggering slightly she held her skirts higher to avoid the gathering waves.

Davie grasped her thin arm. 'Come on, before you sail down the river,' and making sure she did not stumble, led her to the shore.

The women, already walking towards the village, strode out with manly steps despite their wet skirts. Jeannie was not sure how they managed it because the sogginess of her skirt kept catching her legs and slowing her down.

'Cheer up,' Davie tramped along at her side. 'Ma'll be too busy helping Belle birth the bairn she won't notice there's hardly any mussels, and by the time she does I'll make sure your murlin's full.'

Jeannie did not bother to ask him how he would manage that, but she reckoned some of the other baskets might be slightly less full. It wasn't right some of the things Davie got up to, but she would not refuse the extra mussels, for Ma's displeasure was dreaded by all her children.

'D'you think the bairn's born yet, Davie?'

'How should I know? That's women's business.' Davie

lengthened his stride. 'Anyway I expect it is,' he added.

Jeannie giggled. Davie often imitated his older brothers in his efforts to appear a man. 'D'you like Belle?' she asked, and watched with interest as a blush stained Davie's neck and spread to his face.

'She's all right,' he mumbled.

'Ma doesn't like her.' Jeannie hesitated, not sure whether she should or shouldn't like Belle, just because Ma didn't like her.

'Ma wouldn't like anybody who'd taken her Jimmie away from her.'

'That's not true, she wanted Jimmie to marry Ellen Bruce,' Jeannie nodded in the direction of the group of younger women just in front of them.

'I heard her say so.'

'She only wanted that so Jimmie could get a share in the Bruce boat, anyways Belle's a lot prettier than Ellen.'

'See, I knew you liked Belle,' Jeannie skipped out of the way of the hand that Davie aimed at her head. Hoisting her damp skirt up to her knees, she ran to the top of the grassy bank where she could see straight down the river and out to sea.

The mud flats were now completely under water as the tide raced in. Jeannie shivered to think that only minutes before she had been gathering mussels where now there was only water.

The village lay before her, small and constrained by the cliff that rose behind it, the sun dappling the faces of the cottages that sat in its lap. She tried to pick out her ma's house, but they all looked the same at this distance.

Shading her eyes with her hand, for the sun was high in the sky, she looked beyond the small huddle of whitewashed cottages to the river mouth.

'The boats should be coming back now the tide's on the turn,' Jeannie lowered her hand and turned to look at her brother. 'Jimmie'll be anxious to know if he's a da yet.'

'They'll not come back until they're full of fish, no bairn's worth an empty boat. Besides Ma would give them what for if they came back without a catch.'

'You're right, Davie, I suppose I just wished they'd come home.'

Jeannie started to walk down the path towards the cottages, 'At least we can see if Belle's had her bairn yet.'

3

Belle sank deeper into the sleep of exhaustion. The voices muttering in the background turned into the gentle shush of waves rolling up the beach.

Her feet sank into the sand and it trickled round them and between her toes. Jimmie's hand, clasping hers, was warm and firm.

They started to run, whooping and laughing like children. Then he stopped, swung her off her feet and twirled her around before pulling her close to him, so close she could feel the beat of his heart against her breast. She swayed into him, feeling his love and need for her.

It was the most wonderful thing in the world, having someone want you and love you. It was something she had never experienced before.

'Oh, Belle,' he said, looking into her eyes. 'You are the best thing that ever happened to me. Nothing must ever come between us.'

'Nothing will,' she replied. 'I won't let it.'

She savoured the moment, warmed by his love. The love that was hers alone. A love she would never willingly share with anyone.

The shriek of a gull broke into their reverie, accompanied by the clatter of tongues. Belle blinked. She was back in the box bed, lying on hard straw.

The Bonnie Annie approached the river mouth well in front of the other fishing boats, and its skipper, James Watt, sighed with contentment. He was a tall man with weather-beaten features and a grizzled grey beard that he kneaded with his fingers in an attempt to loosen the salt left behind by many dousings with sea spray. He looked with pride at his eldest son, Jimmie, who at nineteen, was turning into a damned good seaman, able to handle the boat almost as well as he could himself.

'Pull that sail round, Jimmie, we're just about at the river mouth and we don't want to come in too close to the rocks.' James Watt looked with satisfaction at their silvery catch. Never had he seen the herring so plentiful, they could almost have scooped them out of the sea with a bucket this time, and they hadn't even lost one net.

'Let me swing the sail, Da?' Angus pleaded.

'No lad, you must wait till you've more experience, and we can't afford to sail too near the rocks. We'd lose everything if we lost the boat.' James looked with pleasure at his second youngest son, only fifteen, still smooth-chinned and desperate to have all the knowledge and experience of older sailors so he could get his own vessel. Not like Ian who slouched in the bottom of the boat and couldn't care less. Still, Ian was only seventeen and might grow out of his fighting and carousing ways.

The small boat swung round in the wind and scudded round the rocky promontory as Jimmie expertly handled the sails. Jimmie was the eldest of James's four sons and his favourite. Of course there was wee Jeannie, who did not count because she was a girl. James would never have admitted it, but he had a soft spot for Jeannie, pity she hadn't been a boy. James smiled with satisfaction, 'Good lad, Jimmie.' That was as much praise as James could bring himself to give.

Salt spray splashed over the side of the boat as the tide caught her, and James laughingly rubbed it out of his beard. 'You'll make a sailor yet,' he shouted to Jimmie, 'that is if you can manage to keep us afloat at the speed you're going. But no doubt, you'll be wanting to see if that wee lass has made you a father yet.'

Angus who had been having trouble maintaining his balance dropped down to join Ian on the bottom of the boat, 'Jimmie's in a hurry, but I don't blame him. I'd be in a hurry too if I had somebody like Belle waiting for me.'

Ian snorted. 'Jimmie's had more lassies than you've had herrings for your tea,' he sneered. 'I don't see Belle's that much different. She's just the one who caught him. She'll have a hard job keeping him though.'

'Away you go. I've seen the way he looks at her. He never looked at any other lassie like that before.'

'That may be so but Belle's not a fisher lass and doesn't know the life. She'll never stand it and before you know it she'll have found somebody else.'

'But she can't, she's Jimmie's wife,' Angus stuttered.

'A flash town tart, more like,' Ian retorted.

James frowned down at his two sons. 'That's enough of that,' he snapped. 'Jimmie and Belle are nothing to do with you two. So hold your tongues.' Turning he stared toward the little cluster of houses cradled in the shadow of the cliff. 'Pull your sail round now, Jimmie,' he ordered curtly, his earlier good humour gone as he worried about what he had overheard Ian saying, for it appeared to him that there was some truth in it.

Jeannie had almost reached the cottages when she caught sight of the boat, sails billowing in the wind, racing up the river with the incoming tide. She rose up on her toes and shaded her eyes. 'Look, Davie! Look! The boats are coming back. Can you see which one's in front? Is it Da's boat?'

Davie frowned, 'They should be lowering their sails by now, they're too far up the river.'

'Is it Da's boat?' Jeannie persisted. 'Is it?'

'Yes, yes, it's Da's boat . . . '

Jeannie didn't wait to hear any more, she was already running towards the cottage, her murlin grasped firmly in both arms to prevent the bouncing mussels from spilling out.

'Ma. Ma,' she gasped as she burst through the door, 'the boats are coming back.' The sun cut through the green tinged gloom in the room, but even so, Jeannie had to blink several times before her eyes adjusted. She could distinguish her ma sitting on the ingle neuk stool, smoking her clay pipe and the village midwife kneeling to bath a tiny baby.

'Leave the mussels outside the door, Jeannie,' her ma's voice was harsher than usual, 'you know better than bring them in the house.'

Jeannie turned, almost colliding with Davie. 'Here, you take them, Davie. I want to see the bairn,' and she thrust the murlin into her brother's unwilling arms. 'Is it a boy?' she asked excitedly, ignoring Davie's muttered objections as he turned to place the basket outside.

'No Jeannie, it's not a boy. It's the bonniest wee lass I ever saw.' The midwife beckoned to her. 'Come and see.'

'You don't have time to be admiring bairns,' Annie snapped. 'If the boats are coming up river there'll be work to do.' Tapping her pipe out on the hearth stone she rose and strode out to the sunlight.

'Ach, Ma. Just a wee look, that's all I want.'

'There'll be plenty of time for that later. Come on, Jeannie.'

'Quick Jeannie, have a wee peep. Your ma won't know the difference if you run fast and catch up with her.' The midwife laid the baby on her knee. Jeannie tiptoed over to her, afraid the baby would start crying. She looked in amazement at Sarah and gently touched her black hair, 'I never knew babies had so much hair,' she said. Sarah turned her head towards Jeannie's stroking finger and the sound of her voice, and it was as if an instant bond had sprung up between the seven year old and the new baby.

'Come on, Jeannie,' Ma's voice broke the spell, and Jeannie turned to run out of the cottage knowing that Sarah was special.

4

When she woke, Belle ached all over. The straw dug in to her back and her heels rested in hollowed out grooves in the mattress. Never had she been so uncomfortable or so sore in all her life. If she regretted anything about her marriage to Jimmie Watt, it was not being able to sleep on a feather mattress. Yet, when she thought about the nights she had spent in the kirk manse, her uncle's house, she would gladly sleep on straw for the rest of her life than return there.

She struggled to a sitting position expecting to see Annie's disapproving face. Belle had hoped that Jimmie's mother would have welcomed her with open arms, taken the place of the mother Belle had never known, been the type of mother she had imagined in her dreams, the mother she thought about and cried for after her uncle's visits to her room. But Jimmie's mother had barely looked at her when he brought her to his home. Belle had covered her ears when they argued about her, thinking of her own mother who, if she'd ever met her, would have enfolded her in her arms and wept tears of joy.

The stool at the ingle neuk was empty. Annie's pipe lay on the hearth where she had left it minutes before, and the midwife was wrapping the baby in a sheet so that only the top of her head showed.

There was a tingling in the tips of Belle's breasts as she looked at Sarah and a strange feeling of warmth and anticipation. She wanted to hold her baby. The baby she had not wanted. She sensed Annie did not like her, because she thought Belle had trapped her son with the baby who had swollen her body and made her look ugly. Her baby.

'Can I have my baby please?' She had meant to be forceful and demanding, but her voice was weak and pleading.

'Ah, you're wakened then,' the midwife fastened the sheet with a pin, held Sarah up to her shoulder and patted her gently. 'It's a bonnie lass you have, and born with the incoming tide. Lucky that is. If it'd been a boy it would've meant he'd make a fine fisherman. Not sure what it means for a lass.' She approached the bed and looked down at Belle. 'You see that you look after her right. Bairns are precious,' and with that comment she laid Sarah in Belle's arms and turned to leave. The sun streaked across the room when she opened the door. Pausing for a moment she looked back at Belle, 'I almost forgot to tell you. The boats are back. Your Jimmie should be home soon.'

Belle's eyes glowed with pleasure. Her arms tightened on Sarah's small body and she hugged the baby to her breast. Jimmie home? She could not wait to see him and show him the baby. Closing her eyes she pictured his face, all kind and concerned and looking at her in that loving way he had. The look that made her feel special and sent butterflies fluttering around her stomach. But now there would also be admiration in his gaze as she presented him with his daughter. Belle frowned momentarily as an unwanted thought forced its way into her mind. What if he was disappointed it wasn't a boy? All men wanted sons after all. No, she would not think it. He would be pleased she'd had a child, it wouldn't matter that it was not a boy.

Sarah nuzzled at Belle's breast twisting and rubbing her mouth against the coarse linen of her nightgown. Belle responded to the strange tingling feeling and started to feed the baby. She pulled the gown off her shoulder and bared one creamy breast, hoping that Jimmie would hurry up.

The room was silent, even the fire seemed to be holding its breath, and Belle started to get impatient. Where was Jimmie? What was taking him so long? Surely he wasn't helping to unload the catch, not when she was here waiting for him. Surely she was more important than fish. A single tear trickled down her cheek. She quietly detached Sarah from her breast and pulled the gown back up on to her shoulder. Well, if he couldn't come and see her she was not going to bother looking pretty for him. Lying back in the bed she stared unseeingly at the dying fire while Sarah lay, forgotten, on top of the rough blanket just out of reach of her mother's arms.

Belle was uncertain how long she lay there or whether she slept, or how long Jimmie had been in the room. She had not heard him enter, but he was there, and so was Annie.

'You're back from the fish then,' she rasped, her tongue clinging thickly to the top of her mouth. 'It's not before time.'

Annie snorted, 'That's a fine welcome to give a man just back from the sea.'

'Ach, Ma. It doesn't matter.' Jimmie turned from his mother to smile at Belle. 'I know she's glad to see me. Aren't you Belle?' Crossing to the bed he knelt and enclosed Belle's hand in his own.

The strength of his fingers and the warmth of his body when he bent towards her wrapped around Belle and she no longer cared what Annie thought of her. Jimmie loved her. Nothing Annie could say or do would alter that.

'Oh Jimmie . . . ' a lump rose in her throat, and she was on the verge of tears.

Suddenly she remembered Sarah and, turning, lifted the baby with gentle hands. How proud he would be, she thought. How clever he would think she was. 'I've named her Sarah,' she told him, lowering her gaze towards the baby and stroking the tiny head with a finger.

'She can't call the bairn Sarah. I've told her that already.'

Belle's head jerked up. She had forgotten that Annie was there and the harshness in the woman's voice made her shrivel inside.

'It's not a fisher name,' Annie added, returning Belle's stare.

'If Belle wants to call her Sarah, then Sarah it'll be.'

Belle smiled. It had been unnecessary to worry that he would side with his mother. He loved her, Belle, after all. She turned to look at Jimmie, love shining out of her eyes, but Jimmie was looking in wonderment at his new baby daughter. He fingered her hair, stroked her soft cheek and examined her tiny fingers.

Belle watched, jealously. This was not the way it was supposed to be. He was supposed to make a fuss of her, Belle, telling her how wonderful she was and stroking her cheek, and smoothing her hair – not the baby's, not Sarah's. Sarah was there to give Belle love. Not take it away from her.

'Be careful,' she snapped, holding the baby close, 'she's delicate, you mustn't touch her, you might bruise her.'

Torn by conflicting emotions she turned her back on Jimmie and started to feed Sarah, but there were tears in her eyes as all her feelings of worthlessness resurfaced How could this be, she thought. How could a child rob her of the love of her man.

5

The women waited thigh deep in water, as the fishing fleet sailed towards the village with the gulls screaming and circling round the boats. They were strong women, as tall and weather-beaten as the men who fished the seas, and as each boat arrived they grasped the prow pulling it ashore while the men attended to the task of securing the sails and oars.

James had been first back, and now he looked up from his task of unloading the fish from the boat that rested on the shingle where Annie had pulled and guided it. It would not be long before the cadgers arrived to haggle over the price of the fish. Their carts were probably already rumbling across the bridge from the town on the north shore of the river. Maybe he should not have sent Annie back to the house, for he was never able to get as good a price as she could. Still, family had to come first and Jimmie's Belle was family now, as he had reminded Annie.

'You'll not be going to the town to sell fish the day,' he'd said, his voice brooking no argument.

Annie had thrown down her creel in annoyance, but she had not argued.

'Get Jeannie to put some of the fish in the creel for our own use, and bring it with you when you come . . . and mind and get a good price for the rest from the cadgers. They'd rob you as soon as look at you.' With that parting remark Annie turned her back on James, and started to walk towards the stone house that had been home to them for the past twenty years.

James sighed as he resumed his task of unloading the fish. She was a good lass Annie. He was sure that once she'd got over her disappointment about Jimmie's sudden marriage she would take to Belle, even if it was only for the sake of the bairn.

Most of the boats had beached by now, and the chatter of the women and girls mingled with the deeper voices of the men as they helped their fathers and husbands to unload them. Some of the women were already strapping on their creels ready to leave for the market in Invercraig, where they could get a better price for their fish than the cadgers gave them.

James looked around for his sons, for if he did not finish unloading soon he would not get the best price from the cadgers.

'Ian!' he shouted, catching a glimpse of his second eldest son. 'Will you leave the lassies alone and get the hell back here to unload the boat!'

'That's women's work,' scowled Ian, 'I shouldn't need to unload. I'm a fisherman, not a labourer.'

'You'll unload if I say you unload, my lad. And you're not a proper fisherman yet, not till you have your own share in a boat. So you'll do what I tell you.'

'I don't see Jimmie here unloading,' Ian sneered. 'Away to see his precious Belle, is he?'

'Never you mind about Jimmie. He has an excuse the day. He'll be needing to see his bairn.'

'I wonder if it would have been the same if it was my bairn that had been born.' Ian's tone was bitter.

'Well it's not your bairn. So just get on with the work.'

James watched Ian bend over the edge of the boat. He was so like Jimmie in looks they could almost be twins, although there was two years between them. But Ian did not have Jimmie's good nature. It was as if there was something eating him away inside. Always since they were children, Ian had wanted what Jimmie had.

The first of the cadgers' carts arrived at the river's edge pulling up parallel to James's boat.

Angus leaped from the cart to the ground clearing the edge of the bank. 'I went to meet Wullie,' he shouted to his father. 'Told him he had to buy his fish from us.'

'You'd no right, lad,' James scolded, 'you should have been here helping.'

Angus laughed, 'You'll not say that if you get a better price because of me.'

James smiled back. He found it impossible to stay angry with Angus, who at fifteen was smaller and stockier than his two elder brothers. This last fishing trip had been Angus's first time out with the boat. And he'd done well. He'd been keen and eager to learn, and always good natured even when things had been tough.

'Come on then, lad. Let's get these fish away so we can go home and see the new bairn.'

Annie sat on the stool by the fire her fingers seeking the comfort of the clay pipe. But it was cold like her heart. She had come home at James's bidding, seeking to help her daughter-in-law, but it had all gone wrong. Belle's treatment of Jimmie had sent a flare of resentment coursing through her.

Now she sat rubbing the clay bowl of her pipe as if that could erase all that had happened over the past few weeks. It wasn't that Annie had not noticed that Jimmie spent a lot of his spare time in Invercraig, the big town across the water, but she had never given it a second's thought. The young lads of the village often went there to visit the inns and public houses, which were livelier than the ones where their fathers congregated. But Annie had not expected Belle. And when Jimmie brought her home three weeks ago, Annie had been shocked. She still hadn't worked out if it had been because Belle was in an advanced state of pregnancy, or whether it had been because she was a townser. Craigden men always married their own kind.

Annie's hands grew damp at the thought, just as they had done when she first saw Belle in her fancy silks. She rubbed her palms on her own homespun skirt, feeling the comfortable roughness of the cloth. But that could not quite erase the urge to know what silk against her skin would feel like.

She fumbled for the pipe lying in her lap. Smoking helped to calm her down and she had needed to smoke a lot lately. Scraping the remnants of the old tobacco ash from the bowl she tapped it on the hearthstone to get rid of the residue. The blow was harder than she meant it to be and now the bowl rocked on the hearth while her hand gripped the severed stem. She watched the gently spinning bowl in dismay, and resolved that Belle would not come between her and her family. Even if that meant she had to accept Belle as one of her own.

Annie looked again at the kneeling figure of her eldest son as he leaned towards Belle and the baby, and at Belle feeding Sarah, with her back turned towards him.

'Come and sit by me and give the lass peace to feed the bairn.' Annie forced herself to smile at Jimmie. He was her favourite son, despite her disapproval of Belle.

Jimmie came and squatted on the floor at her side, 'Is she not a bonnie bairn, Ma?' He smiled up at her.

Annie rested her hand on his head just as she had done when he was a child. 'Aye lad, she's a braw bairn.' Her eyes turned towards the alcove bed where Belle was feeding Sarah, and she frowned. She could almost swear that Belle disliked the baby. Her hand tightened on Jimmie's head. No, that couldn't be. All mothers loved their babies.

James heaved the last basket of fish onto the cadger's cart. He pulled a rope taut over the rear end and tested the knots securing it to each of the side spars. He did not want to risk the fish bouncing off before it got to the market. Wullie jumped on the front of the cart and grasping the reins shook them. The horse strained and pulled while Wullie clicked his tongue in encouragement.

James walked beside the cart as it rocked towards the level ground of the narrow path. 'You're sure you'll get a good price for me then, Wullie?'

'Aye, that I will. I'm heading for the Dundee market.

There's a better price for the fish at Dundee than there is at Invercraig, or Forfar,' and with a final click of the tongue and shake of the reins, the cadger's cart rumbled on its way.

Jeannie looked up from the creel she was pulling over the shingle. 'Is Dundee a big place, Da?'

'Yes, Jeannie lass, it's a big place.'

'Bigger than Invercraig?'

'I'm told it is.'

'Why would they want our fish, Da? Do they not have fishing boats there?'

'No, Jeannie lass, they've only got whaling ships.'

'There's whaling ships at Invercraig.'

'Yes, but there's a lot more whalers at Dundee. They tell me there are as many whalers as there are at Peterhead.'

James had seen the whalers at Peterhead and Invercraig, although he had never been to Dundee. He'd had one trip on a Peterhead whaler when he'd been Ian's age but had been glad to get back to the fishing boats. Still that one journey had been profitable and had given him the stake to buy his share in the *Bonnie Annie*.

He looked round for a bucket and filling it with river water, he quickly rinsed the boat out. He made sure that not all of the fish scales were washed away, for it was a well-known fact that the fish would not come to a clean boat.

6

Belle wanted everyone to like her but, having sensed her mother-in-law's dislike from the first moment she had set foot in the cottage, she was certain that Annie only tolerated her to please her son.

The men of the house though, that was different, and Belle responded to them with coy glances and flirtatious looks.

She had seen the admiration in their eyes, even though her body had been distorted and clumsy, and Belle desperately needed the family to like and admire her. She was sure they would admire her more than ever now that she had lost her burden and regained her figure. Besides, Jimmie would see they thought she was attractive, and that would make him love and desire her even more than he already did.

Sarah stopped sucking, although her tiny mouth still grasped Belle's nipple. Her long lashes gave a final flutter and closed. Belle held her for a moment, desperately wanting to love this baby. Sarah stirred and clamped her mouth even more firmly on her mother's nipple. Belle reacted instinctively, pulling the baby roughly away from her. She quickly regretted her hasty action as a sharp pain shot through her breast. She shuddered. There was something unnatural about this animal process of feeding babies.

Turning over in the bed, Belle looked towards the fireplace where Jimmie sat at Annie's feet. He had no right to be there. He should be beside her. He was hers now. Not Annie's.

Unexpectedly, tears gathered in her eyes and trickled down her cheeks. Her body ached with pains, inside and out, until she did not know what to do with herself to lessen the hurt. She wanted Jimmie. She wanted him all to herself, not shared with his mother or his family. But she had no option, nowhere else to go, except for James and Annie's house.

'What's the matter, love?' Jimmie had risen and come to her side. His large hand caressed her cheek, wiping the tears away.

Belle gazed up at him, enjoying the roughness of his hand on her skin.

'Oh, Jimmie,' she wailed, 'it was horrible and it hurt so much. I just wanted you, and you weren't here.'

'I'm here now, love.' He wrapped strong arms around her and Belle put her head on his chest and sobbed.

'But you weren't here when I needed you. I so wanted to give you a son, and all I've given you is a girl.' Belle's voice was muffled and despairing.

'She's a lovely daughter, Belle. I'm fair pleased and there's plenty of time for sons.'

Belle subsided into fresh sobs at the thought of having to go through all that again to give Jimmie a son. What if the next one was a girl too, another lovely daughter? She did not want lovely daughters, and she certainly did not want Jimmie to love them more than he loved her.

Jimmie held Belle until her crying stopped and, after giving her one final hug, he laid her down onto the mattress. Leaning over her he rescued Sarah from the back of the bed where she slept peacefully, and gently placed her in Belle's arms.

'There now,' he said, as he pulled the rough blanket up and tucked it round his wife and daughter, 'you have a wee sleep. I'll help Ma build up the fire so you can have some soup after you're rested. We've brought some braw fish back with us and I'll pick out the best one for you. Once you've slept and eaten you'll feel better.'

When Belle woke it was evening and Annie had just lit the crusie lamp, although it wasn't yet dark outside. The soup pot bubbled on the fire filling the cottage with a warm, tantalising smell. Laughter and voices resounded in the room as James and his sons related the story of their recent fishing trip to Annie and the younger children.

'You should have got Cadger Wullie to pay you before he left with the fish,' Annie berated James, although there was no anger in her voice.

'Naw, Annie lass, Wullie said he'd get a better price for us if we waited while he took it to Dundee to sell in the market there.' James's voice, a gentle rumble, seemed to fill the small room.

'We'll not get paid till Monday now, for tomorrow's the Sabbath. Had you forgotten?'

'Naw, Annie lass, I hadn't forgotten, but I trust Wullie and so should you.'

Annie sighed, but turned to stir the soup and turn the oatcakes on the griddle.

'Soup's ready to lift. Jimmie will you see if Belle's awake? And you lot,' she glared at her elder sons, 'mind your manners while Belle's with us.'

Belle closed her eyes, feeling more than ever like an intruder, and waited for the touch of Jimmie's hand if only to remind her that he loved her.

'Are you rested, love?'

Jimmie's hand, despite its size, was light on her shoulder. Belle covered his hand with hers and looked up at him feeling the familiar churning sensation at the pit of her stomach.

He gave her shoulder a squeeze, 'I'll get you some soup. We'll soon have you strong and well.'

'Strong enough to carry you to the boat?' Ian mocked. 'There's nothing of the lass. She couldn't even lift one of your seaboots.'

'Hold your tongue, laddie,' Annie's voice was sharp. 'This is not the time to be planning who's to do what. Anyway if she can't manage I'll do it as I've always done. We'll find some other job for Belle to do.'

Belle shrank back in the bed. She had seen the fisherwomen carrying their men out to the boats so they would not get their feet wet before they sailed. Surely Jimmie would not expect her to do that? And yet, she did not want Annie to do it either. Jimmie was her man.

'Never you mind them, Belle. Ma can carry me to the boat, you're too wee,' and so saying Jimmie dipped the spoon in the soup and fed her.

Annie dished up the fish into the well-scraped soup bowls. She was glad they were eating well tonight. It made up for all the times when the catch was poor and they had to tighten their belts.

Reaching for Belle's bowl, she snorted, when she saw it still had some soup in it. 'D'you want to finish this, Davie lad?' Davie, her youngest son, was a tall, lean twelve year old who always seemed to be hungry, and she was sure he would not refuse her offer.

'Shove it over here, Ma. I'll soon make short work of that.' Davie had his spoon ready.

'Hurry it up, Ma,' Ian growled, 'it'll soon be too late for Angus and me to go over the water to Invercraig.'

'Have we not had enough of Invercraig to last us a lifetime,' Annie retorted, with a glance at Belle and Sarah, lying in her bed. The bed Annie and James had shared since their wedding day. The bed where Jimmie had been born, then Ian, followed by Angus, Davie, and Jeannie. And now the bed where Sarah had been born.

'Can I come to Invercraig with you?' Davie had swallowed the extra soup. He was now finishing his herring which Annie had served up with skirlie, the oatmeal and onion mixture that was the staple diet of most of the villagers.

'You're too young, Davie lad, they wouldn't let you into the places we'll be going to.' Angus tousled Davie's hair. 'You'll have to grow a bit yet, lad.'

'You shouldn't be going to them either, I'm thinking,' Annie's voice was sharp. She knew she would never keep Ian away from the town and the drinking dens, but it vexed her that he took Angus with him. Angus was a good lad and Ian would only get him into trouble.

The house seemed quieter after Ian and Angus had left.

Annie and Jeannie gathered up the plates while James toasted his toes in front of the fire and Davie whittled away at a piece of wood with a knife.

Annie paused, her hands full of bowls and spoons, 'What are you making this time, Davie lad?'

'A wee doll for the new bairn, just a welcome,' Davie explained, holding out the half carved shape for her inspection.

Annie laid the plates and spoons on the table, and taking the piece of wood caressed it with her fingers. It brought back memories of other times and other bairns, and she felt ashamed. She had not welcomed this bairn and she should have. This bairn was Jimmie's. Flesh of her flesh, blood of her blood. And blood was important. Blood meant family, loyalty, ties, love and affection. The bairn couldn't help it that she was also of Belle's flesh and blood.

Annie turned towards the box bed in the alcove at the rear of the room. She forced herself to smile at Belle and leaning over she caressed the head of the sleeping baby.

'Sarah,' She tested out the name. It would be the first time there had been a Sarah Watt, and it sounded right.

Annie smiled a happy smile. She looked directly into Belle's eyes for the first time and said, 'I'll look out the cradle for Sarah. James's grandpa carved it and every bairn that's slept in it has had the sea in their blood.'

7

The walls of the house were closing in on her and the only sun Belle had experienced over the past six weeks had been that which sneaked in when the door opened. The boats had been to sea at least four times since Sarah's birth and Belle had not been allowed to step outside the door of the cottage. Her nerves were now at screaming pitch, and she was convinced she'd been condemned to a life of green-tinged gloom.

'You can't go out until you're ready to be kirked,' Annie told her, 'for it's not a changeling you'll be wanting.'

'I don't believe in your silly superstitions,' Belle wanted to retort, but held her tongue. There were so many customs and beliefs held by the fisher folk that seemed strange to her, and she was finding it more difficult than ever to fit in.

'You'll wait to be kirked,' Annie's tone had been final.

Belle bit her lip but knew better than to argue with her mother-in-law. Anyway, how could she tell Annie why she did not want to be kirked, or why she did not want Sarah christened. She had too many bad memories of churches and ministers. Of the things her uncle had done to her, and the penances he had made her perform afterwards for making him succumb to the temptations of the flesh.

Eventually Belle's longing for fresh air and sunshine became too much for her and she agreed to the kirking in order to get out of the house. Now, as she struggled to fasten her best dress, she pushed the thought of the christening to the back of her mind.

The heat of the sun struck Belle like a physical blow when she left the house. Narrowing her eyes against the impact she was not sure if she was crying for joy, or whether the glaring brightness was forcing the water from her eyes.

The villagers were already making their way to the church, up the path that led to the top of the cliff, and Belle could sense their curiosity. It shimmered in the air like the heat waves rising off the cliff, seen but unseen.

The shawl clad figures walked in little huddles that were in some strange way attached to each other, but separate from her. She was not one of them. Their eyes never seemed to meet hers, while at the same time they exuded a barely concealed air of contempt for her, bringing out all the feelings of worthlessness and vulnerability that she was trying so hard to suppress. It was just as well she'd put on her finest dress and daintiest slippers, because this was the only way she could show them she was better than they were in their dull, coarse skirts and blouses, and their heavy, ungainly shoes.

'Belle,' Annie's voice sounded sharp, 'the bairn will slip and fall out of that shawl before you're halfway up the cliff path. Come back in and I'll give you one of mine.'

'Sarah's fine, she'll come to no harm.' Belle forced the words out. She fingered the silk and wool shawl she had wound round Sarah, before strapping her to her breast and thought of the length of time it had taken to arrange the pattern and the fringes to their best effect. She did not want one of Annie's shawls which were horrid homespun things. They were scratchy and uncomfortable and would hide what she was wearing. The clothes she was relying on to boost her confidence.

'I'll brook no argument. I'll not have you kill the child, for that path's steep and your shawl's too silky to hold her. Take it off.'

'Can I wear Belle's shawl?' Jeannie had followed her mother out of the door.

'No you may not, and neither will Belle.'

Belle unwrapped Sarah and removed the silky shawl, reluctantly winding the one Annie handed her round her shoulders and round Sarah.

'That's better,' Annie said, pinning it into place.

The shawl smelled of fish combined with soot from the

fire, and the roughness of it scratched her neck. Belle felt like crying and her resentment of Annie increased. The baby did not seem to mind though, as she snuggled into her mother's breast, sucking her lips and making little mewing noises.

Every stone bit into Belle's feet as she struggled up the dirt path leading to the top of the cliff. Jimmie should have waited for her and helped her to climb the path. Instead of that he had left early with the men, and they were no doubt laughing and joking together with never a thought for her, nor any consideration of how alone she felt.

She looked with envy at the other women as they strode effortlessly upwards to the small church that stood at the edge of the cliff. Annie was just in front of her but the distance was growing between them. Despair clutched at Belle and tears pricked the back of her eyelids. She knew that Annie only tolerated her and would have preferred her precious Jimmie to marry any one of those ungainly women.

'Are your feet hurting, Belle?' Jeannie had already been to the top of the cliff but had run down again to walk beside her.

Belle smiled at the child. She was the only one in the family who seemed to like her and Belle enjoyed the admiration that Jeannie did not bother to hide.

'My feet are just fine, Jeannie,' Belle lied, 'how much further is it?'

'It's not far now. You'll see the church spire in just a wee minute and then it's just a wee bit of a puff and a blow before you're there.' Jeannie grinned at her and raced off again.

Annie was already at the top of the cliff path and Belle could see her talking and laughing with one of the fisher girls. The one who always watched Jimmie when she thought he wasn't looking. Not that it would do her any good, Belle thought, Jimmie was well and truly hers, he had proved that when he married her. He could easily have left her when he knew she was pregnant. She would not have been the first unmarried girl to have given birth in secret, what people called a private birth. She shuddered at the thought. Most girls who had private births either disposed of the baby by overlaying and smothering it, dumping it at the workhouse door, or becoming working girls. That was one of the benefits of living over the water at Invercraig. There were plenty of foreign sailors to keep a working girl busy.

Suddenly her feet did not seem to be so sore, her heart lightened and she looked down at Sarah with the beginnings of affection. She had not had to give Sarah up and she would never need to be a working girl. Jimmie had ensured that when he married her, and for that she would always be grateful.

Jeannie threw herself onto the grassy bank, plucked a blade of grass, stretched it between her fingers, put it to her lips and tried to make the screeching noise that Davie could do every time. But it never seemed to work for her.

She lay back and looked at the sky. She liked to watch the clouds. They made all kinds of patterns, moving and rippling across a blue ceiling. In some ways it reminded her of the sea, only it was different. Ma didn't like her to stare at the sky. Daydreaming she called it. Not the thing that fisher girls should do. Fisher girls should keep busy and not dream their lives away. But Ma would be at the church by this time so she wouldn't know.

Jeannie shut her eyes and chewed the grass. The sun was warm on her face and she could feel the drowsiness coming over her, so it was just as well that Sarah started to cry just before Belle reached the top of the path.

She sat up. 'I waited for you,' she told Belle. 'Ma said it would be all right.'

Belle stopped to catch her breath. 'That was nice of you, Jeannie.'

'You could sit here beside me for a minute,' Jeannie patted the grassy bank. 'It's fine and comfy, and maybe Sarah could do with a feed before we go in the kirk.'

'D'you think we'd have time?' Belle's voice was

anxious. 'I don't want to annoy your ma.'

'Aye there's plenty of time. The kirk bells haven't started yet and the laird's carriage hasn't gone past. I like to see the horses and the carriages, and the grand ladies and gents who sometimes come with the laird.'

Belle sat down beside Jeannie and opened the top of her dress so that Sarah could suckle her breast. 'Well if you're sure we've time,' she said.

8

The Reverend Murdo McAllan was a tall, pale complexioned man, whose face was reminiscent of the cadavers that lay in the vaults at the rear of the building. He was a distant cousin of the laird and knew he should have been grateful for the charge of Craighead Church, but he was not. He would have preferred a church with a wealthier congregation rather than the farm workers and fisher folk that formed his own flock.

Now, as he stood in the shade of the church door waiting for the laird's carriage to arrive, he could feel the familiar build up of sweat beneath his collar. It had been a long hot summer and in his opinion the weather was far too warm for a September Sunday. It could not last.

He ran a finger round his collar and wiped the sweat from his face. Where was that blasted carriage? If it was much longer he would be forced to go and speak to some of the early arrivals who were congregating outside the gate.

The church stood almost on the edge of the cliff just where the river met the sea, although Murdo rarely went near the cliff edge. The sight of the waves on the rocks below did something strange to his insides, however, this was where the fisher folk liked to stand before services started. He could see them now, laughing and gossiping while they looked seawards. Their eyes rarely left the sea, although Murdo could not understand what it was they saw.

He had a christening to perform for them today. He was looking forward to it, for it would give him a chance to preach yet again about the wages of sin.

Murdo liked to preach about sin, and this christening would give him extra pleasure, for the girl who would be standing before him was Belle Findlay, the niece of his colleague, the Reverend Abraham Findlay.

He rubbed his hands down his surplice and gave a shiver of anticipation. Perhaps the reverend gentleman would give up his charge at Invercraig because of the scandal. Mayhap there might be an opportunity for himself when all was said and done.

The laird's carriage had not yet left the big house, and Sir Roderick Craigallan was becoming angry. Lachlan knew better than to look at, or speak to, his father when he was in one of his moods. So he turned to look at the house, as if by doing so his mother and Clarinda would immediately appear. The house looked as it always did, slumbering in the autumn sun, the half-drawn blinds shading the windows like drowsy eyelids.

Out of the corner of his eye Lachlan could see his father's frown deepen as he consulted his fob watch yet again. The young man leaned against the carriage, making sure he stayed out of the way of the horses' hooves; he did not relish another kick from them. He was still sore from the last one.

His father started to pace, stopping now and then to run his hands over the horses. Lachlan still did not look at his father or speak, for he knew that his father had more time for the horses than he had for his own son.

At last the women emerged from the house and Lachlan could relax, for his father's ill temper never sustained itself in the presence of his wife, Catherine. Lachlan was always careful only to smile at his mother when his father was not looking, for he was keenly aware that his father was jealous of any attention his mother gave him. 'Spare the rod and spoil the child,' had been a phrase that had echoed throughout his childhood, always to be answered by his mother, 'He's just a child.'

No rod had ever touched Lachlan's body and nothing could convince his father he was not spoiled.

The two women arrived, and the laird grasped Catherine's hand and elbow to help her into the carriage.

'Look lively, lad,' he snapped, making Lachlan start.

'Help your cousin into the carriage.'

Lachlan had expected his father to assist Clarinda, but he did not argue. He never argued with his father. He just wished that occasionally his father would treat him with some respect.

He approached Clarinda and, tentatively holding out his hand, avoided looking into her supercilious eyes. She was heavier to support than her slim frame suggested and for one horrible minute he could feel her sway as she transferred her weight to the carriage. He held his breath. He could imagine the reaction of his father if he let her fall.

His father climbed into the carriage before him and sat down beside Catherine, leaving Lachlan no option but to sit beside Clarinda.

His mother smiled encouragingly at him. She was a small, round woman with pleasant features and brown hair just peeking out from the brim of her bonnet. Lachlan could not imagine her as the beauty she was said to have been in her youth. Not like Clarinda who was slightly taller, slim and really beautiful.

Lachlan would have liked her better if she had been less beautiful and more friendly.

The carriage rattled down the back drive towards the rough, cliff-top road that led to Craighead church. Dust spurted upwards from the carriage wheels as it gradually gained speed, and Lachlan, holding the edge of his handkerchief to his nose, stared out of the carriage so that he would not have to look at Clarinda.

The carriage slowed a little as it passed a girl and a woman, sitting at the side of the road. Lachlan found himself looking at the woman who was younger than he had first thought. Noticing the curve of her breast as she fed the baby in her arms, a dull ache of desire gripped the pit of his stomach reflecting its way downwards into his loins.

The young woman stared at him before she lowered her eyes, and covered her breast. Her hair, a mass of brown curls with the faintest glint of red where the sun caught it, fell forward, covering her face.

Lachlan forced his eyes away from her. He did not need to look at his father to know that he was being glared at, it was obvious from his own rising embarrassment and confusion, and his overwhelming feeling of guilt. This was the effect his father always had on him.

He had been aware from an early age that there was nothing he could do to please his father, who had always made it plain that he did not measure up. As a result Lachlan paid lip service to following the family rule book, but privately went his own way, and this was one of the reasons he was being sent to London.

It was not the first time nor would it be the last that Lachlan wished he was able to stand up to his father.

9

Belle buttoned her dress and strapped Sarah to her in the shawl. She could still feel the young toff's admiring gaze and the warm feeling that had coursed through her when their eyes met.

'Who was that in the carriage?' She deliberately made her voice casual as she looked down at Jeannie who was still lying on her back in the grass. It would not do to let Jeannie see her interest in the young man who had looked at her with such longing in his eyes.

'That was the laird's carriage,' Jeannie spat out the piece of grass she had been chewing.

'Yes, but who was in it?'

'The laird was there, and the laird's lady. She was the older one. I don't know who the other lady was, but she was probably with the laird's son. They say the lassies have to watch out for him. They say he got one of the maids at the big house in the family way and that the laird's going to send him away.'

Jeannie stood up and brushed the grass from her skirt. 'We'd better get going to the kirk or the minister'll have rare fun getting on to us for being late. One thing's for sure though, he'll not be saying anything about the laird's family. He knows better.'

Belle was thoughtful as they walked towards the church. The laird's son, no less, and if she was not mistaken he fancied her.

She would have liked to sit in a carriage and be able to nod to all the fisher folk and the farm folk. Annie would not have despised her if she had been a lady. Instead she would have thought herself lucky to have Belle as a daughter-in-law, and everyone would have looked up to her. Even the minister would not dare criticize her.

But she was not a lady and she would never sit in a carriage and, although the laird's son might fancy her, it could never amount to anything because they were not from the same class.

Murdo heard the rattle of the wheels as the dust cloud moved nearer. He observed the groups of farm labourers and their women folk turning to watch the progress of the carriage, although, as always, the fisher folk disdained to look. A proud, uncouth lot, the fisher folk, thought Murdo, not respectful like their country counterparts.

His lips formed their usual grimace as he moved forward to welcome the laird's party.

Sir Roderick alighted first.

There was a delicate grace in his movements that belied his size, for he was a stocky bull of a man who looked as if he would be more at home in the farmyard than the drawing room. He was reputed to be fair and just, although getting on the wrong side of him had never been recommended, and Murdo knew his place.

Lachlan followed him. He certainly was not the man his father was and Murdo found it difficult to be civil to him. He had little patience for the laird's son, with his foppish ways and womanising habits. He sighed, if only Lachlan had not been the laird's son he could have used him as the topic of many a sermon.

Murdo could feel the sweat running down his back as he stood in the full rays of the sun. He wanted to get back into the shade of the church, but dared not do so until the laird was ready to enter.

He gripped his hands behind his back and struggled to maintain his smile as he waited for the ladies to be helped out of the carriage.

The laird turned, 'Ah, Murdo, my man! You haven't met my niece Clarinda, have you?'

Murdo surreptitiously wiped his hands on his robe before

raising her hand with the tips of his fingers and, bending towards her knuckles, dryly brushed them with his lips.

The church was cool and, after the brightness of the morning sun, Belle had to blink several times before her eyes adjusted to the gloomy interior. She did not want to be here and it had been an effort for her to enter the church but she held her head high, even though there had been something in the minister's gaze, when he'd looked at her in the churchyard. It had made her uneasy and brought back unwelcome memories of her uncle. Now, as she followed Jimmie and his family to a pew she could feel the minister's eyes watching her, and it made her want to turn and run out again.

The pews in the central area of the church were of rough, unvarnished oak and Belle's silk dress did not protect her from the cold hardness of the seat, although she doubted if Annie or any of the fisher girls would notice the discomfort. Their thick, rough skirts probably provided them with more protection.

Jeannie wriggled in beside her and Belle smiled her appreciation of the child's interest, although the poor child was plain beyond belief. Belle was not accustomed to feeling any kind of kinship with women or girls, but Jeannie was no threat to her, and she certainly needed a friend in this village, so she grasped the child's hand and squeezed it with a warmth that was genuine. Maybe she would be able to help her look prettier. She would have to watch out for Annie though, for Annie would not like it.

The organ music reminded the congregation they were in God's house and should show proper respect. Belle, however, let her thoughts drift to pleasanter times while her arms cradled Sarah.

The Reverend Murdo McAllan's voice droned on, and Belle in her inattentive state only vaguely heard references to fornication and other sins too heinous for her to want to hear. When the time came to take Sarah to the font for the sprinkling of the baptismal waters she moistened her lips and held her head erect so that her hair flowed down her back. She had met men like the Reverend Murdo before and nothing he could say or do could ever affect her. She smiled at him to display her lack of concern about his vituperous sermon and took pleasure in his evident discomfort.

Sarah cried as the cold water sprinkled over her brow and face. Belle held her close to her body trying to soothe her, but the crying continued and Belle was unable to console her. She grew hot and flustered, aware of the minister's thin-lipped smile that seemed to say to her, 'Be sure your sins will find you out.' Heat crept up her neck towards her face but she held her head high as she returned to her pew. After she sat down, she pressed Sarah's face into her breast and rocked with her.

At the end of the service the congregation emerged to the fresh air and heat. The laird and his party led the way followed by the farm-workers who tipped their bonnets to him, and the more independent fisher folk who nodded briefly but showed no other signs of subservience.

Belle held tightly to Jimmie's arm. She was determined that he would walk her down the path to her mother-in-law's home and not leave her to make the journey on her own as he had done earlier.

She could feel Annie's eyes on her and knew she had displeased her in some way, but she did not care.

They passed the laird and his party and Belle glanced surreptitiously at Lachlan, hoping he would notice she was taken, for she was already fantasizing that he was in love with her.

10

That night Belle and Jimmie made silent love for the first time since Sarah's birth. Jimmie's touch was gentle, although his hands were rough on Belle's skin. She pressed herself against him, for Belle knew what he wanted and was willing to provide it so that she would be loved. Belle needed to be loved and her uncle had taught her well in the ways of pleasing a man.

She murmured in Jimmie's ear and nibbled at his lobe. She had to make sure he thought he was pleasing her, for truth to tell there was no pleasure in it for Belle; again, the outcome of her uncle's teaching.

His arms held her tight and safe and she ignored Annie sleeping in the truckle bed at the other side of the room.

The bed creaked and the straw in the mattress rustled every time Jimmie thrust himself into her but the curtains enclosing the boxed in bed ensured their privacy. Belle almost wept with joy because with every thrust Jimmie was proving his love for her, and with every submission she also proved her love for him.

Later, as they lay in each other's arms, Belle felt strangely restless. She had been accustomed to her own room in her uncle's house and now she was aware of every noise and creak in the crowded cottage. She could hear Annie's soft snores from across the room, the restless turnings of Jeannie in the truckle bed just beyond the bed curtains, and the rustling sounds of Jimmie's father and brothers as they slept among the nets in the loft.

Turning in the bed she put her arm around Jimmie and nuzzled at his ear with her lips. 'Jimmie,' she murmured, 'we have to get a place of our own. We can't stay here much longer.'

'Why not? Ma said it would be all right. We can stay as long as we need to.' Jimmie's voice was fuzzy with sleep.

A tidal wave of anger surged up within Belle. Annie would like that. She would love to keep her precious son under her own roof where she could keep an eye on his new wife so she would not step out of line. Well, Belle was not going to put up with that. She bit back the retort that trembled on her lips. She would have to be careful for Jimmie loved his ma.

'Don't you see, my love. It's not fair on your ma and da if we stay here. We're sleeping in their bed and the house is overcrowded already. Besides, it's not easy to love you here. We have to be so quiet.' She flicked her tongue inside his ear feeling a surge of satisfaction as he moaned and turned to take her in his arms again. 'Hush, my love,' she said. 'We don't want to waken anyone.'

Jimmie's grip on her tightened, 'There's a wee house at the end of the village that's used as a store. I'll go see the laird about it.'

Belle's heart gave a little flip as he mentioned the laird, and she remembered Lachlan, who had looked at her so longingly. The memory lingered for a moment making her tingle with the warmth of it before she thrust it out of her mind. Her life was with Jimmie, her love was for Jimmie, and she allowed him to pull her into his embrace.

Jimmie had inherited his father's ability to waken when the tide was on the turn. He could hear his ma moving around and the stirrings of his brothers in the loft. He knew the time had come, for the boats could only leave Craigden with the outgoing tide.

Belle lay beside him. Her face flushed with sleep and her arm thrown over his chest. Jimmie smiled as he looked at her for he still could not quite believe that she was his. Gently, he lifted her arm and wriggled from her embrace. It would be hours before she would waken. He brushed his lips over her forehead and she stirred and smiled. Pulling open the curtain that enclosed the alcove he slipped out of the bed, and taking one last look at her, pulled it closed again so that the faint light from the crusie lamp would not waken her.

'Is Belle not getting up?' Annie's voice was harsh. 'Is she not going to see you to the boat?'

'Don't wake her, Ma. Let her sleep on. She's tired.' Jimmie kept his voice low.

'I see. You're going to spoil her are you. I suppose you'll be wanting me to carry you to the boat as usual.'

'I'll wade out myself if you don't want to do it but I'll not have Belle wakened.'

'Don't be silly laddie. You'd only get wet and that's not good for a fisherman on his way to the sea.' Annie stared at the closed curtains of the box bed, 'Why you wanted to marry a useless townie I'll never know. You should have married one of our own kind.'

Jimmie thought of the large, big boned fisher girls, who no longer attracted him. He liked Belle's smallness of frame and delicate features, although he was just as aware as his mother that she would never be able to carry him to the boat like the other women did. 'She's not useless. She's just not big enough to carry me to the boat. Maybe she could do something else?'

'Aye, maybe laddie, but what d'you think that might be. She hasn't done anything yet that I can see.'

'Give her a chance, Ma. She's only just had the bairn.'

'Well it's time she got over it, and now the bairn's been kirked she should be ready to work.'

James Watt descended the ladder from the loft in the same sure footed way that he moved about his boat. 'What are you two squabbling about. You'll have the whole house wakened.'

'Can you not guess what they're fighting about?' Ian followed his father down the ladder. 'There's been nothing but trouble since he brought that tart home.'

Jimmie glared at Ian. 'I'll not have you call Belle a tart.'

'I'll have no fighting in this house, and mind your language in front of your ma,' James growled.

Annie ladled porridge from the pot hanging over the fire, and thrust a bowl into their hands. 'Eat your breakfast or you'll miss the tide.' Still holding one bowl, she looked around. 'Where's Angus?' she demanded.

'I'm here, Ma,' Angus peered down from the edge of the loft. 'Davie's wakened as well and wants to know if he can go out with the boat.'

'He's a lot brighter than you are, laddie, but he's still too young. Tell him to go back to sleep.'

'Aye, Ma. That I will.'

11

Annie led the way to the river's edge. The tide was high making the small boats swing back and forth with the strength of the water. She looped her skirt above her knees and tucked it into her waistband. Bracing herself against the coldness of the water she stepped into the river.

'I'm ready, James.' She waited for him to climb on her back. Her body stiffened in expectation of his weight for he was a well-built man, tall and strong, as most fishermen were. She loved him with every part of her being. She had been carrying him to his boat for the past twenty years, and would probably still do so for the next twenty years, because for all the grand talk of the laird about the pier he was going to build it was not even started yet.

The water was up beyond her knees before Annie reached the boat, and she could feel it pulling at her as it swirled round her legs. She half-turned so that James could dismount. As he transferred his weight he turned and held her by the shoulder. Looking into her eyes, he said, 'You're a grand woman, Annie, and a braw wife. Don't think I dinnae appreciate you, but don't be hard on Belle, she's just a bit lass. She's a lot to learn yet.'

'If you say so, James. I'll try, but I can't help feeling Jimmie would have been better to marry Ellen Bruce. She has a fancy for him, you know.'

'It's too late for that now, Annie, but have you seen the way Ian looks at Ellen. Mayhap she'll be part of the family yet.'

Annie could feel her legs becoming numb. 'I'd better get the laddies on board. It's time you were away.' She turned and waded back to the bank, and carried her sons, one at a time, to join their father on the boat.

'We'll be back later today,' James shouted to her as they cast off. 'We're only going down the coast a bit.'

Annie watched as the small boat swung round with the tide and raced seawards. Her skirt, clinging wetly to her legs, sent a chill racing through her body making her yearn for the comfort of her little cottage and a soothing pipe of tobacco. Loosening her skirt, she rubbed her legs with her petticoat and turned towards home.

Jimmie watched his mother striding away towards the huddle of cottages. He could sense an air of disapproval in her firm, erect movements, just as he had sensed her disapproval as she carried him to the boat. She had not said anything, but he could feel it in the tenseness of her body and the abrupt way she had detached herself from him.

He sighed, wishing his mother could accept Belle, could see her as he saw her. If only his mother could see the kind, loving person that Belle was, and not just the outward flippancy. He would do anything if only the two women that he loved more than anything else could accept and like each other.

The boat swayed out to meet the river current forcing Jimmie to grasp the mast in order to steady himself. He stopped watching his mother's retreating figure and turned his face towards the sea. Excitement mounted in his chest. The movement of the boat, the feel of the spray on his cheeks and the wind in his hair, made him forget everything else. The sea was his first love. It was his life. The only life he had ever wanted.

He looked at Ian slumped in the bottom of the boat. He loved Ian as a brother, but Ian always seemed so discontented and they always ended up quarrelling and fighting. Jimmie was never sure how the arguments started but they always ended with his brother stamping off in a rage. Jimmie was sure that Ian had no love for the sea and would seek his fortune elsewhere if he could.

Angus lay curled up beside the nets. He was willing and

keen to learn, but he was still young. Jimmie liked having Angus on board because it helped him to realise how experienced he had become. Soon he would be as adept as his father at handling the boat and maybe he could start thinking of getting a boat of his own.

'Aye lad, you've stopped dreaming then.' His father had already stowed the anchor away. The boat rocked and spray splashed over the bows as the outgoing tide caught it. 'Never mind the sails until we reach the sea. The tide's strong enough for us to clear the river mouth and we don't want the wind taking us onto the rocks.' James rubbed his beard absent-mindedly as he gazed seawards.

Jimmie grinned at his father. He admired him and wanted to be just like him. Fingering his smooth chin, Jimmie wondered if it was time he grew a beard. 'D'you think there'll be fish the day?' he asked.

'Of course there will, lad. What for would there not be fish? It's been a good season.' James laughed. 'I know what's up with you. You'll be needing to get home to that wee wife of yours. Well, we'll be home before you know it, and with a fine big catch.'

The sea seemed to reflect in their eyes as both men, father and son, gazed seawards.

Annie hesitated as she reached the house. She looked towards the sea, straining to catch sight of the *Bonnie Annie* as she sailed towards the fishing grounds. She thought she saw the dark shape of sails at the river mouth, but the moon had slipped back behind the clouds and it was difficult to be sure.

The house was silent and still as she entered, with only the glimmer of the fire throwing strange shadows around the room.

Belle, hidden behind the curtain that covered the entry to the bed alcove, hadn't stirred. Annie could almost imagine the girl was not there and with that thought uppermost in her mind she had to fight against the sudden, desperate urge that threatened to overcome her, to climb into the bed that was rightfully hers and cuddle down into the warm hollow that James would have left.

Shrugging her shoulders, she sat on her seat beside the fire and pulled her shawl around her. This was her sleeping place for the time being. She could not join James and the boys in the net loft. It wouldn't be right, particularly now the boys were becoming so grown up.

Jeannie turned in her sleep. She looked small and peaceful as she slept on the truckle bed. Annie's expression softened, for Jeannie was her youngest, the only girl in a family of boys.

She had almost given up hoping for a girl when Jeannie had come along. James had thought she'd wanted another boy, but he was wrong. Fisher families needed girls. After all, who would look for mussels, bait the hooks and sell the fish, not the men, for sure. Jeannie was still small but she was wiry and active. She would be all right. Just give her time.

Annie tried to get comfortable on the chair. It was still the middle of the night, too early to start the chores. Monday was not her favourite day, for the boats could not sail on the Sabbath and had to wait for the first tide after midnight.

She watched the flickering flames until sleep crawled into her mind and her eyes closed. She was lying beside James in the box bed, feeling his warmth and the fisherman smell of him. If she reached out she knew he would respond, because he still saw her as the tall, young girl she had been when he married her, and not as the work-weary woman she had become, old at the age of thirty-nine.

A surge of longing crept up through Annie's skin making it tingle. She wanted him. She wanted his caress and his lips on hers. Her arm went round him, and she woke with a start as it touched the cold wall. The fire had dwindled. There was no James, and no warmth, and no comfort.

Confusion swept over her. It had felt so real, but there was nothing there. She still sat on the chair before the dying fire. Jeannie still slept on the truckle bed, and Belle still lay in Annie's bed.

Despair sat heavy on her heart. She would have to talk to James. They would have to do something about Belle and Jimmie.

12

It was dawn before Belle woke. She could hear Sarah making soft mewling noises and knew that the baby's lips had puckered in a sucking action. Pushing the blankets aside Belle raised her foot until it reached the shelf, just wide enough for the cradle, at the foot of the bed. She wriggled her foot until it touched the cradle and prodded it so that it rocked gently. She knew Sarah liked the movement, and it might give Belle a little more time before she would have to feed her.

She leaned over and pulled the curtains aside. The dawn light had filtered into the room, although it made little difference to the shadows at the back of the hole in the wall bed.

The fire was blazing but the chair beside it was empty and there was no sign of Annie. She must have risen and left the house. Belle was thankful for that because Annie never gave her any peace.

Jeannie was sitting on the side of her truckle bed trying to comb her hair, although it was not having much effect. It always looked straggly no matter what she did. Jeannie liked her, she could sense it, besides she had often felt the child's fingers touching her hair or her dress. There was also the hungry look that Jeannie had when she watched her, an expression that was not quite envy but something akin to it. Sympathy for the child who often followed her around, welled up in her and she ached to help her.

'Are you going to feed Sarah?' Jeannie asked. 'Can I watch?'

Belle turned towards the cradle. She supposed she had better feed the baby, although her breasts were sore from the constant suckling. Thankfully, apart from the pain, Sarah was an easy baby to feed and seemed to be grateful for anything her mother could give her. She did not cry much either, probably because the baby was aware of her mother's displeasure when she did so. It pleased Belle that Sarah was a fast learner, because it saved her a lot of trouble.

Jeannie perched on the side of the alcove bed, watching, as Belle lifted the baby and commenced to feed her.

'She's a bonny baby,' Jeannie stretched her hand out to stroke Sarah's hair. It was not as long or as thick as it had been when she was born, and it seemed to be losing its lustrous black colour. 'I think her hair's turning brown,' she said to Belle. 'More like the colour of your hair.'

Belle looked. 'I think you're right. I hadn't noticed.' The baby, snuggling into her body, was warm and soft against her breast and, as she wriggled even closer, a surge of emotion welled up within Belle until she almost choked on it.

Belle sat on a rock near the river mouth waiting for Jimmie to sail back to her. Annie and the rest of the women had gone to the mussel beds, and Jeannie was minding Sarah. The village had been deserted when she walked through it. She had been glad of the peace and the lack of prying eyes, aware that she was the subject of much gossip and speculation since Jimmie had brought her to his home.

She dabbled her toes in the water enjoying the swishing motion as it eddied round her feet. Little waves whispered their way through gaps in the rocks making soft shushing noises and occasional slapping sounds where there was no opening for them to escape through. She leaned back, supporting herself by her hands as she turned her face into the breeze. Her hair streamed out behind her in a wild jumble of curls and she laughed with delight, enjoying the fingers of wind sifting through the strands. The feeling of abandonment and freedom was intoxicating.

Lifting her skirts above her knees she plunged her feet deeper, gasping at the coldness of the water swirling round them, but she did not care and kept them submerged until they became numb. Her eyes constantly watched the sea and she wondered how long it would be before the boats returned but, although she saw sails on the horizon several times, the boats never came any nearer.

Belle was not sure how long she sat there, enjoying the feel of the water, the smell of the dulce, and the soft shush, shush of the waves, before she became aware of a slight rustling noise behind her. She realised she was no longer alone and turned to see the gaunt, black clad figure of Reverend Murdo McAllan standing on the path above the foreshore. He was standing with his hands clasped behind his back and she had the feeling he had been there for some time.

Belle had only seen him once before, in church, and he had called her a harlot. She had not liked him then and she did not like him now. There was something about him that made her fear him.

The minister's eyes were staring at her legs. If it had been anyone else Belle might have revealed a bit more as she removed them from the water. But now, anxious to cover herself up, she soaked the bottom of her skirt as she scrabbled for her shoes.

'Have you no shame,' the minister's voice seemed breathless in the wind. 'Sitting on the rocks and displaying yourself. What would your uncle think?'

'My uncle! What do you know of my uncle?' Belle demanded. Her cheeks burned. She did not like to think about her uncle. That was all in the past.

'Oh yes, I know your uncle, the Reverend Abraham Findlay who has the best parish in Invercraig. He is an influential man, and a man of standing in the community. What would he think of his niece now?'

'I don't care what he thinks of me,' Belle's voice was defiant. 'I've left all that behind me and I won't be going back.'

She gathered up her skirts and ran down the foreshore afraid to look back in case the minister was pursuing her.

It wasn't fair, she should not be reminded of her uncle now, not when she was so happy and things were starting to work out for her. Her uncle couldn't spoil it, could he? He couldn't come and take her away. Not now she was married. She could hear Murdo's voice echo in her mind, 'An influential man.' She shivered. She would kill herself before she would let him take her back to the manse. She could not go through all that again.

13

Lachlan tapped at the door of his mother's sitting room. He had always run to her when something worried him.

The problem was that his father had demanded he propose to Clarinda, and marry her before the year was out. But he was not attracted to Clarinda, nor yet ready to become a husband. Apart from that, she terrified him, and he was convinced she would rebuff his proposal. If she did, he would have to crawl back to his father and admit defeat. He shuddered as he imagined his father's reaction to that. This was a time when he needed his mother to pat his hand, smooth his hair and tell him it would be all right; the way she used to do when he was a boy.

Entering the room, at his mother's invitation, his heart lightened as she turned to smile at him. She would understand. It was going to be all right.

'Ah, there you are Lachlan,' she said. 'I was just thinking about you.'

He crossed the room and taking her hand in his, kissed it. 'You never change, mother,' he said, as he sat on the stool at her feet. It was his favourite position. Ever since he could remember he had sat there and buried his face in her skirts when his father was angry with him and, although he was too old now to seek refuge in her skirts, at least he could sit beside her.

'Are you looking forward to London?' Catherine's hand smoothed a lock of hair from his forehead. 'You will arrive well before the Christmas festivities start. It should be exciting for you.'

'Yes, mother,' he hesitated. 'But you know I wouldn't go if you didn't want me to.'

Catherine's eyes clouded over and Lachlan could not tell

what she was thinking. 'Of course you must go. It will give you the opportunity to get to know Clarinda better. We have high hopes for both of you.'

'I'm not sure I'm ready,' he looked away from her, 'marriage I mean, with Clarinda.'

'Of course you're ready. You're nineteen now. Your father and I were younger than that when we married.'

'It's not that, mother. I don't feel I know Clarinda well enough. She's so . . . cool towards me.'

Catherine smiled at him. 'I didn't know your father very well either when we were betrothed. My father chose him for me and that's as it should be. You and Clarinda, it will be all right. Just give it time.'

Lachlan did not want to give it time. He dreaded a life with Clarinda, all duty and dullness, and no excitement. For a moment he thought of the fisher girl in her silk finery, so out of place among the other fisher girls from the village. He did not want to get married to Clarinda, or anyone else. He valued his freedom too much.

'Are we so poor that I have to marry Clarinda?' he asked.

'Hush my boy, you shouldn't talk of money.' Catherine looked away from him.

Lachlan rose from the stool and walked to the window. He could see the rhododendron lined drive from there, with its avenue of autumnal greenery. It was all so familiar and comfortable. If he went to London with Clarinda, he would not see the flowering next spring and summer.

He dreaded London. He knew where he fitted in here. He was the laird's son. People looked up to him and he was safe. He was not so sure about London society, although there might be some pretty girls. But would they want him? Or would they look on him as some kind of country bumpkin? His conviction that he was gauche and awkward in company made him unsure how he would fit in with society ladies, and he wished he could stay at home where the serving girls he courted did not look down their noses at him.

Lachlan turned to face his mother. 'What if Clarinda

won't have me? What if she refuses?'

'Clarinda will not refuse you, my son. There has always been an understanding, ever since you were children. You are a Craigallan, and you must honour that understanding and court her. She will not refuse.'

Lachlan was not so sure about that. Clarinda had hardly glanced at him since her arrival a month ago. He had offered to walk with her in the gardens, but she had shown no interest.

'The country is so uninteresting, not like London where there is so much to do. And the weather here is so chill,' she had said, although Lachlan thought it pleasantly warm.

He wanted to tell her about the beauty of the flowers, the sound of birds singing in the trees, the smell of freshly turned earth, but he did not know where to start. He did not know how to talk to her or engage her interest.

'It worries you, my son, this courting of Clarinda.' Catherine was watching him. 'It is like everything else in life, take it slowly and easily. Get to know her and it will come right in the end.'

'If you say so, mother. You know I'd do anything to please you. But what if it doesn't work out? What if I disappoint you?'

'You will never disappoint me, Lachlan, never.' Catherine caressed his hair and he leaned toward her hand enjoying the feeling of being a child again.

Clarinda tapped her foot impatiently. 'No, no, you silly girl. Have you never packed a trunk before? You fold the dress this way so that it will not crease so much.'

'Yes, ma'am,' Meg refolded the dress.

'I declare, I should have brought my own ladies' maid with me. It's bad enough having to come to the wilds of Scotland without having to do without the niceties of life as well.' Clarinda prided herself on her manners and her self discipline but since she had come to Scotland both seemed to have deserted her somewhat.

'Can I trust you to get on with the packing while I go and see how my aunt is managing?'

Clarinda swept into her aunt's room. 'I declare if I had stayed in the room with that maidservant for one more minute I think I might have boxed her ears.'

'That is most unlike you, Clarinda. You are usually so calm.'

Clarinda could feel Aunt Beattie's questioning glance and she coloured slightly. 'I suppose it's just being here. The month has passed so slowly, and it has been so dull. There is nothing to do, and even at this time of the year the weather is so cold that I have to wear mittens in my room.'

'You know as well as I do that the point of the visit was for you to meet Lachlan. A little discomfort should not put you out of sorts.' Her aunt's tone was kindly but firm.

'Lachlan! He's no more than a country bumpkin. His clothes are not fashionable and his manners leave a lot to be desired. He is not even gallant.' Clarinda brushed an imaginary speck of dust from her skirt.

'He will inherit the title. Is that not worth something?'

Clarinda smiled. 'It is the only good thing about him.' She had to admit she rather fancied being Lady Craigallan. 'I suppose one does not have to see too much of a husband,' she said thoughtfully.

'There should be a period of courting, and getting to know one another. One should not rush into these things. Make him wait,' she said, smiling up at her niece, for in comparison to Clarinda, Beattie was quite a small woman.

Resisting the impulse to pat her tiny aunt on the head, Clarinda returned the smile. Her height had always given her a feeling of superiority and when she was with Aunt Beattie she felt even taller. Clarinda was adept at picking up unspoken feelings and knew she made Aunt Beattie uncomfortable, but she enjoyed the discomfiture of others, even those she loved. So she always stood straight and made sure that when she was with her aunt she could look down on her.

'I suppose you are right.' Clarinda was in no hurry. She

would be quite happy to keep Lachlan waiting for ever if need be. She was confident that he would never have the backbone to pursue another lady of quality, and he would certainly never consider marrying one of his serving wenches.

She smiled quietly to herself as she returned to inspect the packing of her trunk, thank goodness she was returning to London today.

Lachlan was restless. He paced up and down the library, stopping from time to time to take a book from one of the shelves and just as quickly replace it. He had hoped his mother would have been more sympathetic, perhaps saying he did not have to go to London, that he did not have to court Clarinda, and that she would talk with his father and make it be all right. But she had not done any of this. Instead she had reinforced his father's plan for him.

He knew that Hamish would be getting the coach ready, even though they did not want to leave too early. The first stage of the journey would only take them to Dundee where they were to spend the night with cousin Letitia before leaving on the sailing packet tomorrow.

Lachlan had been to the stables this morning to look at Clarinda's large travelling coach. It was magnificent, if somewhat plain. Not like his father's coaches which had the family crest emblazoned on the doors. But then Clarinda did not have a crest to use, not unless she married him. Lachlan suspected that Clarinda would quite like a crest on her carriage.

He had a sudden urge to go and sit by the river and watch the tide rushing to the sea. He wanted to walk on the rocky banks and the shingle of the foreshore and listen to the lap of the waves and the screams of the gulls. The river sang to him and he envied the weather-beaten fishermen who had no worries other than how big their catch of fish would be.

There was a part of the garden where it was possible to see the back-sands, that large inland lake where the women harvested the mussels when the tide was out. He had often stood, unseen, among the trees watching as they waded in with their skirts hitched up to their waists. There was a grace in their movements, almost like a ballet, as they moved their feet in the sand looking for mussels.

It was not the first time he had wished he was not the laird's son. He would have been happier as a fisherman's son or a farmer's son.

The farmers would be harvesting their grain at this time of year. The scythes would be glinting in the sunlight and the men and women would be hooking the hay to pitch it into newly evolved haystacks.

He could almost taste the musty smell of the hay, see the men with sweat glistening on their muscles, and hear the buzz of the women chattering and laughing.

The urge was strong, but even stronger was Lachlan's fear of his father. He knew that if he went to the farms or the river he would arouse his father's wrath.

Elsie's laughing eyes and happy smile invaded his memory and he wondered where she was. Not that it would make much difference because those eyes had saddened with the disgrace he had brought to her. At the end there was no longer anything he could do to help her, except to ensure she had sufficient money to start a new life.

His father had not refused his request to provide support for Elsie, but had made plain his displeasure. 'There are plenty of women in Invercraig without having to bring disgrace to a decent family,' he had told Lachlan. Elsie's father was one of the laird's tenants.

The library was closing in on Lachlan. He could hardly breathe. Opening one of the large windows he stepped over the sill onto the grass outside.

Lachlan stood for a moment inhaling deeply. He would miss this smell of earth and plants, the feel of grass under his feet, and the bushes that swayed and murmured in the freshening breeze. It was as if they were saying, 'Stay Lachlan, stay.'

14

Annie watched Belle running along the shore as if the devil were after her. The girl looked afraid and vulnerable, and Annie felt a momentary sympathy for her. Maybe if she had been more charitable the girl might have settled in better.

'Are you all right, lass?' Annie said as she went to meet her. 'You look as if you've seen a ghost.'

Belle's strange green eyes seemed to look at Annie without seeing her. Then, it was as if the girl had given herself a mental shake and she realised who Annie was. 'I'm fine,' she said. 'I went to the river mouth to see if I could see the boats coming back but it was so desolate there I thought I'd better get back.'

'You're not used to being on your own, are you lass? You were never born to it, so how can you understand. The sea now, it has its own voice. It has a rhythm, if you listen it'll speak to you. You can never be alone when the sea's there.' Annie looked at Belle as she spoke, but it was obvious the girl did not understand what she meant. She sighed, 'Come along with me, lass. I have a wee job for you.'

The older woman and the young girl walked towards the cottage in silence. Jeannie sat on a stool at the door, her hand on the wooden cradle at her side. 'Sarah's been good, Belle, and she never cried once.'

Annie smiled at her. 'That's good, Jeannie lass. You must have the magic touch. Or maybe she just likes the cradle.' Annie bent down to peer at the sleeping baby. She was bonny enough despite her dark hair. 'Just like a wee gypsy lass,' Annie murmured.

'The boats are in sight.' The cry came from the river's edge.

'Hurry, Belle lass, over here.' Annie lifted the lid of a kist at the back of the room. She lifted out a blue and white striped petticoat, a blue woollen skirt and blouse, and a blue shawl. 'I was keeping them for Jeannie but she won't be needing them for a while yet. Try them on, they should fit you fine.'

Belle did not object but her face was expressionless as she tried the clothes for size, and Annie couldn't tell what she was thinking.

'You don't mind Belle getting the clothes I was saving for you, do you Jeannie? It'll let her get started to learn the fishwife's trade. She's going to need to know what to do if she's going to be a good wife to Jimmie.'

Belle wriggled inside the unfamiliar clothes. The roughness of the material chafed, and it was as if an army of insects was crawling all over her. It took all her will-power to resist the urge to scratch and tear at her skin.

She smiled weakly at Annie who had been kind to her for a change. It would make life easier for her if they could get on together, so Belle did not want to do anything to jeopardize the tentative friendship that Annie seemed to be holding out to her.

'My, you look more like a fisher-girl now,' Annie said turning Belle round to view her. 'You're still not very big mind, but I don't suppose you'll grow any more now. You'll have to do.'

'I've never seen you look so bonnie,' Jeannie danced round her. 'You look better in the dress than anyone else in the village.'

'D'you think so, Jeannie?' Belle gave a little twirl and decided that she would have to get used to the itch if she looked as bonnie as Jeannie said.

'Strap the bairn to you with the shawl,' Annie said, 'and we'll away to meet the boats, and then I'll tell you what you're to do.'

Jeannie danced round Belle as she followed Annie to the river's edge. The child chattered to her most of the way but

Belle was not listening. Annie was hailing and greeting the other women who were also on their way to meet the boats. Belle wished she could do the same, but knowing she was not accepted by the women she dreaded what they would think of her in the strange, new clothes, and could not help wondering if they would mock her. She sensed them watching her, although their gaze always focused on something else when she turned to look at them.

The boats raced up the river, their sails flapping in the wind until almost the last minute when they seemed to collapse onto the decks with a resounding crack, leaving only the bare masts pointing skywards. The smell of fish hung in the air, and the gulls wheeled and screamed around and over the boats, as they anticipated their share of the catch.

Annie kilted up her skirt and waded in to pull the boat nearer to the shore, while Belle hesitated wondering what she was supposed to do. She did not think she would be much use at pulling the boat in because it looked heavy, and she did not want to appear a fool in front of the other women. And anyway she had Sarah strapped to her. So she did nothing.

Jimmie splashed his way to the shore without waiting for the boat to be pulled in. He ran to her, clasping his hands round her waist and lifting her up. He held her for a moment and then spun her around. 'My I've missed you,' he said.

Belle blushed. 'Mind the bairn, and put me down, Jimmie, everyone's laughing at me.'

She struggled in his arms but he just laughed and kissed her. 'I don't care, Belle. I love you and I don't care who knows it.' He held her for a moment and then released her. Standing back he studied her for a moment. 'You're surely intending business, Belle. You're all dressed up for it, and I've never seen the clothes look so well as they do on you. It fair suits you.'

A warm feeling of satisfaction crept over Belle. She had not been sure of the costume, but it met Jimmie's approval so it must be all right. 'Your ma said she had a job for me, but she hasn't told me what it is yet.'

'Is that right, Ma? Have you managed to find something for Belle to do?' Jimmie strode towards Annie helping her to give the boat its final pull onto the foreshore.

Annie let her skirts down, giving her legs a quick rub at the same time. 'I thought Belle would manage to take the laird's share of the fish to the big house, and then go to the farm and trade for some meal, potatoes and eggs. Jeannie's come with me many a time, so I thought she could go with Belle and show her where to go and what to do. You'll manage that, won't you, Jeannie lass?'

'Aye, Ma. That'll be no bother.'

Belle smiled with relief. A nice walk to the big house did not sound so bad.

15

Jeannie skipped up the path, pulling at bushes and swishing at the grass with a stick she had found. The basket of fish she carried did not seem to hamper her in the slightest.

'Aren't the flowers bonnie, Belle, and d'you smell the grass and the plants? I'm glad I've come with you instead of Ma, for the smells of the market in the town are not nearly so nice. D'you see the rabbits, Belle? They make a grand stew. Davie often comes out here after dark to catch them, but he'd be in awful trouble if he got caught.' Jeannie hardly stopped for breath as she chattered.

Belle did not feel the need to answer and concentrated on walking instead. Her new shoes made her feet sting and she was sure she would have blisters on her heels before long. The strap circling her shoulders cut into her skin and the creel bounced painfully on her back because of the weight of fish in it. Her head ached with the strain and she did not know how the child managed to carry her murlin of fish and still prance about.

All it needed now was for Sarah to wake up and start crying. Belle glanced down at the sleeping baby fast asleep in the shawl and wriggled in an effort to reposition her, but the creel's strap held the shawl firmly in place.

The rough road had been uphill until they left the village behind. It was level now, so maybe the going would get easier.

'How far is it to the big house,' gasped Belle, trying to catch her breath while she balanced her creel on the stones of the wall that bordered one side of the path.

Jeannie stopped swishing her stick for a moment. 'It's just a wee bit further on. There's a path not far from here that takes you there.' She leaned against a tree. 'Just wait until you see the house. It's awful big, and awful grand. There must be thousands of rooms in it, and they have fancy curtains at all the windows. And the kitchen's bigger than any room I've ever seen, and it's got a great big fireplace with lots and lots of ovens. As well as that there's lots and lots of pots and pans hanging on the walls, and they sparkle and shine.' The child's eyes widened as she spoke. It was as if she could not imagine how anyone could need so much.

Small rustling and chirping sounds broke the silence as birds hopped about in the branches of the trees, and crickets whirred in the undergrowth. A rabbit crossed the path in front of them and Jeannie lunged after it with a whoop and a swipe with her stick.

Belle braced herself for the weight of the creel as she removed it from the wall and started to walk up the path again. The sooner they got to the big house the better, she thought. She would get rid of some of the fish and her creel would lighten, and maybe, just maybe, she would get a seat in this grand kitchen.

Belle was not sure how much longer they walked because she was busy concentrating on putting one foot in front of the other. It was the only way she could keep going.

The house was larger than any house Belle had ever seen. She had imagined it might be like the villas that lined the highway to the north of Invercraig, but they were small by comparison. The building before her stretched upwards to where a myriad of chimneys squatted on the roof, and lengthways to accommodate the rows of windows winking and gleaming in the September sunshine.

'My Jeannie, it's like a castle,' Belle said as they came to where the path curved in two different directions. 'Which way do we go?'

Jeannie skipped down the path to the left. 'This way, Belle. We can't go to the front of the house. It's not allowed, although I'd fair like to see it. Davie's seen it and he says it's awful grand.'

The air was heavy with the smell of manure as they walked through the courtyard at the rear of the building.

There were rustlings and soft neighings as horses peered through half open doors, and Belle took care not to walk near them. A large black coach stood in the middle of the courtyard as if waiting to see which horses were to be hitched to it.

Jeannie ran round it, 'That's the biggest coach I've ever seen,' she shouted to Belle.

The coachman poked his head out of one of the stables. 'Don't you touch, young missy,' he roared in a loud voice. 'I've spent all morning polishing that coach and I don't want your dirty fingers on it.'

'My fingers aren't dirty,' Jeannie retorted. 'Anyways, where you going all so smart and posh?'

'The young master's off to London with the ladies today, as if it's any business of your'n.' He led a large brown horse out of the stable and started to manoeuvre it between the two shafts at the front of the coach. 'Away with you and not be upsetting the horses.'

Jeannie laughed as she ran over to Belle. 'That's old Hamish, he looks after the horses He's not nearly as bad tempered as he sounds. Isn't that right, Hamish?'

'Be off with you,' he growled.

An arch led out of the stable courtyard into a cobbled area, and the buzz of voices, and clatter of pots and dishes, signalled to Belle that she had arrived outside the kitchen. The noise intensified when they entered a stone lined lobby which was cold and dark. She shivered, and had to wait a moment for her eyes to adjust before she could follow Jeannie into the kitchen.

The warmth that met her as she walked through the door was a welcome relief, and above the clamour she could hear, 'It's the wee fisher lass. Where's your ma the day? You've brought someone else.'

'This is Belle,' Jeannie said. Pulling down a corner of the shawl, she added, 'And this is Sarah. Is she not bonny?'

'Get back to your work, you bunch of skivvies. You don't have time to admire bairns.'

The maids scattered back to their jobs as the plump

woman who had spoken glared at them. She waited until they were busy again and turned to peer into the shawl at Sarah. 'She is a bonny bairn,' she smiled at Jeannie.

Jeannie smiled back, 'Sarah's my cousin, and Belle's my auntie.'

'Your auntie, eh?' the woman looked Belle up and down. 'You'll be young Jimmie's wife, I take it?'

Belle nodded, uncertain of this forceful woman and aware that the kitchen had suddenly gone quiet.

'Well if you're coming with the fish it'll be me, Mrs Ross, you deal with, not that rabble. Just mind that. And mind you come to me before the rest of your round. I've to get the pick of the fish. Understand?'

Belle nodded again and was glad when Mrs Ross made her selection and she was able to escape from the kitchen.

'You never warned me about her,' Belle accused Jeannie.

'Oh, she's all right when you get to know her. Come on, Belle, we still have the farm to go to.'

As they set out on the path towards the farm Belle could hear the rumble of the coach wheels as Lachlan and Clarinda set out on their journey.

PART TWO

1834

16

1834

A cold, windy April followed the long hard winter. A winter where the snows had come early and lain long, and the boats had been unable to take to the sea because of the wildness of the waves. The people of Craigden had become serious and sad-faced as hunger pinched their bellies, and it seemed as if the fish would never come again, nor would the sea accept their boats.

Sarah, clutching Jeannie's hand, watched the water bubble and race towards the river mouth as the inland tidal basin emptied. With the splash of the spray tingling her skin, the taste of salt on her lips, and the scream of gulls echoing in her ears, she shivered with fear and delight. There was something about the river and the sea that both fascinated and repelled her but she felt safe with Jeannie, who at eleven was bigger and cleverer than she was.

Jeannie turned away from the river, 'Come on Sarah, I'd better get you home before Belle starts to shout for you.'

'Do I have to?' Sarah had learned to talk early and had never used childish expressions. Not quite four years old she was a sturdy if somewhat serious child with large sad eyes. She did not want to return to her mother, preferring Jeannie's company, for her young aunt was more of a mother to her than Belle was.

Sarah had learned at an early age that her mother was inconsistent and not able to love her unconditionally. Even as a baby Sarah had learned to be quiet, for Belle could not tolerate crying. She picked up her cues from Belle, and would smile to order, gurgle to order, and stay out of her way when this was necessary. If it had not been for Jeannie, Sarah would never have known what love was.

'Yes, you have to,' Jeannie's smile transformed the plainness of her features. 'I'll have to get back to my ma too, she'll be looking for me to help her.'

Sarah considered this and felt sorry for Jeannie, because if there was one person who terrified her more than Belle it was her granma. Still, Jeannie did not seem to bother too much about granma, maybe it was different because Annie was Jeannie's ma. She shrugged her shoulders and looked up at Jeannie, such matters were too complicated for her to think about.

The two girls turned away from the river's edge, Sarah, small and sturdy her dark hair tied with a piece of string – gypsy hair her granma called it, whatever that meant – and Jeannie, tall for her years, and thin, with long brown hair that tangled in the wind.

'Come home with me,' Sarah pleaded.

'No,' Jeannie's voice was firm, 'my ma would give me what for if she knew I'd been spending time at Belle's house when I'm supposed to be doing chores,' she paused, 'you'll be all right on your own,' and giving Sarah a push, Jeannie turned in the direction of her own home.

Sarah watched for a moment, then slowly walked to the one-roomed shack at the end of the village. The small house, little more than a shed, was set apart from the other houses just as Belle was, part of the village and yet not part of the village. It had been used in the past as a bothy and a net store and, although Belle often sneered at it, both she and Jimmie had been glad to get it, because it gave them freedom from Annie's house. Sarah liked the compactness of the house except for the times when Belle was angry with her, for at those times there was nowhere for her to hide in the one small room.

The door was ajar and, as Sarah approached, she could hear her mother's angry voice.

'It's your fault we have no money.'

'Now Belle, you know that's not true. The fish . . . '

'Fish! Fish! That's all I ever hear. The fish aren't biting! The sea's too heavy! The boat's can't go out! Can you not do anything except fish?'

'You know fishing's my life, Belle. I can't do anything else.'

'You could go to the factory in the town,' Belle's voice was flat.

'Oh, Belle. I'd never get my own boat if I did that, and you know fine I couldn't be cooped up in a factory.'

'You'll never get your own boat anyway. Not when you've to share the catch with your father and your brothers. Maybe it's the whaling you should try.'

Sarah turned silently away and walked back down to the river's edge. She blinked the tears from her eyes, for she did not like to hear her mother and father argue.

17

Sir Roderick led the way down the bridle path from the house to the village. He made an imposing figure sitting astride his horse, proud and erect, and in complete control of his mount, while Lachlan, his son, was having difficulty controlling Raven.

Lachlan jerked the reins angrily as a splash of mud spattered his fine buckskin trousers and the horse reared up, spattering him again. It had been foolish to select Raven, he should have taken a more placid horse from his father's stable, but he had wanted to impress his father and mother, and prove to them they had a son worthy of the name Craigallan.

Lachlan's father, reaching the road at the bottom of the incline, reined in his horse and turned in the saddle to wait as Lachlan's horse slithered down the muddy slope to join him.

'Not the same as riding in London, is it?'

Lachlan looked ruefully at his muddy trousers, 'I'd forgotten the country was so muddy. Give me London any day.'

'You've been away too long, that's all. You'll soon get used to it again.'

The two men rode on in silence. They did not really look alike, Lachlan was taller than his father with a slimmer build and a softer more refined appearance, probably the result of four years of London grooming. Sir Roderick was a more robust figure, stocky in build, and with the look of a farmer, it was only his bearing that suggested he might be more than that, as indeed he was.

The Craigallans of Craigallan Castle were an old family, and the laird was the seventh Lord Craigallan in the line. He and his predecessors had all been men of the earth, unsophisticated men living their lives within the confines of their estates. Sir Roderick, however, had other plans for his son which was why he had sent him to London four years ago, over-riding his son's protestations that he did not want to go. Lachlan had soon settled to London life, which was just as well, because he intended him to be the one who was going to be instrumental in expanding the Craigallan business interests, after he brought new money into the family when he wed Clarinda. The only dissatisfaction Sir Roderick had was that Lachlan had not yet done so.

'Don't waste your time in London,' his father had instructed him when he left. 'Enter society and cultivate the business men. Meet the shipowners and the traders. Above all make contacts.' Lachlan had nodded his agreement, although he was not happy about his father's plans for him, and his return had been triggered by a bad run of luck at the tables rather than any business success.

As Craigden came into sight Lachlan could feel a surge of excitement. He had forgotten how the place affected him. He could remember playing with the village children when he was a boy, although it used to annoy his father. However his mother had never minded and had thought it would broaden his outlook on life. It was there in the village he had first learned about the differences between girls and boys, and had first felt the attraction to women who were not of his class.

'Do you think Clarinda might visit if I ask Catherine to write and invite her?'

Lachlan wondered, not for the first time, if his father could read his mind, and this was his way of reminding Lachlan that he had a fiancee. 'I doubt it, father, Clarinda's not too keen on the country she finds it too quiet, and besides she would not want to miss the London season.'

The two men lapsed into silence again and Lachlan wondered, as he had done many times previously, what his father was thinking. If only his father would show him some signs of affection or approval, Lachlan knew he would have done anything for him. Instead of that the constant disapproval, which convinced Lachlan of his father's hatred for him, prevented him from trying to gain that approval.

The village was quiet, and Lachlan noticed that the boats were pulled up on the shore out of reach of the racing tide. The only person in sight was a small child standing at the river's edge. She turned just as the horses were passing her and, drawing back in alarm, slipped over the edge of the embankment on to the gravel below with the river racing past just inches away from her body.

'Well, don't just sit there, boy,' his father rasped. 'Go and get the child before she slips into the river.'

Lachlan felt his cheeks grow hot at his father's reproof, however, he dismounted and slithering down the bank gathered her into his arms. She raised frightened eyes up to his and stared at him as he scrambled back up to the path. He set her on her feet and turned to remount.

Sir Roderick swung himself off his horse, and knelt beside Sarah. 'Where do you live, little one?' he asked in a gentle tone.

She stared silently at him, the tears trembling on her lashes.

'It's all right lass. I won't hurt you,' and lifting her up he placed her in the saddle of his horse. 'I won't let you fall off,' he reassured the trembling child. 'Just point to where you live and I'll take you there.'

Following his father and the child to the hovel at the edge of the village, Lachlan waited while Sir Roderick knocked on the door. He could not understand why his father had not just left the child where she was, unless it was because he was the laird and had to take an interest in his tenants. Dismounting, he stood behind his father. He felt safer off Raven, and was sure the horse shared his father's contempt for him.

The door was opened by a young woman who was as unlike Clarinda and the women of Lachlan's acquaintance as it was possible to be. There was an air of wildness and passion in her eyes, and he was unprepared for the sudden urge that overwhelmed him. Lachlan felt his manhood stir and clasped his hands behind him for fear he would succumb to a sudden mad impulse to sink his fingers into the tangle of brown curls that framed her face and cascaded over her shoulders to flow down her back. He had a feeling he had seen her somewhere before, but could not remember where.

'Are you the child's mother?' Sir Roderick gruffly addressed the woman. 'She has had a fright. She almost fell into the river.'

Lachlan wanted to add, 'I rescued her,' but his tongue seemed to be sticking to the top of his mouth and he cleared his throat instead.

'Thank you for bringing Sarah home.' Her voice was deep and warm, and her eyes, green as a turbulent sea, were fixed on his, although she was addressing his father.

Heat spread through Lachlan's body and his clothes seemed to have tightened on him. He wished Sir Roderick was not there, and hoped his arousal had not been noticed by his father, although he was sure it was obvious to the woman. His father started to turn towards him so Lachlan swung himself back into the saddle and, despite his discomfort with Raven, was glad of the horse's bulk to hide his aroused state.

18

Belle watched the two men ride away. It was almost four years since she had last seen Lachlan, but she had not forgotten him. At that first meeting she had been sure he was attracted to her, just as she was sure now that the attraction was still there. She could feel it in the air and in her body, and her body never lied to her. There was a spark, a current of emotion that seemed to flash between them when they met which left her confused and restless. She knew deep within herself that he was the laird's son and she was a fisherman's wife and that there could never be anything between them. But her emotions told her otherwise.

'What did the laird want?'

She had not heard Jimmie come up behind her as she stood at the door and she had almost forgotten he was in the house, he had been so quiet. However, she knew he would not have wanted to speak to the laird, although he would not want to admit that to her. He was a proud man, her Jimmie, and he had never forgotten the time he'd had to go cap in hand to Sir Roderick to ask for their house.

'He brought Sarah home. She seems to have been in some sort of an accident at the riverside.' Belle placed her hand on Sarah's shoulder and felt the child shift restlessly under her touch.

'Aw my wee pet, are you hurt then?' Jimmie knelt down beside Sarah and took her into his arms.

Belle frowned at Jimmie. After all she was Sarah's mother and she should have been the one to comfort her, but she had not been able to do it. It was as if there was an invisible barrier between herself and the child. A barrier she was unable to breach. She felt a wave of irritation engulf her, and snapped, 'Of course she's not hurt. She just slipped down the river bank. She'd have been all right even if they hadn't been there.' Her eyes shifted to the distant figures. She did not like to see Jimmie fussing over Sarah and preferred not to look.

'You should look after her a bit better, Belle. She's a bit too wee to be down by the river on her own.' Jimmie gave Sarah a hug and the child smiled up at him.

Belle's stomach churned with the sick feeling she always got when Jimmie criticized her. She knew he was right but that did not help, and it bothered her that she had problems relating to her own child. She wondered whether her lack of feeling for Sarah was the reason Jimmie loved his daughter so much, but she could not help thinking that it was not natural for a father to dote on his child like that. Father's were not supposed to bother with children, they were supposed to keep their love for their wives. Maybe if he did that she'd be able to love Sarah.

Belle answered in the only way she knew how, 'She's looked after well enough. Not like those fisher brats, who are down at the river almost before they can walk. Anyway she was with your sister, Jeannie. She was supposed to be looking after her, if it's anyone's fault it's hers.' Belle turned, and grabbing Sarah's hand pulled her away from her father. 'It's time you were in the house, my lass, where you won't get up to any mischief.'

Jimmie followed Belle and Sarah into the house, 'Aw Belle, what are we fighting about.' He fondled her hair, 'You know I love you, but you get me so mad sometimes.' He put his arm round her waist and pulled her to him.

The strength of his arms around her felt good. He had forgotten Sarah in his desire for her, and that was as it should be. Belle felt the usual warmth in the pit of her stomach and wanted him to hold her close and make love to her.

Remembering Sarah, who was watching them with her solemn eyes she turned, and said, 'Sarah, away you go out and see if you can find some firewood, your da and I have something to talk about.'

She waited until the child left the house before yielding to

Jimmie's embrace. His arms felt good as they held her body firmly against his own but they reminded her he was still only a fisherman. 'You will think about the whaling, won't you Jimmie?' she murmured against his shoulder. 'After all you'll never get your own boat without money, and you'll never get money if you stay on your da's boat.'

'Later, Belle. I'll think about it later.' Jimmie's voice was muffled as he kissed her neck.

'No, Jimmie. Not later, think about it now.' Belle leaned back from his embrace conscious that her movement pressed her hips more firmly against him. She moved her body, feeling the heat from his loins. 'Now, Jimmie, now,' she murmured, and reaching up she nipped his ear between her teeth.

Jimmie groaned as he pulled her towards the bed in the corner of the room.

She sat on the edge of the bed and, just as he pushed her backwards into its depths, she said, 'Just one whaling trip, Jimmie, just one so we can have our own money and so we don't have to rely on Annie any more. Then we'll get our own boat and you can fish for the rest of your life.' Her body was stiff as she waited for his answer.

'Aye, Belle,' he murmured, 'as long as it's only one trip.'

Her body softened and blended into his. 'You promise?'

'Aye. I promise.'

'Mind now. A promise is a promise.' Her arms circled his body and she matched her movements to his, abandoning herself to the passion she felt rising within her.

19

A thin straggle of trees grew at the base of the cliff almost reaching the edge of the village. Wind whipped round Sarah's skirt as she ran for the cover of them, because if you moved quickly it was possible get there without anyone seeing you. She hoped the bigger boys were not there, for this was where they had their dens, and where they tried to climb the grassy cliff out of sight of any interested parent. She did not like the fisher boys much. They laughed at her and called her a townie, even though she had never been out of the village. Usually she only came here with Jeannie, but Ma had said she had to gather firewood, so she'd had to come alone.

The trees sheltered her from the wind and Sarah wandered among them looking for twigs and small branches. She supposed Ma meant wood to light the fire with because she was not big enough to carry anything larger. It did not matter anyway for no matter what she collected and took home, it would never be good enough for Belle.

Sarah piled the twigs she had gathered into a heap, and lay down on her stomach under a tree. From where she lay she could see the path and the river beyond it. She liked to watch the river as it raced down to meet the sea, and wondered what it would be like to go out in the boat when Da went to catch fish. Closing her eyes she tried to imagine she was in a boat, tossed and driven by wind and waves, but it was no use. All she felt was the wind whipping round her skirt.

Granda often said the sea was like a fast woman, wild and fickle, and not to be trusted. He also said that if a seaman wasn't careful he would sleep forever in its depths. The fisherman's cradle he called it. Granma didn't like it when he talked that way and told him to hush up and that he was tempting the devil. Sarah wondered about that, not sure what she meant, but then Granma often said strange things that did not make sense to Sarah.

The river was running fast and Sarah knew that when it emptied it would leave a large mud lake behind it. That was where Granma and Jeannie went to collect mussels to bait the lines. Sarah would have liked to have gone as well but Granma said, 'No!' in that stern voice she had. Granma never gave any reasons when she said, 'No!' so Sarah was sure it was because Granma did not like her.

Granma didn't mind her going with Ma to sell the fish though. Ma had to dress up in the fisherwoman costume when Granma sent her to sell fish to the big houses. Ma didn't like the clothes, but Granma insisted, and Sarah liked to see her in the blue striped skirt with the white petticoat peeking out below. 'It scratches my skin,' Belle would complain.

'Hmph,' Granma would snort. 'If that's all you have to bother about you're not doing too bad. I haven't yet seen you carry your man to the boat, nor are you able to walk to Forfar to sell in the market. You won't even walk to Invercraig market and that's only two miles.' Sarah could tell by the look in Granma's eyes that she did not like Ma. She liked Da though. When he visited her she would feed him soup or any other tasty bit that was going.

Sarah did not mind going to Granma's house when Da was with her. Granma was different then, sometimes she would even smile, and Sarah, her hand tucked into the safety of Da's fist, didn't feel so scared of her.

The faint thudding of horses' hooves, which Sarah had been aware of for some time, seemed to be getting nearer. She slid behind the tree for she did not want the two men to see her again. They might take her home and Ma would be angry.

Sarah watched them from her hiding place until they cantered past and it was safe to stand up. She had not liked the men, particularly the thin one, the one who stared at Ma.

She was sure he was not a nice man, not like Da. Sarah hoped Ma would stay out of his way for there was something in his look that upset her and she was sure that he would hurt Ma if he had the chance.

The sticks and twigs she had gathered filled her arms and she hoped Ma would be pleased with her. Maybe she would smile at her the same way she smiled at Da. Sarah quickened her steps and, half-running, half-sliding, made her way out of the wood and onto the path that led to home.

Her steps slowed as she reached the house and tilting her head to one side, she listened. Always she approached the house in this manner, as if she could judge her ma's mood by the feel of the air and the smell of the wind. Satisfied, she pushed the door open.

'I've got the sticks, Ma.' Sarah held the bundle of twigs out to Belle who was humming to herself as she placed the wooden bowls on the table.

'Lay them in the hearth, Sarah,' Belle did not look up.

Sarah looked at Ma out of the corner of her eyes as she laid the sticks on the hearth-stone. She was sure she had been a good girl. Hadn't she done what Ma asked her to do? Maybe it wasn't enough, maybe she needed to do more.

20

Jimmie and his father pulled hard on the oars of the small boat as they fought the river current which was threatening to pull them off course. Water splashed over the bow as the angry tide swirled round the small island which sat in the middle of the river, and the two of them were breathless and sweating as they approached it.

'We should've asked Ian and Angus to come with us,' Jimmie paused to spit on his hands. The boat swung as the current caught it again, but he grasped his oar with both hands and forced it back on course.

'After we've rounded the point it'll be easier,' James panted. 'The tide'll carry us part of the way to Invercraig, and we can row to the harbour.'

'Aye,' Jimmie muttered. He looked uncertainly towards the Invercraig side of the water where the whaler was berthed. What on earth had possessed him to sign on? He should have ignored Belle and gone back on his promise. But a promise was a promise and Jimmie knew he could not have gone back on his word.

He concentrated on the oars. In, out, lift and pull. The water sucked at them as he counted the strokes, and he could feel the sting of the spray on his cheeks and the taste of salt on his lips. They drew level with the island and both men concentrated on their oars, pulling hard to round the point and stay clear of the shore. The tide caught them, swinging the boat round and upriver. They let the current carry them until they were level with the harbour and then without a word they started to row again, each in unison with the other.

The three-masted whaling ship creaked and strained at its mooring as they rowed around it heading for the section of harbour where it was safe to tie up. The ship loomed over them and Jimmie was glad when they pulled clear.

Jimmie heaved his oar into the boat, as they neared the dock where several other small boats were moored, while James manoeuvred the boat closer.

'Be ready with the rope,' James said, while he stroked the water with his oar until the boat was almost touching the side of the quay.

Jimmie grabbed the iron ring protruding from the wall and quickly threaded the rope through, knotting it until it was secure. He grabbed the bundle containing his possessions, and keeping one hand against the quay wall stepped from boat to boat until he reached the steps carved into the quayside.

His father scrambled up the steps after him, and both men stood for a moment while they looked around. Jimmie's hand tightened on his bundle. He wasn't sure he liked so much noise and bustle. There seemed to be people everywhere. Men like himself with their bundles clutched to them. Other men were balancing barrels and sacks on their shoulders as they made their way towards the ship. Carts lined up with produce of all kinds. Cows and sheep tethered in pens, waiting their turn to board. Soaring over everything, the babble of tongues.

'Aye lad. It's not like Craigden now, is it.' James stroked his beard as he always did when he was troubled.

Jimmie forced a smile. He did not want his da to worry about him. 'I'll be all right, Da. It's a good ship, the *Eclipse*. They say they catch more whales than any other whaler, and that means a bigger share of the catch for the men. One voyage and I'll be able to get my own boat.'

'I hope so lad. I hope you won't be disappointed.'

'You'll look after Belle and Sarah for me. Won't you Da?'

'Don't you go worrying over Belle, lad. Me and Annie'll see she's all right.'

'Well, I'd better go now, Da.' Jimmie held out his hand and both men clasped each other's arm, hands on elbows.

James leaned towards Jimmie and threw his other arm

round his son's shoulders to clap him on the back. 'Take care, son,' he said, his voice strangely husky.

'I will, Da. I will.'

James turned and clambered back down the stone stairs. Reaching the bottom he stepped over the vessels moored there until he reached the rowboat. Jimmie felt suddenly desolate as James lifted his arm in a salute and turned away making ready to cast off.

Straightening his shoulders, Jimmie walked towards the ship. It was bigger than any boat he had previously sailed in, and it would travel a greater distance.

He'd heard tales from men who had sailed with the whalers, and of the strange white world they went to. Ice and snow, and freezing cold, and whales, larger than anything they had ever seen before. Jimmie experienced a surge of excitement that started in his stomach and ended up in his throat. His step quickened and his hand tightened on his bundle. Soon he would be able to recite his own tale of adventures in the Greenland seas.

'Come, Sarah. We'll walk to the river and watch your daddy's boat sail off to sea.' Belle held her hand out to Sarah. The child's eyes were dark and serious, but she put her hand in her mother's as she had been instructed. What a strange child she is, thought Belle. Still, she always does as she is told, so I suppose that's something.

Sarah's hand felt small and warm as it rested in her mother's grasp, and Belle felt an odd pull at her heart. It was funny, sometimes she felt she disliked the child and yet at other times there was this odd sensation, as if she was learning to love her.

Belle held her head high as she walked through the village, passing the fisherwomen sitting at their doors shelling mussels and gossiping between themselves. She knew they did not accept her, and she felt their eyes on her and heard their voices go quiet as she passed. She stared straight ahead, because she no longer cared what they thought of her.

The huddle of houses was soon left behind, and Belle pulled her shawl closer and caught her breath, as the April wind buffeted her. She had not walked to the mouth of the river since she had been frightened there by the minister, soon after her arrival in the village. She remembered his threats and the feeling of menace she had experienced as he'd stood watching her. The fear came bubbling up again but she closed her mind to it, because it was more important for her to be there when Jimmie's ship sailed. Besides, she was sure she could deal with the Reverend Murdo if he made his appearance.

The gravel crunched under her feet for there was no sand at this side of the river, only rocks, stones and gravel. Sometimes she missed having a beach to walk on, and the feel of sand between her toes. Her childhood memories from living in Invercraig included the sandy beach where children played and lovers courted. She looked at Sarah, trotting beside her. Sarah, who had been conceived among the sandy dunes, but who had never played on a sandy beach. But then, Sarah was a strange, serious child who never seemed to play in any case.

Belle stopped to look over the river towards Invercraig, but the island still blocked her view.

'Just a little bit further,' she said to Sarah, 'and then we'll be able to see Daddy's ship.'

She turned her face into the wind enjoying the sensation of it whipping through her hair. It instilled a feeling of abandonment within her and she had a sudden urge for Jimmie, for his touch on her skin, his lips on hers. She wanted to lie in his arms and allow him to love her. But he would be gone for many months. It was too late to say, don't go. Far too late.

Tears streamed down her face. She should not have asked him to go but what option did they have if they were to escape from the poverty of their situation. With a boat of his own Jimmie would be something in the village and she would have more status as the wife of a man who owned his own boat.

Belle perched herself on a rock at the river mouth. She remembered sitting on this self-same rock the last time she had been here. She had dangled her feet in the water while she watched for the fishing fleet to return. Now she took off her shoes and let her feet hang over the side. The coldness of the water made her gasp and she pulled her feet up to rest on a ledge where the spray merely tantalised her toes.

She reached over and pulled Sarah to her. The child was heavier than she thought and she almost dropped her. And for a moment she almost wanted to drop her, but she held Sarah firmly until she was sitting beside her. 'There's room for both of us on the rock,' she said, her eyes fixed on the ship moored at the other side of the river.

21

Ian lay on the cliff top and watched Belle. He had seen her walk through the village with Sarah, and he had followed them.

The first time he saw Belle, he had been with Jimmie. He'd known then that he wanted her, but he did not have a way with the girls like Jimmie did, and it was him she noticed. She had looked at his brother through half-closed eyes, as if she had not wanted him to know she was watching. But Jimmie knew. He always seemed to know when a girl was interested. As far as Ian was concerned, Belle didn't even seem to know he was there, and Ian would have died for her to look at him the way she looked at Jimmie.

Ian had taken the cliff-top path keeping pace with Belle as she walked along the shore. The path was rough, and several times a stone or some gravel would rattle down the cliff face, but Belle never looked up. He'd lost sight of her when he skirted the church and the manse, bending low so that the Reverend Murdo would not see him. He did not want any sermons from him. But now that he had reached the point where the river flowed into the sea and the cliffs turned to look seawards, he stopped and lay on his stomach to watch her.

He liked to see the wind catch her hair and blow it round her shoulders and face. She was so small and delicate he could almost imagine she would break if he caught hold of her. Ah, if only he could hold her. He glared across the water to Invercraig, where the whaler sat tied to the jetty, and then spat on the grass. I hope you never come back, Jimmie. I hope you rot in hell in the whalers' graveyard, then maybe I'll have a chance. Why should you get everything? It's always been the same all our lives, you're the favoured one, you're the lucky one. But what about me? Isn't it my turn now?

He rested his forehead on the grass and thought about Belle. He could almost see her capricious green eyes sparkle with invitation, but they had always sparkled at Jimmie and never at him.

Annie was shelling mussels when James returned from Invercraig. Her left hand plucked the mussel from the pail at her side while the knife in her right hand deftly split the mussel and scooped the flesh out into the basin on her knees, and with a flick of her fingers the empty shell was tossed into the growing pile of other empty shells. She could usually empty her mind while she performed this familiar task, but today it was troubled.

Her fingers flashed between pail, shell and knife as she watched James stride up the path from the river. Jimmie would be away then, away with the whalers. Away to that dangerous territory from where so many did not return. And if they did return they were changed, infected by the excitement of the whale chase and anxious to return to face the dangers again.

The clay pipe clamped between her teeth gave her no comfort as she sucked hard on the stem, for the wind had extinguished it some time before. Annie was used to the wind. She had lived most of her life in the fishing village and always proclaimed it would take more than a puff of wind to ruffle her. The only time she worried was if there was a gale and her men were at sea.

She removed the pipe from her mouth and tucked it into the pocket of her skirt. 'He's away then!' Her voice was flat and harsh. She did not look at James as she spoke. She could feel an unfamiliar prick at the back of her eyes and did not want to disgrace herself by shedding tears.

'Aye, lass. He's away, but the ship doesn't sail until the afternoon tide, mayhap we'll take a walk to the river mouth to see it sail.'

'You'll not be going to sea the day?' Annie's fingers were busy as they shelled, scooped and flicked.

'Aye, lass, but not till later, this morning's for you and me.'

Annie's fingers stopped working and she looked up. She could have sworn there was a sentimental note in James's voice, but his face was as expressionless as her voice had been when she'd spoken to him.

'You're a fine man, James Watt. I was lucky when you took me.'

'Nay, lass. I was the lucky one.' James stretched out his hand and stroked her hair. 'You haven't had an easy life. I wish it could have been better.'

'I wouldn't have wanted any other kind of life, James Watt.' Annie reached up and took her husband's hand in her own. 'Come away in now, and stop being daft. I'll get you a glass of ale.' She placed the basin of mussel flesh on the ground and laid her knife beside it. 'Jeannie can finish the shelling.'

22

The *Eclipse* creaked and strained at its mooring as if anxious to be at sea. The deck was only slightly higher than the jetty despite the size of the ship, for the tide was only just starting to rise as the sea flooded upriver towards the inland basin. Jimmie knew the ship would sit much higher in the water once the tide's task was complete, and then they would sail with the outgoing rush of water that would help them to clear the river in record time.

Making his way towards the whaler, shouldering through the crowd of traders and observers, he could not help but be impressed by the sheer size of the ship in comparison to the *Bonnie Annie*. Three masts soared upwards like trees reaching towards the sky. They were impressive as they stood in all their nakedness, Jimmie could only imagine what they must look like when they were clothed with sails.

The gang-plank vibrated to the thud of feet as a stream of men hefted the supplies aboard. Groups of men with bundles and sea-boxes stood at either side of the plank awaiting an opportune moment to board.

Jimmie stood watching the activity, unsure about the procedure for boarding. He had signed on earlier in the week at the harbour office of the owners and all they had said was to report this morning. He looked around him and noticed that some of the men seemed to be gravitating towards a table further up the jetty. He joined them and waited his turn.

The seaman standing behind the table licked the point of his pencil. 'Name?' he demanded.

'Jimmie Watt.'

'Ah. You'll be the greenman that's signed on for three voyages.' The seaman ticked a name on his list. 'Stand over there. You'll board once the provisions are on. Next?'

Jimmie's mouth opened but nothing came out. Three voyages? There had been a mistake surely, he had only signed on for one voyage. He waited until the next man had given his name and been ticked off the list, then stood in front of the table again.

'You still here?' The seaman glared at him. 'I told you to wait over there.'

'But there's been a mistake,' Jimmie explained. 'I only signed for one voyage.'

The seaman checked his list. 'Says three voyages here. Anyway, greenmen are never taken on for any less than three voyages, and you signed the articles, didn't you?'

Jimmie nodded, 'Aye, I signed.'

'Well that's that then. Three voyages it is. Stand over there now.'

Jimmie joined the group of men. Three voyages. He was sure he had only agreed to one voyage, but he had not read the paper he'd signed because his reading wasn't too good. He should have had Belle with him, she could read. Maybe the man in the office had mistaken what he had said, but it was too late now, if he'd signed for three voyages he would have to stick with his bargain. A man's word was his bond.

'You fell for it then?' The man next to him grinned. 'That's how they got me. Told me it was one voyage and got me to sign for three. Oldest trick in the book. Keep their finger over the three when they get you to sign the papers, and by the time you find out it's too late. Still, I haven't regretted it. It's been a good life. Good money too if you're lucky . . . Ben Stimson's the name. And you are?'

'Jimmie Watt.' A calloused hand gripped his and shook it hard.

'Pleased to meet you, Jimmie Watt. You stick by me and I'll see you're all right.'

Lachlan and Raven had reconciled their differences. Lachlan accepted the horse was his own master and no longer tried to impose his will. In response, Raven responded to Lachlan's gentler touch. The pair were now headed homewards after watching the *Eclipse* set sail.

'Lachlan, my boy,' his father had said while they breakfasted. 'I want you to go to Invercraig and keep an eye on my factor.'

Lachlan had paused while he decided between the kidneys and the herring. The serving spoon hovering over one silver dish, and then the other. He hated decisions, much preferring things to take their course. Sighing gently he spooned some of each onto his plate.

'Why would you want me to watch the factor?' he asked. 'Is he not honest?'

'If a man knows he is being watched he will be honest,' Sir Roderick answered, 'and I have no wish to pay for another man's pleasures.'

'How will I know if he is being dishonest?'

'You won't, but he will think you know and that is what matters.' Sir Roderick returned to the sideboard for another helping of fish.

Lachlan chewed slowly while he observed his father. 'What would you want me to do to convince the factor that I would know?'

'He will have a bill of lading which he has to check off as the supplies are delivered. You will be at his side while he does this and inspect the bill of lading when he is finished.'

'I won't know what I am inspecting.' Lachlan ate his last mouthful. The fish had been good. Maybe he would join his father and have some more.

'That won't matter. The important thing is just to give the impression you do understand.' Sir Roderick smiled at him. 'We have to protect our investments and I have a pretty big share in that whaler.'

Lachlan was in good spirits when he arrived at Invercraig harbour where the *Eclipse* sat at rest. He sat astride his horse watching the crowd and it seemed to him as if the whole town was there. Women in their fancy coloured dresses waiting to wave goodbye to their fathers, brothers or lovers. Suppliers and tradesmen of all sorts. Horses and carts queuing while they waited their turn to unload. Bags of flour, barrels of ale, boxes containing all sorts of supplies, and seamen waiting in groups to board the vessel that would carry them off to hunt the whale and provide much needed profits for his father to boost his fortunes.

Looking around, Lachlan was unable to see the factor anywhere. He tethered Raven to some railings at the rear of the harbour, well away from the jostling crowds, and made his way through to the table where the sailors seemed to be signing on.

'I'm looking for the factor, Wullie McPhee,' he said in what he hoped was a voice of authority.

The seaman was busy ticking names on a list. 'And who might it be that's looking for Wullie McPhee?' he enquired without looking up.

'Lachlan Craigallan, and I'll have less of your impudence,' Lachlan snapped. He was used to the independence of the fishermen at Craigden but not to the insolence he detected in this man's voice.

The seaman raised his head, 'Oh, it's yourself is it. Wullie's where he should be, at the top of the gangplank. Wouldn't have thought a toff like yourself would have wanted to go aboard, though.'

Lachlan turned towards the *Eclipse*. His father would not have put up with such insolence nor would the seaman have offered it to him, but he was at a loss about what to do or how to handle the situation.

The gangplank creaked and swayed as he climbed it and he had the horrible thought that he might fall over the side into the blackness of the water that sucked the boat forwards then spat it backwards after it struck the harbour wall.

Safely at the top he introduced himself to the factor. 'My father sent me to supervise the loading,' he explained.

'Och, I wondered what'd happened to the laird. He's usually here to inspect.' Wullie looked Lachlan up and down. 'So you're the laird's laddie are you. Well you'd better stand over there while the provisions are loaded. It's busy the now and we'll be going hell for leather until the loading's done.'

Lachlan tried to look knowledgeable and interested as Wullie counted, inspected, consulted his lists and ticked off the various items. But as the day wore on he found it difficult to stifle his yawns and his attention wandered. He surveyed the crowds looking for familiar faces but he had been away too long and they all looked like strangers. Some of the women were quite attractive, but no more than pretty. Certainly not worth the effort of trying to make their aquaintance.

He thought of Clarinda waiting for him in London. They had been promised to each other for the past four years but she seemed to be in no greater a hurry than he was to be wed. As he tried to visualize her cool beauty another face pushed its way into his mind. A face that was framed by a tumble of dark curls, a mouth that was full of invitation, and eyes the colour of the sea, as changeable as the weather.

This was foolishness, this girl was not for him. She had a husband who, by the look of him, was not going to let her out of his sight.

It was as he turned his attention back to the loading of the vessel that he caught sight of the girl's husband, waiting with the crew to board the ship.

Now, as he and Raven left the harbour he was deep in thought. He had waited until the ship sailed and there was no doubt about it, Jimmie had sailed with it. Maybe he would manage a little dalliance after all, before he returned to London.

23

Jimmie clambered down the ladder after Ben. The focsle was larger but more enclosed than he had expected. The swinging oil lamps cast weird shadows into the gloom and the sound of water lapping against the hull had a far off echo, as if the ship was detached from the water Jimmie knew it rested on.

When he sailed in the *Bonnie Annie*, Jimmie could always feel the wind in his hair and the spray on his cheeks. Never before had he felt so enclosed on a vessel, and he missed the sense of freedom and exhilaration that usually swept over him prior to sailing.

He threw his bundle of clothing onto one of the bunks that lined the interior of the focsle. This would be his quarters for the next six months so he had better get used to it.

'All hands on deck!' The call echoed down into the depths of the ship.

'We'd best get up top, lad.' Ben was already running towards the ladder.

Jimmie followed at a trot feeling the excitement start to well up in him again. It was time to sail.

'Stay close to me,' Ben muttered, 'and you won't go wrong.'

'Aye, that I will.' Jimmie was relieved to have Ben's example to follow. He did not want to seem ignorant in front of the whalers because he had never sailed in anything bigger than the *Bonnie Annie*. The sails he had rigged in the past had been small compared to those that were furled on the massive masts that towered above him, and casting off had been a simple procedure compared to what would be required for this vessel.

Men were already clustered round the capstan ready to wind up the anchor, while the mooring ropes were being loosened and thrown onto the deck.

'Man the sails!'

Ben pushed him forward. 'Best do this now coming out of harbour. Then you won't be afrighted in a storm. Just do what I do.'

The ratlines were not as formidable as they'd first appeared to be. Jimmie concentrated on moving his hands and feet up the rope rigging. They swayed with him as he climbed but as long as his grip was firm and sure he felt safe.

'You're doing fine.' The voice was level with his ear. Ben had moved from the ratlines to the yardarm – the massive wooden beam supporting the sails.

The rope rigging cut into Jimmie's hands as his grasp tightened. He hadn't noticed how Ben had transferred himself to the yard, but knew he would have to follow.

'Lean towards the yard and sling one arm over it . . . that's right. Now rest your body on it and put your other arm over . . . you're nearly there. Now what you do is move your feet to the footrope below the yard . . . see, that was easy, wasn't it?' Ben grinned at him. 'Knew you could do it. You have the look of a born seaman.'

Jimmie clung to the yard. The deck was far below and he had no wish to fall.

Ben started to move along the yard. 'Just one foot at a time. Slide along. You'll be fine. You're past the worst.'

Jimmie was not so sure, but he did as Ben instructed and they were soon as far along the yard as it was possible to go.

'Now wait for the signal and when it comes loosen the ropes and let the sail go. Keep your body pressed to the yard and you'll be fine.'

The man who had followed Jimmie along the yard, shouted, 'First time aloft?'

'Aye,' replied Jimmie. He looked around him. There seemed to be men all over the rigging.

'Set the mainsails.' The cry sounded from the deck, and the sails dropped and swelled as the boat moved down the river.

'Set the topsails.'

'Set the gallants.'

The ship swayed and rolled as the men started to move back along the yard. Invercraig was left behind and Jimmie could see the cottages of Craigden at the other side of the river. Belle would be there watching the ship sail. How proud she would be if she could see him now.

The tide was high when James and Annie left the house to walk to the river mouth. Annie was as tall as James and had a stride that matched his. She would have liked it if he had taken her hand in his the way she had seen Jimmie do with Belle, but that was daft. Such things were for the night and the privacy of their own bed.

'Can I come too, Ma?' Jeannie came running behind them, her hair whipping in an untidy mess round her face. 'Davie and Angus went to Invercraig to see the ship away but they wouldn't take me and I wanted to see it too.'

'You've finished the mussels, have you?'

'Aye, Ma. They're all done.'

Annie nodded her head with satisfaction. She was a good lass, Jeannie. A good worker. Another two or three years and she would be able to go off to the market or round the farms with her own creels instead of looking after Sarah so Belle could go. Jeannie would do better than Belle, Annie was sure of that.

Jeannie ran on in front, stopping every now and then to skim a pebble across the water, or to take aim at a nearby seagull.

Annie smiled at James. 'Jeannie's turning out just fine.'

James grunted in reply but she could tell he felt the same. Sometimes it was as if their thoughts and feelings were tied together, as if each was one half of a whole. On an impulse she reached out and clasped his hand. He turned to look at her and she knew he was surprised by the sudden show of affection. His grey beard twitched and his eyes creased at the corners as he smiled at her. The two then walked on in silence.

Annie was not sure which of them she saw first, Ian on the cliff top or Belle sitting on the rock at the mouth of the river. She frowned. She had seen the way Ian looked at Belle, just as she'd seen the antagonism between Jimmie and Ian escalate. She hoped Ian wouldn't make trouble now Jimmie was gone, maybe she'd better have a word with him. He had been walking out with Ellen Bruce and it was time they were thinking about getting wed.

Sarah had spotted Jeannie and came running to meet her. 'Jeannie! Jeannie!' she screamed with delight.

Jeannie bent down and hugged Sarah. They could almost have been sisters, Annie thought.

Belle stood up and waited until they reached her. 'We've been waiting for the ship to sail,' she said, her eyes filling with tears and her body starting to shake.

Annie felt a sudden surge of emotion. Belle was little more than a child herself, 'Have you been here all morning?' she asked.

Belle nodded mutely.

'Poor child. You're frozen. Here have my shawl,' and so saying Annie removed her shawl and wrapped it round Belle's shoulders.

'The ship, Ma. The ship. It's sailing.' Jeannie swung Sarah round. 'Look Sarah that's your da's ship. He's away to hunt the whales.'

Annie watched the large ship slide down the river and take to the open sea. Her eldest son was on board, the first to leave the family to seek his fortune in far off waters. Her arm tightened on Belle's shoulder. Jimmie had left them with a responsibility and she was determined he would not be disappointed.

'Come away home, Belle. It's time you and me were friends.'

The ship's sails fluttered on the horizon like far away seagulls as the family made their way back to Craigden.

24

The *Bonnie Annie* left the river for the fishing grounds not long after the *Eclipse* sailed, although the whaler was long since out of sight.

'We'll not be back until morning,' James said as Annie carried him to the boat. 'That'll give you an early start for the Invercraig market.'

'Aye,' Annie replied. 'I've asked Belle to stay over tonight so she can start her round at the same time.'

'That's my lass. I knew you'd take to her sooner or later.'

Annie turned to wade back to the shore. She wasn't sure about that. She had tried hard to like Belle, but there was just something about her. Well maybe this time. Belle had seemed so vulnerable when they'd been at the river mouth, but when Annie had put her arm round her the girl had seemed to draw back a little before succumbing to the gesture.

There was plenty to do when Annie returned home but she could not help noticing that Belle just seemed to mope around while Jeannie looked after Sarah. She pushed down her irritation, the girl was just missing Jimmie, that was all.

After supper Jeannie and Sarah bedded down on the truckle bed. The larger girl tucking her arm firmly around the smaller one so she would not fall out. Davie climbed up to the net loft as usual while Annie and Belle shared the alcove bed.

Annie was conscious of Belle's slight frame lying next to her and could not help thinking that she would have preferred it to be James who lay there. She hadn't bothered to pull the curtains shut, which would have sealed the bed off from the room, and now she watched the flicker of the firelight as she lay, back to back with Belle, trying to sleep.

She rose the next morning, unrefreshed. After lighting the fire and making the oatmeal porridge, she served it in the wooden bowls to a sleepy-eyed Davie, a thoughtful Belle, and the two girls who had risen before Annie and whose laughter had wakened the whole household.

'Will you two scallywags sit at peace and eat your porridge.' Annie couldn't help smiling at their exuberance as she made them sit at the table.

The two girls giggled as they ate, and even Davie managed to wake up enough to share in their laughter. However, Belle seemed impervious as she splashed her face with cold water from the bucket that Annie kept in the room.

'You'd better get your porridge, Belle,' Annie said, trying hard to keep the pleasant tone in her voice. 'The tide's on the turn and that means the boats will soon be back, and we'll have work to do.'

Jeannie's spoon rattled off her bowl as she scraped the last mouthful of porridge out of it. 'Can Sarah and I go down to the riverside to watch for the boats, Ma? We'll come back and let you know as soon as we see them.'

'Aye, I suppose so,' Annie replied, 'but you'd better ask Belle if Sarah can go.'

'Can she, Belle? Please say she can,' Jeannie pleaded. 'I'll look after her. I'll see she doesn't fall in.'

Belle dried her face on the edge of her skirt. 'Mind and look after her then,' was all she said before seating herself at the table.

The two girls scrambled off their stools and ran towards the door, Jeannie, grabbing Sarah's hand as they ran, shouted over her shoulder, 'You coming too, Davie?'

Davie's bowl was empty, his elbows on the table and his chin in his hands. 'Ma,' he said.

'Yes, Davie lad? Is it more porridge you're wanting?'

'No . . . aye, that as well.' Davie looked up at his mother.

'What is it, Davie?' Annie stopped spooning porridge into his bowl. It was not like Davie to be so hesitant.

'I want to go to the fishing with Da. Angus got to go when he was fifteen, and I'm sixteen now. You just won't let me go. Why, Ma?' Davie stopped for breath. 'The *Bonnie Annie*'s a man short now with Jimmie gone. Da'll need me. I could be a scum boy first and I'd learn quick. Please, Ma? Please?'

Annie put the pot on the table. Davie, her Davie. The last of her sons. Fear of the sea was part of her existence. She lived with it every day of her life. She dreaded the storms. Her heart beat fast when it was time for the boats to return and the *Bonnie Annie* was not in sight. She often thought of James lying in a watery grave with his sons for company. Cradle of the deep they called it because so many fishermen slept their last sleep in its depths. Old legends claimed that was why the sea was salty because there were so many women's tears shed over it. And now Davie wanted to be with his father on the *Bonnie Annie*. All her men in one boat.

'Aye, maybe it's time,' was all she said. The lump in her throat would not allow her to say anything else.

'Thanks, Ma,' and so saying Davie raced out of the door after the girls, leaving the bowl of porridge uneaten on the table.

Annie slumped onto her chair by the fire and pulled her pipe out of her pocket. She stroked its bowl and gazed absently into the flames as they spurted and flickered, seeming to echo the turmoil of her thoughts. She had forgotten Belle was there and only faintly heard the girl's voice, as if it was coming from a distance.

'Are you all right, Annie. You look a bit queer.'

'Aye, I'm fine, lass. Just having a wee rest before we go to the boats and take the fish to market.' Annie did not stop to think how odd this sounded for she never rested and never seemed to need to rest.

25

Jeannie's grasp on her hand was warm and firm, and Sarah felt safe. She ran alongside the older girl, determined to keep up with her and felt happy because she was with Jeannie whom she adored.

The morning air felt sharp and Sarah caught her breath, but still she ran on because she did not want to slow Jeannie down. The path was rough under her feet and she concentrated on not stumbling.

Little plumes of smoke trickled out of the cottage chimneys, scenting the air with the faintest aroma of burning. Doors opened to welcome daylight into countless gloomy rooms, and there was the hum of voices and the clattering sound of activity as the village awoke.

Davie caught up with the two girls. 'You might have waited,' he grumbled.

'Ach. You were taking too long.'

Jeannie slowed down a little when they reached the river bank where the sea had started its daily run up to the inland basin. Sarah was glad, for her legs were starting to wobble.

'We'll wait here,' Jeannie said. 'Sit you down, Sarah, and look out to sea. Soon you'll see Da's boat coming home.'

Davie scrambled down the river bank until he stood on the pebbles of the foreshore. He was a tall, gangly lad, not yet reached manhood, although he was now sixteen.

He bent to pick up a stone and sent it skimming over the water.

Jeannie joined him and Sarah scrambled after her. She was not going to let Jeannie out of her sight. She wanted to stay with her forever.

'Can I try to skim a stone?' Sarah bent down, picked up a pebble and threw it. It plopped into the water and sank.

'Never mind,' Jeannie said. 'It's only Davie can make a stone bounce when the river's running so fast. Even I can't do it.' She threw a stone into the water and it too plopped and sank.

Davie had stopped skimming stones and now stood, his hand shading his eyes as he looked out to sea. 'I can see sails. You'd better run and tell Ma the boats are coming.'

'You mind Sarah then,' Jeannie said, 'and don't let her fall in.' She turned and sprinted towards the cottage.

Sarah watched her go. She hadn't wanted Jeannie to leave her, but she did not seem to have any choice but to stay. She frowned at Davie. He was so big, but he was kind too. Not like her other uncles who teased her and sometimes made her feel like crying. Only she did not cry and would not cry. What was the use in that?

The village women were starting to gather by the time Jeannie returned and soon they were joined by Annie and Belle. The women's eyes were turned seawards and they chatted as they waited.

As the boats came nearer the women started to prepare. Creels and murlins were stacked against the river bank in readiness to pack the fish and take them to market. Hems of skirts were lifted and tucked into waistbands. Shoes were kicked off as they prepared to enter the water to pull the boats in and help their men ashore.

Sarah watched, her eyes wide. The first boat arrived and Annie splashed out to meet it while her ma just stood and waited. She could not understand why her ma never waded into the water but she did not dare ask.

When the boats were beached the business of sorting out the fish started. Creels were filled and strapped on the women's backs while the smaller murlins were balanced on each hip, the straps that held them criss-crossing round the women's waists.

'That's it then,' Annie turned to Jeannie. 'You and Sarah can take our share of the fish home. Davie, make sure you help them. Belle, you know your round. The big house first, then the farm, and then the manse. I'll see to the Invercraig market. I should get good sales there because the fish have been scarce this year.'

Annie set off at a trot while Belle followed at a more leisurely pace.

'Why is Granma running?' Sarah wanted to know.

'It's so she'll get to the market early. The sooner she gets there, the more she'll sell.' Jeannie was already piling fish in a basket. 'Come and help me, Sarah. The fish'll not bite you.'

Sarah lifted one of the fish. It felt cold and slimy and she almost dropped it. But Jeannie was handling them confidently, as if it was the most natural thing to do, so Sarah clasped the fish with both her hands and placed it in the basket. She turned to lift another one. They weren't so bad to touch, not really.

'Ma's not running,' she stated matter of factly.

'That's because she's not going to the market. She's got her round. She'll get rid of her fish no matter what time she gets there.'

Sarah watched the receding figures and turned back to the fish. She felt important. She was helping Jeannie. She was working.

26

Lachlan had not been sleeping well since his return home. Tossing and turning he dreamt of Clarinda with her maddeningly aloof ways, but then she changed into the fisher girl with the strange inviting eyes. He reached out his arms towards her but touched nothing and felt nothing, except pillows and sheets.

Sleep eluded him after that and now he lay in the early morning dawn, awake and yet not awake. His bones ached and try as he would he found it impossible to be comfortable. He was loath to leave the warmth of his bed but knew that he would experience no relief from his discomfort until he did so.

The room was chilly, and he shivered as he pulled his breeches on. He remembered Clarinda's refusal to come with him.

'It's far too early in the year. It will be cold and there is no social life to speak of. You may give my regards to your parents but tell them I prefer to remain in London.'

The decision was made. Clarinda stayed in London and Lachlan travelled north.

He wondered if Clarinda thought he might be disappointed at her refusal to come home with him and wondered if she missed him. He wondered if she loved him at all. They had been engaged to be married for four years, but nothing seemed to progress beyond that. She was no more in a hurry than he was. But now he had started to question within himself whether she would ever make that final commitment and if she did, would he be ready.

London was no place to try to think, there were too many activities and distractions. So, he had returned home to the peace and quiet of his childhood surroundings. Here he would make his decision and return to London to either marry Clarinda or beg for his release.

There was only the hum of distant activity from the kitchens as he left the house and stepped onto the grass. It was damp with early morning dew, and his feet hardly made an impression as the grass sprang back into place. He entered the wooded area where the clamour of birds grew louder and the smell of leaves and earth seemed overpowering. He breathed deeply. He had not realised how much he had missed the country.

That was one of the many differences between himself and Clarinda. She had no love for the countryside and no interest in the creatures or the land, for her interests were mainly in London, that great heartless city that was as cold and emotionless as Clarinda.

He could not understand why she disliked the country so much. What kind of person could not appreciate the warmth and the vibrancy of nature and appreciate that the land was the heart of everything?

Leaves brushed his face as the tree branches reached towards him, welcoming him home. Crickets chirruped in the bushes, and the undergrowth rustled as the invisible inhabitants of the wood fled from his approach. He remembered catching a cricket and keeping it in a box, but it had died and he had been overcome with grief. Ever since that time he had disliked caging any living thing. Maybe that was why he had avoided the final commitment to Clarinda, afraid he would be imprisoned in marriage and something inside him would die.

The track, unused since he'd left for London, had become overgrown. He remembered running down this very path, his need for Elsie burning within him. But now grass and weeds threatened to obliterate the narrow track, just as Elsie had been eradicated from his life. He wondered where she was now and whether she had managed to keep the child she'd been carrying. His child. A momentary feeling of guilt touched him, but he shrugged it off. It was not his fault he was the laird's son. If he had been a farm worker he would have married her, but girls like Elsie were not for him. He was destined for Clarinda.

Rhododendron bushes separated the wood from the back road that led up to the farm. He lifted aside the branch of one of them and crept into the shade of the bush. The branches formed a leafy tunnel that opened out into a small clearing, cool, shaded and private. It was here that he had made love to Elsie, each exploring the other with increasing passion, protected from prying eyes by the bushes.

He lay down on the mossy bed in the centre of the bush and thought of what had been and what might have been.

Belle meandered up the back drive towards the big house. It was early and she was in no hurry, besides the creels were easier to carry when she took her time.

The morning was calm and clear and Belle thought of Jimmie, sailing in a big ship with white sails towards the whaling grounds. It was at times like this that she wished she was a man and able to do what men did. She longed for adventure instead of having to sell fish in order to make a few pennies. She would not have needed any urging to go off whaling. Not like Jimmie whose heart was in the smaller boats and his home and child. Her face became troubled as she thought of Sarah, for sometimes Jimmie seemed to be fonder of the child than he was of her.

Horses neighed softly as she passed the stables in the courtyard but, apart from the clatter of pails somewhere inside, no one was to be seen. She was glad. She did not like old Hamish, the coachman, and the stable lads often shouted rude remarks to her.

She jangled the bell pull at the back door and waited until someone came. Jeannie usually marched straight in but Belle did not think that Mrs Ross would stand for her doing that, for the old housekeeper had made it obvious to Belle that she did not like her.

'Well, don't just stand there, girl. Come inside.'

Belle followed Mrs Ross down the corridor and into the

kitchen.

'Let's see the fish then.' Mrs Ross held up first one fish then the other. 'I've seen better. Are you sure you came to me first?'

'I always come here first.' Belle glared at Mrs Ross. 'The fish have been scarce, it's the best you'll get at this time of year.'

Mrs Ross stiffened and her face turned white with annoyance. 'You'd sell more fish if you were less impudent,' she snapped, and selecting some of the largest fish she slapped them down on the kitchen table.

Belle laughed softly as she left the kitchen. Mrs Ross had been so annoyed she had turned her back and had not noticed one of the maids slipping a biscuit into Belle's hand as she left.

She nibbled the sweet biscuit as she strolled through the courtyard, it made a nice change from Annie's oatmeal bannocks. The coach-house door was open and Belle could see Hamish polishing one of the carriages.

'It's a lovely morning, Hamish,' she called out.

Hamish stopped and looked up in surprise. 'What's so lovely about it,' he grumbled, but she could see he was pleased she had spoken to him.

Reaching the back road she turned in the direction of the farm. She always looked forward to taking her fish there, for Mrs McKenzie, the farmer's wife, was pleasant and always gave her a tankard of milk and a chunk of home-made bread. Sometimes she spoke of her daughter, saying that Belle reminded her of happier times and that if her Elsie'd had a man like Belle's Jimmie, she wouldn't have suffered her misfortune.

'Be thankful for your Jimmie,' she'd say. 'As long as he's with you no harm will come to you.' Belle could not imagine what harm could come to her so she'd smile and nod.

Belle hummed to herself as she walked. The creels were lighter since she'd left the big house, although since she had become accustomed to carrying them she did not mind their weight. Just as well, she supposed, because she would probably get some potatoes and vegetables from Mrs McKenzie. She never left the farm with her creels empty.

Belle quickened her step. She was looking forward to a gossip with Mrs McKenzie and could almost taste the milk, still warm from the milking.

27

Lachlan lay beneath the rhododendron bush thinking of Clarinda, although it made him confused and angry because he could not decide whether he wanted her or not. If only she was more like Elsie who had been soft and loving. In his imagination Clarinda responded to him with a passion that belied her coldness, but he despaired of that ever happening.

He was not sure if it was part of his dream but he could hear a girl humming. Elsie used to hum when she was happy, but it couldn't be her. The humming grew nearer, so he crawled out from under the bush and, skirting its edge, came out onto the lane.

The girl's skirts swayed as she walked up the lane and he caught his breath as he recognised her. However, as soon as she saw him, she stopped. He could almost feel the tension crackle as she stood there, legs spread and the creels resting on each hip. She had the startled look of a rabbit caught away from its burrow, not knowing whether to stay or run.

The silence seemed endless. Even the birds were quiet, as if holding their breath while they waited to see what happened. Lachlan searched his mind for something intelligent to say that would not frighten her away.

She turned her eyes from his and studied her toe while it traced patterns in the dust of the lane. Lachlan felt she was poised for flight. He had to break the silence.

'I say. I'm sorry if I frightened you,' he said. The words hung in the air between them, somehow seeming less than effective.

She looked up, studying him. And after what seemed to be an eternity, she smiled. She seemed to have made up her mind that he was harmless. 'I'm not frightened, sir,' she said, 'just startled.'

Her voice was deeper than he expected with a throaty quality that excited him. He had an urge to pull her into the bush and make love to her there and then, but was afraid. This was no maidservant who would giggle and succumb to him immediately. He had to be careful.

'I had intended to walk up to the moor. There's a fine set of standing stones there.' Lachlan had not walked to the moor for years but it seemed to be a good idea and would give him the excuse to walk with her. 'Perhaps I could accompany you as far as the farm. It is the farm you're heading for, is it not?'

She looked sideways at him. 'If that is your wish, sir.'

She had hesitated slightly over the 'sir,' and Lachlan was not sure if she was mocking him or tempting him.

'If we are to walk together you may call me Lachlan,' he looked away from her, uncertain of her reaction.

'If that is your wish, Lachlan,' she repeated softly.

'And pray, what shall I call you?' he asked.

'My name is Belle . . . Lachlan,' her words seemed to caress him.

'Belle,' he echoed. 'That is a lovely name for someone as beautiful as yourself.'

Lachlan. His name was Lachlan. Belle had known from that very first day he was attracted to her. Just as she had known they were destined to meet and, dare she think it, love each other. It was fate. It just had to be fate.

It was obvious from his reaction to her that he expected her to be modest so she kept her eyes lowered and her voice respectful. When all the time her body was crying out to him. Take me. Hold me.

Somehow she knew that if she said one word of invitation he would respond to it. She could almost smell his desire for her. But if she bided her time she might get the dream, the silks and the satins, the nice house with servants to wait on her, a horse and carriage, like the one she had seen in the courtyard. Everything she had ever dreamed.

'Ah, Belle,' Jimmie's voice sighed through her mind. 'Always wanting what you don't have. But when I come home from the whaling you'll have it all.'

Belle's footsteps faltered for a moment. She was fond of Jimmie and he loved her, but it did not compare to the desire she felt for this tall young man who was now walking by her side on the dusty lane. Jimmie was salt, but Lachlan was wine.

'Are you tired?' Lachlan was looking at her with concern and Belle realised she had stopped walking. He put out his hand and gripped her arm.

'No. Not really. I was only thinking.' Belle, conscious of the heat of his fingers, realized she was trembling. She gazed into his face and swayed towards him. His soft brown eyes, like a doe's, reflected concern for her.

'You're trembling.' He traced a finger across her brow and down her cheek, sending a delicious shiver coursing through her. 'Are you sure you feel well? You're so warm.'

Belle felt as if she was burning up. The slow fire that had started in her stomach now pulsed through her with an intensity that threatened to consume her completely. Always her body let her down. It had been the same when she had first met Jimmie, the desire had built up so quickly it had frightened her, although Jimmie had always thought that he had been the one to seduce her. She could not let it get out of control this time, not now, not here, not in the middle of a dusty road with the farm just round the next bend.

'I'm fine,' she lied. 'The road is rough and I stumbled slightly.' Detaching herself from Lachlan's grip she continued walking up the road towards the farm.

They walked in a pulsating silence until they reached the junction where the road divided. One fork leading to the farm and the other to the moor.

'Come with me to the moor, Belle,' Lachlan gazed at her. 'You can see all around the countryside and out to sea from the top.'

'I'm sorry. I have to sell my fish. They'll be waiting, you see.' Belle bit her lip. She wanted to go with him, but there was no way round it, she had to go to the farm. 'Maybe another time.'

'After the farm, come with me. You won't regret it.'

'I don't know.' Belle turned down the farm road. Her thoughts were in turmoil, churning round and round. She daren't look at him again or she would drop her creels and run to him.

'I'll wait at the standing stones. In case you change your mind. Just follow the road to the top.' Lachlan was already striding up the lane.

28

Lachlan frowned to himself as he strode towards the moor. She had responded to him. He had felt it. He could not be mistaken. So why hadn't she come with him?

If she had been one of the farm girls she would have been rolling in the hedge with him within a few minutes, however the fisher folk were different from their farm neighbours. They were a proud lot, and the girls didn't usually share their charms with anyone other than their own kind.

Many a time he had fancied a little dalliance with one of those tall, proud women, but had always been rebuffed. Belle was different though, she was small and dainty, and he could sense the fiery nature and the smouldering promise that lay behind her eyes. She just needed awakening and he was sure he could kindle those dormant passions.

The road narrowed to a path as Lachlan climbed upwards to the rise of the moor. The standing stones were a familiar landmark, a circle of large oblong boulders marking some pagan ceremonial site. Lachlan had always felt an affinity for them. They seemed to release him and confirm his baser, heathen instincts, and he could feel at one with the earth here. He didn't have to be someone he did not want to be.

The turf was springy and soft under his feet as he left the path and approached the circle. He stood for a moment, his hands flat on one of the boulders, making his communion with the elements. Then resting his forehead on the cool stone he looked downwards to the farm. Life went on as usual. The farmer was following his plough in one of the fields followed by a flock of birds as the earth was turned. Belle was probably inside the farmhouse gossiping with the farmer's wife, and smiling and laughing while she handled her fish and struck her bargain. Her left cheek dimpled when she smiled and her eyes lit up. He groaned to himself because his need for her was so great.

He slid to the ground and sat with his back resting on the stone. There was a good view of the farm and he would be able to see her leave. She would turn either to the left or right. If she turned right it would mean she was not coming to him. But if she turned left it would be a signal that she wanted him as much as he wanted her.

The metal jug rattled off the side of the pail as Mrs McKenzie scooped up a measure of milk. 'Here lass, it's just fresh from the cow,' she said to Belle as she poured it into the tankard. 'No doubt you'll have a fine thirst and hunger after walking up from Craigden.'

The hunger Belle felt was for neither food nor drink but she was not going to admit this to the farmer's wife. 'Aye, that's right,' she said, grasping the tankard with both hands.

The smell of fresh baked bread permeated the kitchen as the older woman sawed a piece from the loaf she had just taken from the oven. She laid it on the wooden table in front of Belle. 'Eat up, lass. You could do with some flesh on your bones. There's nothing of you.'

'Thanks.' Belle pulled a chunk from the bread in front of her and placed it in her mouth. She was hungry after all and she chewed appreciatively, washing it down with a swallow of the warm milk.

'Tell me about Jimmie, then.' Mrs McKenzie sat down opposite her. 'He's off to the whaling, I heard.'

'Aye, he left yesterday.' Belle stopped chewing. 'How did you know?'

'Ah, there's not much as goes past me,' Mrs McKenzie's sharp blue eyes twinkled.

Belle felt suddenly uncomfortable, imagining the woman could read what was in her mind and see what was in her soul. She shrugged off the feeling. No one could see what was in her soul or know the dark secrets hidden away that even Belle no longer thought about. All that was in the past, and it was a past she would never reveal.

'This bread is good,' she said. 'I always look forward to your baking.' She gazed out of the open door towards the fields. 'Sometimes I wish my Jimmie was a farmer instead of a fisher. I might have had a house and kitchen like this and have been able to bake bread and keep cows.'

'Aye, lass, but like as not you wouldn't have been any happier. You have a good, hard-working man and don't you be forgetting it. He's maybe away to the whaling just now, but he'll be back and looking to you for comfort. Seems to me he'll deserve all the loving you can give him.'

Belle glanced suspiciously at the older woman. 'What do you mean? Of course I'll be waiting for him, and he knows it. Why would it be any other way?'

Mrs McKenzie drummed her fingers on the table and her eyes looked troubled. 'I didn't mean anything, lass. It's just that I can't help thinking about my Elsie and how she was tempted off the straight and narrow. No good comes of hankering after someone who's not of your own class. Believe me I know.' She stood up and started to clear away the plates and tankards. 'Well, some of us have work to do, so I'll bid you goodbye.'

Outside the door Belle pondered on Mrs McKenzie's words. Had she seen Belle and Lachlan walking up the lane together, and were her words meant to be a warning? Or was she simply mourning her lost daughter?

Belle walked slowly towards the fork in the lane and hesitated with her hand on the fence post. She looked back towards the farm house but no one was in sight. Tracing her toe in the dust of the lane she considered which way she should turn. Right towards the manse to sell her fish, towards the safety of the known, towards doing what was right, towards duty and loyalty to her man and family. Or left towards the moor, towards Lachlan, towards the unknown, towards adventure, towards ecstasy.

29

Sadness clouded Mary McKenzie's eyes as she watched Belle stop at the end of the farm track, and it was as much as she could do to prevent herself from running after the girl. She mouthed the words, 'Don't do it,' but no sound came out.

Visions of Elsie floated through her mind. Elsie, so full of life, always laughing. Elsie walking up the lane with the laird's son, just as she had seen Belle walking up the lane with him before she came to the farm with her fish. Elsie running up towards the moor to meet him just as she knew Belle would do.

Elsie had been so sure the lad would stand by her. 'He loves me,' she'd told her mum, but that had not saved her from the sinner's stool at the Kirk.

'He won't stand up to his father,' she had said later. 'They've given me money to go away,' and so Elsie had gone.

'No good will come of it, lass,' Mary McKenzie whispered as she watched Belle turn towards the moor. 'Your Jimmie's worth ten of him despite his fine clothes and fancy ways.'

She turned back into the kitchen and, sitting on a stool, buried her face in her apron and sobbed.

The wind fingered Belle's hair and it streamed behind her as she sped up the lane towards the moor. There were no trees or bushes bordering this part of the lane and no soft rustlings and birdsong. The wind whispered through the grass as if it had a secret to tell her, and rabbits showed her their tails. Belle was in too much of a hurry to notice.

Oblivious to the roughness of the road and the stones that scattered as her feet struck them, she could only think of Lachlan waiting for her.

Many thoughts had gone through Belle's mind as she'd stood at the end of the farm track making up her mind. The main one was her love for Jimmie but that was a different kind of love and did not give her the feeling of excitement she experienced when she thought of Lachlan.

She thought of Jimmie's large, gentle hands and how it felt when he caressed her with them. Then she imagined Lachlan's hands on her body and hair, and shuddered with the emotion it aroused. It was that thought which turned her towards the moor.

Jimmie's image receded in her mind until it was as if he had never existed. She could not remember what he looked like. There was only Lachlan.

The stone circle was larger than Belle had pictured it. Boulders rose upwards to the sky casting long, brooding shadows on the grass, while the place looked as if it had never seen another human being. Belle was reluctant to step off the path. A sense of magic pervaded the scene, a hint of long past rituals, and she knew instinctively that once she stepped onto the grass her life would never be the same again.

Belle hesitated. The creels balanced on her hips suddenly felt heavy reminding her of her responsibilities. Her body sagged as if under a great weight and she turned to face towards the sea and the village that sheltered unseen below the cliff. She knew she had to return and that she must not take that step onto the grass.

The stone circle was no longer deserted. Lachlan stood up as if emerging from the earth, and Belle stepped onto the grass.

Lachlan watched Belle as she hesitated, and closing his eyes he willed her to come to him. He could not lose her now when he almost had her.

She seemed to be in a trance as she walked towards him. Coming to a stop she stood, her hands resting on her creels and her eyes studying his face. Her striped skirts still swung slightly, brushing against her bare legs. She appeared to be waiting for something, a signal, a touch, a word. He was not sure what.

He watched her, wanting her so badly it hurt.

'Unstrap your creels.' His tongue clung to the roof of his mouth making his voice thick and rough. He watched her hands fumble with the fastenings, willing her to hurry but knowing she could not because her hands were shaking too much.

She looked up at him and he could almost swear there were tears in her eyes. 'Let me help,' he muttered as he reached over to pull at the straps. Fish scattered on the ground as the creels fell away but she did not seem to notice. His hand closed over the softness of her wrist and he heard her give an involuntary gasp as she leaned towards him. He was so close to her he could smell the sweetness of her breath and see the green flecks in her eyes.

Placing his hand on the softness of her face he caressed it, his fingers tracing the line of her cheek and then down over her mouth. Her lips were warm and slightly moist, moving to meet his hand as she lifted her head towards his touch. Drawing her behind the boulder he pulled her to him with his other arm. He could feel the slightest resistance but when he bent to kiss her he did not find her lips unwilling.

Glancing quickly around, he pulled her towards the central stone. A large flat slab that might have been a table or an altar. He pushed her against it so that her back was arched over the stone, and raised her skirts over her waist. She wore no drawers and this enflamed him even more, so that the pressure within his own tight trousers was too much to bear and he had to loosen the buttons on his front flap until he was fully exposed.

Feverishly his hands explored her belly and thighs, stroking, poking and prodding, and finally prising her open, for the final relief of losing himself within her. As he thrust fiercely with his loins he entwined the fingers of one hand in her hair and tugged her head back, while at the same time he bared her breasts with his other hand until he could kiss and suck at her.

Her eyes darkened and her cheeks flushed, but he no longer saw her. All he could see was Clarinda's fair beauty and her supercilious smile. He pounded harder. He would show her he was a man, not the nincompoop she thought he was, and he thrust harder and harder, enjoying the hurt he was subjecting her to.

With a final shudder he was still, and raising his face to hers he could see a tear trickle from the corner of her eye. He stroked it away with his finger. She really was the most unusual and beautiful girl he had ever seen, with her long brown curls and those glorious greeny-brown eyes. It was a pity she was not from his own class, for he could easily give up Clarinda in favour of her.

He raised himself from her and watched as she straightened her skirt and fastened her bodice. Her eyes were downcast and he could not tell what she was thinking. Perhaps he had hurt her. He hadn't meant to, but for some strange reason he had been unable to forget Clarinda, even when he was making love to Belle. 'I have to leave now,' he heard himself say, 'but we will meet again, you and I. You would like that, wouldn't you?' and with that he straightened, fastened his trousers, dusted himself down, and left.

30

Belle, still dazed from the encounter, felt flattered that he was attracted to her. She had expected a little romantic dalliance but what she had not expected was the violence of his lovemaking or the passion it had aroused in her.

She shook down her skirts. She could still smell the maleness of him and feel the stickiness of him and she wondered if her gait would reflect the pain she felt.

He had left so suddenly. 'It's better I go first,' he'd said. 'We mustn't be seen.'

The isolation of the moors engulfed her and she felt more alone than before. The sun slipped behind a cloud and the tall boulders surrounding her projected a menace that had not been there before. The sacrificial slab in the middle, where she had given her all to Lachlan, filled her with foreboding. It was as if she had been part of some pagan ceremony. She half expected to hear chanting and see white clad priests appear to claim her soul.

The stone circle loomed over her and closed in around her. Belle knew she had to escape it and, gathering her skirts up, she ran. Once outside the circle she felt safe and she looked around for her creels. There would still be time to finish her round.

Now that Belle had left the silence of the circle the raucous screams of birds, squabbling around the creels, filled her ears. She ran towards them flapping her arms and shouting. Clouds of gulls rose in a flurry of wings and squalls as if they were mocking her with their cries of 'Too late, too late.' Sinking to her knees she looked in dismay at her empty baskets. The fish were gone. However, the gulls had not found the vegetables to their taste and they had scattered these over the grass.

Belle gathered up the turnips and potatoes Mrs McKenzie had given her, placing them in the creels which she strapped on with shaking fingers. There would be no fish for the minister today. Likely he would complain and then she would have to think of what to tell Annie.

The road down from the moor was longer than she remembered and there was no Lachlan at the end of it. He had disappeared just as suddenly as he had come to her and she remembered all the stories she'd heard of how he seduced country girls and left them with child.

She stopped and leaned on a fence. Had he left her with his child? She shrugged the thought away. It was not as easy as that. After all she and Jimmie been trying for a son for the past three years, and nothing had come of it.

She determined to forget Lachlan. Jimmie was her man and she should stay true to him. And yet, she was as out of place in Jimmie's world as she would be in Lachlan's.

Belle was dusty and hot by the time she stumbled into the village, although the wind, whipping the edge of her skirt and the ends of her hair, was still chilly. Muted sounds came from the river's edge. The rumble of men's voices, the laughter of children, and the swish of water as the boats were cleaned.

The women had not returned from the market yet and Belle managed to creep into Annie's cottage without anyone seeing her. She tipped some water into a basin from the pail that sat at one side of the fireplace, and splashed it over her face. Then lifting her skirt she sloshed a handful between her legs.

'Now that isn't a sight I usually get to see.' The voice came from the loft.

Belle dropped her skirt round her ankles as Ian descended the ladder.

'Don't be so modest, Belle. It's not your nature, is it?' He grabbed her round the waist and pulled her to him. 'I've seen you look at me when Jimmie wasn't watching. You want me, admit it.'

'Let me go, Ian,' Belle panted, aware of the strength of

his arms and the hardness of his body. 'I'm Jimmie's wife, and you know it.'

'Aye, but you'll never stay faithful to him. Not now he's away. And, if you're going to dally I'd rather it was with me than anyone else.' Ian held her tightly. 'You see, Belle. I know you. I know what you are, what you feel, and what you want.'

'What do you mean?' Belle wondered if somehow or other Ian was aware of what she had done. Had he seen something, or did he know something?

'You're a woman with needs, Belle. I can sense them and smell them. Now I want to taste them.'

'What would your ma have to say to that if I told her, and I will tell her if you don't let me go right now.' Belle felt Ian's grip on her slacken, so she wriggled free. 'I won't tell her, Ian, if you stay away from me. But if you touch me again, you'll be sorry.'

Ian laughed. 'If that's the way you want it, Belle, but you'll come to me yet. Wait and see if you don't.'

Ian opened the door and swaggered out, leaving Belle shaken and breathless.

Belle sat down on Annie's stool and stared into the almost dead embers of the fire. Thoughts swirled round her brain. Images of Jimmie, and Lachlan, and now Ian, darted in and out of her mind until she could not distinguish one from the other. She couldn't sit still. She wriggled on the stool, and then she paced the cottage. She had to do something to calm her mind.

She raked the ashes from the fire. Set the paper and sticks and watched the last of the embers nibble and lick round them until the sticks flared into flame.

The black cauldron was quite heavy but she managed to hang it from the swey hook and, pouring the rest of the water from the pail into it, she swung it over the fire.

Maybe if she made the soup, Annie would not be angry with her when she returned from the market.

31

Lachlan crept up the stairs, let himself into his room, and threw himself onto the bed. He felt dirty and dishevelled and was glad no one had seen him enter the house. He could almost see his father's eyes accusing him, as they'd done over the Elsie business.

What was he to do? He was promised to Clarinda but when he closed his eyes it was Belle he saw. Proud and erect in her rough blue skirt and striped petticoats. Her long brown curls, a tangled mass, with just the faintest hint of red when the sunlight caught them. And those strange hypnotic eyes, sometimes brown and sometimes green, they seemed to change with the weather.

Lachlan moaned. The thought of her was arousing him again.

He opened his eyes and concentrated on willing her image to go away.

He stared at the mouldings on the ceiling and tried to visualise Clarinda's face but it wouldn't come. He could not understand it because it had been Clarinda's image that had been foremost when he had been making love to Belle.

A feeling of shame crept over him. He had been too rough with Belle. He had wanted to punish Clarinda, but instead it had been Belle he had punished. The girl would probably never look at him again.

He had told her they would meet again. But how? How would they meet again, and how would he keep it from his parents? They would not tolerate another scandal, particularly one involving the fisher folk.

Maybe he should go back to London before any more harm was done. Marry Clarinda and be done with it. After all it was what his parents expected.

Belle's image floated through his mind, and he knew that a return to London was impossible.

Sarah piled the stones in a heap, trying to get them as high as she could before they fell down again. She liked playing on the foreshore for there was something about the river that seemed to call her. She liked the way the waves bubbled up the channel when the tide was coming in, and the way they seemed to rush to the sea when the tide turned. There were also times when the water seemed quiet and calm, when the birds seemed to float and dream instead of being tossed hither and thither with the motion of the waves.

The river was quiet just now, as if it sensed the fishermen were home and it was giving them a calm surface so they could clean their boats in peace.

Granda had finished washing his boat out and was now leaning against it, chatting to Davie. Jeannie was further down the river where the stones turned to small rock formations. She was poking the rock pools with a stick, looking for small crabs.

'You stay there,' she'd said to Sarah. 'You'll just slip on the rocks if you come with me.'

Sarah would have preferred to examine the rock pools as well but she always did what Jeannie told her to do. Anyway, Jeannie would soon be back because she never left Sarah alone for too long.

Sarah tired of playing with the stones and wandered up the river bank. She could see Invercraig at the other side. She had never been there and wondered what it was like. Granma was over there selling the fish. Sarah hoped she would be in a good mood when she returned for she was a bit scared of Granma Annie, who was always so frowning and stern.

As she turned, Sarah saw her ma walking down the path by the side of the river. She crouched down so she was hidden by the river bank because she did not want her ma to take her into the house. She'd much rather stay outside with Jeannie.

She was still crouched there when she heard the door of the house slam. Peeking over the top of the bank she watched Ian hurry down the path and head in the direction of the town.

Sarah wasn't sure whether she liked her uncle Ian or not. Sometimes he teased her and played with her but at other times he was grumpy. He looked grumpy now, so Sarah stayed out of sight.

When it seemed safe she ran along the foreshore towards Jeannie, only stopping when she got to the edge of the rocks.

'When are you coming back,' she shouted to Jeannie. 'I can't get the stones to pile up.'

Jeannie straightened. 'Just stay there, Sarah, and I'll bring you a wee crab to look at.'

Sarah hopped up and down. 'I've never seen a crab before. Is it like a fish?'

Jeannie jumped and stepped over the rocks. Sarah wondered how she managed to do it without falling. When she was bigger she wanted to be just like Jeannie. Jeannie was so clever.

Jeannie reached the pebble foreshore. She smiled at Sarah and held her cupped hands towards her. 'Now remember, Sarah, you must just look. Don't touch the crab in case it nips you.'

She opened her hands, and Sarah stood on tiptoe to look at what she held.

The crab was tiny, with the smallest claws. 'Why doesn't it nip you?' she asked Jeannie.

'Because I know how to hold it, and anyway it's just a baby. Look I'll put it back in a pool and it can go and look for its ma.'

'Why would it want to look for its ma?' Sarah asked. 'Doesn't it have an Auntie Jeannie?'

'Everyone needs their ma,' Jeannie told her.

Sarah looked at her with doubt in her eyes. If Jeannie said so it must be right, but she didn't feel she needed her ma. She did need Jeannie, though.

32

Annie plodded her way home, down the street that led from the market with its stalls and noise and smells. Although her boots were stout, the cobbles were rough under her feet, and her tiredness made her stagger slightly as she walked.

She still had some fish in her creel, but maybe she would find a sale for them on the way home. The gentry who lived in the big houses lining the road leading to the bridge might send a servant out to buy from her. Annie preferred to sell her fish in the market and usually managed to sell or trade everything, so she did not want to have to admit to James that she had not sold all her fish.

'Fish. Fresh fish.' Annie's voice was slightly hoarse from her day's haggling in the market. She walked down the incline towards the bridge calling outside each house she came to, but no one stirred.

'I thought that was you, Annie.' Ellen Bruce fell into step beside her. 'I see you didn't manage to sell all your fish.'

'Aye, lass, I've seen better trade.'

'Too many fishwives, that's what did it. Did you see that bunch standing near the entrance to the market square? They had the best stance and caught folk as they arrived.'

'Aye, lass, I saw them, but they were strangers to me. They weren't local, that's for sure.'

'Cadger Wullie told me they were down from Arbroath. Damned sauce. What's wrong with their own market?' Ellen's cheeks brightened as her indignation rose.

'Not much we can do about it, lass.' Annie plodded on, head down.

Ellen darted her a sharp look. 'It's not like you to be so accepting, Annie. Are you feeling all right?'

'Just tired, lass. Just tired.' Annie shifted her creel to a more comfortable position.

'It's not like you at all,' Ellen repeated.

They had reached the bridge and Annie had not called in at any more of the houses. What did it matter, she thought, what did any of it matter.

'Your Jimmie, he's left for the whaling, hasn't he?' Ellen's voice was contemplative.

Annie was silent for a moment. 'Aye, lass, he has.'

'You'll be missing him then, and your man will be one short in the boat.'

'It won't be so bad,' Annie said, ignoring the lump that seemed to have arisen somewhere in the vicinity of her throat. 'James'll be able to start Davie now. There was no room for him before and he's anxious to learn the fishing.'

Annie and Ellen crossed the bridge in silence. Ellen was the first to break it. 'Annie, I don't quite know how to put this, but you know my da struggles a bit with his boat because there's only Tom to help him.'

'Aye, lass, I think everyone knows that.' Annie thought of Ellen's brother, Tom. He wasn't half the man her sons were, and she pitied Big Jim Bruce. He maybe owned his own boat but he did not bring back the size of catch her James did.

'Well, I'd been meaning to speak to you for a while. You see with all the sons you have I'm sure it must be a hard job to manage when James only has a share in his boat.'

'We manage fine.' Annie's voice was stiff with pride.

'I'm sure you do,' Ellen said hastily, 'but what I meant was there's not much future for all of your sons.'

Annie bristled, 'What do you mean, Ellen Bruce?'

'Hear me out, Annie. All I wanted to say was that my da would welcome a bit of help with his boat, and there might be a small share at the end of it, if someone came and worked with him, and the arrangement worked out.'

Annie thought for a moment. 'Are you asking for one of my sons, perchance?'

'Aye Annie, that I am. I'm giving you first offer.'

'Which one would you be wanting, then?'

'Well, it's too late for Jimmie. What about Ian?'

Annie looked at Ellen. The girl wasn't slow, she had missed out on Jimmie, and now she was angling for Ian. Annie smiled a long slow smile. She did not mind in the slightest, Ellen would be a good match for Ian and he'd make something of himself when all was said and done.

'If Ian agrees that's all right with me,' she said.

The two women smiled at each other. A bargain had been struck, although neither would admit it.

Ian stamped up the riverside path. He had wanted Belle so badly. He still wanted her but couldn't risk his ma finding out, and Belle had threatened to tell.

She was such a beauty, and he could not get her image out of his mind. That mass of brown curls, those glorious eyes that were the colour of the sea, and the smallness of her body that simply accentuated her curves. He could still see her, standing there with her skirts raised and splashing water on that part of her he would have given anything to possess.

Belle was having none of him, however. She had rebuffed him and threatened to tell Ma.

It wasn't that she was pure, he was sure of that. Just as he was sure that it would not trouble her too much if she was unfaithful to Jimmie. Maybe she was playing hard to get? Yes that must be it. Maybe he should play her at her own game and make her want him. He would have her before much longer, he was convinced of that.

Ian reached the turning towards the town without knowing how he got there. He walked over the first small bridge to that area of ground that sat in the middle of the river, and followed the rough road towards Invercraig.

He knew where there were plenty of willing women. Belle wasn't the only girl around and it was time she knew that.

His thoughts were so deep he did not notice the two women walking towards him, until Annie shouted.

'Ian, just the very person we want to talk to.'

Groaning under his breath, Ian turned towards his mother. She would want to know why he was heading for the town so early. He wanted to ignore her but knew he daren't.

'What is it, Ma?' He looked straight into her eyes expecting the inevitable questions.

'Relax, laddie. Ellen has a proposition for you.'

'A proposition is it?' He stared at Ellen. 'Well, you'd better tell me what it is.'

'Just like I said to Annie, my da needs some help with his boat. If you were willing to come and work for us there might be a small share at the end of it. If the arrangement worked out.'

Ian leaned on the wall bordering the road. He looked Ellen up and down. 'That's a handsome offer,' he said, his voice laden with insolence. 'Are you sure it's me you want?'

The colour rose upwards from Ellen's neck, staining her cheeks with a healthy glow. 'It's first offer you're getting. You don't have to take it if you don't want.'

'I never said I didn't want it, but you took me by surprise. I'll need to think on it.'

'Well, don't think too long or I'll offer it elsewhere.'

Ian laughed. 'My, you're real attractive when you're angry. I'll have to anger you more often. Come on I'll walk you both back to Craigden.'

Ian's thoughts were busy on the road back. It was a decent offer and it could result in a share of the Bruce boat. Even Jimmie hadn't achieved that yet. Ian would not have to go off whaling to earn money to get his own boat, all he would have to do would be to take Ellen Bruce, for he had no illusions about what the offer might include.

He glanced at Ellen. She was an attractive woman, tall, clear-eyed and strong enough to carry him to the boat. She would make an ideal wife for a fisherman. 'I'll give you my answer tonight when I call round to see you.'

33

Annie's spirits revived and she strode along the river path with Ian and Ellen following in the rear. She had feared that Ian would spoil the opportunity Ellen was offering with his surly behaviour. However, he had cheered up, and was now walking with her.

James and Davie were lounging against the boat, but they straightened and came to meet her.

'How was the market, lass?' James inspected the creel.

Annie wanted to reach out and stroke the frown from his face but hadn't the strength to raise her arms.

'Not so good, James. There was a crew of Arbroath fishwives down for the day and they had the best stance. I should have gone to the Dundee market instead, it's not that much further.'

'Ah well, lass. You weren't to know they'd be there.'

Annie turned away as she felt the tears prick the back of her eyes. James was such a good man. He would never even think she had failed him. 'I'll go and get the soup pot on, everyone will be hungry.' Turning, she stumbled towards the house.

The smell of soup assailed her nostrils as soon as she opened the door, and she stared in amazement at Belle. 'You've made the soup,' she said, as she sank down on her stool in front of the fire.

Belle seemed ill-at-ease. 'I had an accident and got home early, so I thought I'd better make good use of my time.'

'What kind of an accident?' Annie felt a surge of warmth towards the girl.

'Well, I tripped on the top road, and banged my head on a stone.' Belle had turned her back on Annie, and she seemed to be in some distress.

'Are you hurt, lass?'

'No, I'm fine, but I was dazed for a time and the fish had scattered.'

'Well!'

'Well, you see it's like this . . . the gulls got the fish.' Belle's shoulders shook and Annie wasn't sure if she was crying.

It had been a bad day all round for fish. The market had been bad and Belle had lost her fish. What would happen next?

'You didn't get your round done then,' Annie sighed. 'Never mind, lass. You'll do better next time,' and so must I, she thought, or we'll all fall on hard times. Just as well Ian's taken care of.

Belle spun round. 'I got most of it done,' she said. 'It's only the minister who didn't get his fish. But like as not he's the one who will complain the most.'

Annie got up and hugged Belle. She had hardly ever touched Belle before, but the hug felt good. There was something vulnerable and child-like about the girl, and she suddenly understood why Jimmie loved her. 'You're a grand lass, Belle, and you're not to worry. I'll take care of the minister.'

'Jeannie,' she shouted. 'Jeannie, where are you?'

'Here, Ma. I'm here.' Jeannie ran up the path towards the house, with Sarah following close behind.

Annie parcelled up some fish from her creel. 'Run up the cliff path and take this to the minister. He didn't get his fish today.'

Jeannie grabbed the parcel and ran towards the cliff path.

Annie grasped Sarah's arm as she prepared to trot behind Jeannie. 'No, my wee lass, you stay here with your ma. She's made a grand pot of soup for us.'

Belle stirred the soup. It hadn't been so bad after all. Annie believed her story and had actually been sympathetic. Belle could still feel the warmth of the hug from Annie, maybe they could get on with one another after all.

Belle turned to face her mother-in-law. 'Will you taste the soup? I'm not sure if I've salted it enough.' She held the ladle towards the older woman and watched as Annie took a sip.

'It tastes fine, lass. I couldn't have made better myself.'

A warm glow crept over Belle and she had the strangest feeling. This must be what it was like to be cared for by someone, without having to pay the inevitable price for their love. She felt the urge to please Annie, to seek her approval.

'You look tired, Annie. The market must have been busy.'

'Aye, lass, it was a long trek for very little business the day,' Annie sank down onto the stool.

Belle observed the tiredness in Annie's eyes and the lines on her face. Lines she had not noticed before because Annie always seemed to have so much energy. She had meant to sit back when her mother-in-law returned from the market but now she found herself saying, 'I'll make the skirlie and fry the fish so you can rest. It'll maybe not be as good as you make it but it'll be eatable and it'll fill them all up.'

The pot of soup on the swey hook was quite heavy to swing round but Annie had always managed to do it without any effort, so Belle made no complaint. Balancing a large flat pan on the griddle she swung it over the fire and, waiting until the pan was hot, she threw a knob of dripping into it. While the dripping sizzled Belle sliced the onions given to her by Mrs McDonald and added them to the smoking fat. The oatmeal followed and Belle stirred the mixture energetically so it wouldn't stick to the pan.

Pulling the griddle to one side, Belle swung the soup pot round until it was hanging just in front of the fire, so that both would stay hot. Grabbing another handful of oatmeal she threw it on the table. 'Hand me a fish from the creel,' she instructed Sarah, who had been watching her mother cook. 'And another one,' she said as she flipped the fish onto the oatmeal, coating first one side then the other. 'Now just keep the fish coming until I tell you to stop.'

Belle piled the oatmeal-covered fish on the edge of the table, and brushing the spare oatmeal into her hand she sprinkled it into the skirlie pan. 'That's it done then,' she said, wiping her hair off her forehead with an oatmeally hand, 'I'll get them fried while the men are supping their soup.'

'You've done a braw job,' Annie congratulated her. 'We'd better get the men in now. Sarah, my wee lass, will you run and tell your granda and uncles to come for their dinner.'

'Granma says to come for your dinner.' Sarah had run all the way to the river bank where James and Davie still lounged against the boat. They seemed to be listening to something her uncle Ian was telling them, and Sarah could hear their laughter, although not what they were saying.

'She says to come now. It's ready.'

'Aye, we're coming.' Granda smiled at her. He always had a smile for her, not like Granma who was often bad-tempered.

'My ma made the dinner today. She made soup and skirlie, and she's going to fry the fish.' Sarah expected them to be impressed.

'Maybe we should give dinner a miss today.' Uncle Ian never had anything nice to say about her ma.

'It's good, even Granma said it was good,' Sarah stamped her foot.

'Of course it's good, Sarah, my wee pet. It has to be good if your ma made it.' James smiled at her and Sarah smiled back. She would have liked to hug him but the only person Sarah ever hugged was Jeannie.

Sarah skipped up the path towards the house and the men dutifully followed her.

'They're all coming, Granma but Uncle Ian was horrid. He said he didn't want any dinner.'

'I'm sure he'll want his dinner, my wee lass. He was probably teasing you. Ian's a real tease sometimes.'

Belle started to ladle the soup into the wooden bowls, laying each one on the table in turn.

Sarah frowned. She usually sat with Ma when she was at Granma's house but she knew that Ma wouldn't want her when she was so busy. She looked round the room wondering where she should sit. If Jeannie had been there she would have gone to her but Jeannie wasn't back yet.

She felt a hand close round her wrist and she looked up to see who was pulling her. Granma smiled back at her. 'Come and sit with me, Sarah, lass, and we'll both be out of your ma's way.'

Sarah was not used to Granma being nice to her and was not sure what to do, so she allowed herself to be pulled onto Granma's knee. It wasn't too bad though. It was comfortable enough, but not cosy and warm like Jeannie's knee. Sarah could always feel Jeannie's love when she sat on her bony knees.

Jeannie came rushing in when the meal was almost over. 'Have you saved some for me,' she shouted.

'Aye, lass, there's plenty left. We didn't let Davie loose on the remains until you came back. Did you give the minister his fish?'

'Aye. I gave him his fish, but I don't want to go back there on my own again. I don't like the minister, Ma. He took hold of my hand and wouldn't let it go.'

Sarah slid off Annie's knee and ran to Jeannie who picked her up and swung her round. 'You should have come with me after all, Sarah.'

Jeannie sat at the table and gobbled the soup, quickly followed by the skirlie and fish. Sarah was always amazed at how much Jeannie could eat because she was so thin, and she wished she could eat as much and just be like Jeannie.

'Will you be staying the night again?' Annie asked Belle.

'Thanks for the offer, Annie, but Sarah and I had better go back to our own house tonight. We can't stay here all the time. You've got your own family to think of.'

'Can Sarah stay? Let Sarah stay,' Jeannie butted in.

Belle looked doubtful. 'Sarah should come with me,' she

said. 'Your ma's got enough to do as it is.'

'Please, Ma? Can Sarah stay? She can sleep with me on the truckle bed, there's plenty of room.'

'The bairn can stay if she wants,' Annie said, gruffly.

Jeannie took hold of Sarah's hands and swung her round in a circle. 'You want to stay and sleep with me, don't you?'

The room was spinning, but Sarah managed to look at Jeannie and smile. She would go anywhere and stay anywhere if Jeannie was there. She would even stay with her dreaded granma.

34

As usual, Belle was glad to get out of Annie's crowded, stuffy house. The living room was so small it was never long before the walls closed in on her, squeezing and pushing against the amount of bodies the room contained, leaving no space to breathe.

Outside the air was fresh and sweet and, as she left, Belle quietly closed the door on the heat and the smell of fish and flesh. She made her way through the village to the path that ran alongside the river bank. The water, black in the evening gloom, lapped on the stone shingle reminding her of evening walks with Jimmie. She turned to face the sea and wondered what he was doing. 'We stop at Lerwick first,' he'd told her, 'for supplies and some more men.' Maybe he was at Lerwick now. There would be women at Lerwick but her Jimmie wouldn't bother with them. He was a good man, her Jimmie, and she knew he would never look at anyone else.

It had been an eventful day and Belle hummed to herself as she continued her walk home. She felt free and untrammelled, Annie liked her and Sarah wasn't hanging round her skirts making a nuisance of herself. She did not think about Lachlan, she had blotted him from her memory. He had been an adventure and an experience, but he had left her with hardly a word, and Belle was not prepared to waste her thoughts on him.

The Bruce house was the last one in the village and, as Belle passed it, she remembered Ian ranting about Ellen Bruce and the offer she had made him of a share in her da's boat. Belle thought he had been trying to impress her and she had responded by saying, 'That's nice Ian. I'm pleased for you.' And Belle had been pleased for him because it meant he would not pester her again. He would be too busy with

Ellen Bruce.

The patch of ground between her shack and the Bruce house was dark with shadows. The earth was shingly and covered with a coarse grass that was sharp to the touch, so Belle never took short cuts across it, preferring to follow the path.

The door faced the river and the only window looked towards the wood farther up the path. There was no window looking towards the village but Belle did not mind. The villagers had not been particularly welcoming towards her so she had no interest in looking out on the cluster of cottages they lived in.

Closing the door behind her, she removed her clothing until she was down to the greyish-white shift she slept in. She pulled the rough grey blanket aside and got into the bed which was little more than a box. Jimmie had made it, lovingly nailing the base to the sides and then filling it with a straw mattress. 'Someday you'll have feathers, my love,' he had said. 'And a proper brass bed, I promise you.'

She dozed off with the sound of Jimmie's promises drifting through her mind. The knocking at the window roused her and at first she was not sure if it was in her dream. However it sounded again.

Gathering the blanket together in her hands, she wrapped it around her shoulders and walked to the window.

'Who is it?' she whispered.

'Belle, I need to speak to you. I need to apologize.'

It sounded like Lachlan but it couldn't be. Belle shook her head. Maybe she was still dreaming. If she was dreaming it would not matter what she did.

'I'll open the door but be quick. I wouldn't want anyone to see you.'

A shadow slipped past her. 'I understand that, Belle, so I left Raven in the wood where he wouldn't be seen.'

'Raven?' Belle queried.

'My horse.'

The silence between them clung to the darkness like a living entity and there was only the sound of their breathing.

'Why have you come?' Belle felt foolish. It was obvious why he had come, he wanted more of what she had given him that morning. Was it only that morning? It seemed so distant now and she had done a lot of thinking since then.

Lachlan seemed to be having trouble speaking. 'I've come to apologize.' His voice was so low she could hardly hear him.

'Apologize?' No one had ever said they were sorry to Belle and she had never expected them to.

'Yes. I should not have hurt you this morning . . . it was wrong of me. But Belle, I wanted you so much, I couldn't help myself.'

Belle shivered, she felt tender towards him. He was just like a little boy saying he was sorry for stealing apples.

'You will forgive me, won't you? Say we can start from the beginning and I'll never hurt you again. I promise.'

Belle lifted her hand and laid it on the side of his cheek. 'Of course I forgive you.' She had never forgiven anyone before and it felt good.

Belle's hand was warm and gentle on Lachlan's cheek. He placed his own hand on top of it and lifted it towards his lips so he could kiss her palm.

'I'll leave if you want me to but I'd rather stay.' He could hear her breathing deepen, although it was too dark to see her expression. Would she still want him after the way he had treated her that morning.

'Stay.' Her voice was husky and it excited him.

He put his arms round her. She seemed to be wrapped in some kind of horse blanket. Gently he eased it off until it lay on the floor and she stood before him in nothing but a simple shift.

'Oh, Belle,' he groaned, burying his face in her hair.

'Hush, now,' she said, and led him to the back of the room.

He could feel the edge of the bed and he wanted to take her right there and then, but he had promised to be gentle so he kissed her forehead, and her face, and then worked his way down her neck towards her breasts. He felt her nipples harden under his tongue and she gave a small, strangled groan. She pulled him down into the bed where he fondled her until he could contain himself no longer.

This time their lovemaking was slow and gentle, and Lachlan resisted his baser, animal impulses. No vision of Clarinda came to him and he gave her no thought. There was only Belle. Sweet, sweet Belle. So loving and giving, and so eager for him.

At last they were spent and lay in each others arms like the lovers they were, neither wanting to give up the other. Hours passed. Long tender hours, until at last Belle said, 'You'd better go before it gets light.'

He brushed her lips with his. 'Can I come back, Belle? Please say you want me to come back.'

'I wouldn't have taken you to my bed if I didn't want you to come back.' She smiled up at him. 'But you'd better go now and be careful you're not seen when you return.'

35

Ian woke early. He was to join the Bruce boat today and he wanted to make a good impression.

Ellen had taken him to meet her father the evening before and the older man had looked him over as if he was an animal about to be bought. 'I suppose you'll do,' he had said grudgingly.

'Now, Da. You know you need a man for the boat so that you can stay out at sea longer and bring home better catches.'

'Aye, aye. I know that fine, but it doesn't make it any easier. I'll have to pay him, you know.'

'Aye, and a share in the boat if it works out.'

Ian enjoyed watching the old man squirm. Bruce had a name for being grippy, and no doubt the thought of parting with money or shares vexed him a great deal.

After the details of his employment with old Bruce were finalized, Ian and Ellen escaped to walk by the river.

Ellen was silent and Ian realised he would have to make the first approach if he was to protect his investment.

'You're sure this is what you want?'

'Aye, Ian. It's what I want.'

He reached out towards her hand, and taking it he clasped it firmly within his own. It was a strong hand, warm and unresisting within his grasp. He wondered, fleetingly, what Belle's hand would have felt like but pushed the thought away. This was not the time to have his mind confused with longings for someone else. The prize was too great.

They walked in companionable silence, listening to the lapping waves, the crunch of the pebbles below their feet and the far off rushing noise of the sea that called and beckoned to both of them, for the sea was in their blood.

Ian wondered how much Ellen anticipated from him tonight, but decided it was better not to rush things. She would expect him to try her out before they wed though, for every fisher lad had to ensure the fertility of his bride before he married her. A childless marriage was of no use to any fisher family.

'Will you come in?' Ellen asked when they returned to her house.

'Not tonight,' Ian said, 'I think your da's seen enough of me for today.' He pulled her round until her eyes were on a level with his own. 'You're a handsome woman, Ellen Bruce. A man would be lucky to have you for a wife.'

She leaned towards him and brushed his cheek with her lips. 'You're not so bad yourself, Ian Watt.'

Ian was left looking at the closed door. He touched the spot she had kissed and if she had still been there he would have pulled her into his arms because it had felt good.

He glanced towards Belle's wee house, just visible in the gloom. For a moment he thought he saw a fleeting shadow hovering outside her door but when he looked again it was gone. A shadow over the moon, he told himself, that's all it was, but there was a doubt in his mind.

Annie ladled out the porridge. 'Eat that before you go,' she instructed Ian who seemed anxious to be away.

'You fuss too much, Ma,' Ian grumbled, but he lifted the bowl and spooned the oatmeal into his mouth. Clattering it down onto the table he turned and slammed out of the door

'He never even sat down for it,' Annie muttered to James, who had held his bowl out for a refill.

'The laddie's eager to get away and get in old Bruce's good books. He'll not want to spoil his chances.'

'Aye, you're right there. But it seems like I'm losing all my sons. There's Jimmie away to the whaling, and Ian off to join the Bruce boat and maybe get himself a wife into the bargain, and my wee Davie away to the sea.' She smiled at her youngest son and ruffled his hair.

'Och, Ma. I'm not a bairn anymore.' Davie squirmed under her hand.

'No, I suppose you're not, but you'll always seem a bairn to me.'

James looked up from his porridge bowl. 'You have to let them go sometime, Annie. You can't keep them tied to you forever.'

'Aye, I know that, but it doesn't come easy, and now there's only Angus and Davie left. How long will it be before they want to leave.'

Angus looked up from his plate, 'I don't want to leave you, Ma, but I'll want to get my own boat someday.'

'And how will you manage that, may I ask?' Annie clattered the bowls together. Later, after the boats had left she would take them to the river and wash them out.

'I'll manage somehow,' Angus muttered, as he turned to pull on his sea boots.

'I won't leave you, Ma.' Davie ducked as Annie's hand reached out towards his hair.

'Nor me, Ma.' Jeannie had popped her head out from under the blankets.

'Hush, Jeannie, you'll wake wee Sarah.' Annie bent over the truckle bed and tucked the blanket under her daughter's chin. Sarah was lying in the crook of Jeannie's arm still sound asleep. It would have been nice to have had another daughter, but Jeannie's birth had been difficult and James was so scared of losing her, he had told her, 'There'll be no more bairns. I'd rather have you than all the bairns in Christendom.' Annie never told him, and never would, that she missed his loving and the making of bairns, for once James made up his mind that was an end to it. She sighed and turned away, for the men had their boots on and were ready to leave.

Jeannie tightened her arm around Sarah. It was nice to feel the small body cuddled into her own, she would have liked Sarah to stay with her but knew that she would have to return to her own home and her own ma.

Jeannie frowned as she thought of Sarah's ma. She liked and admired Belle but she did not like the way Belle treated Sarah. Her own ma was sometimes brusque but Jeannie knew that Annie loved her. She wasn't so sure that Belle loved Sarah.

Maybe Ma would let Sarah stay a few more days if she asked her. Jeannie's eyes drooped shut and she rested her cheek on top of Sarah's head. Yes, that was it. She'd ask Ma as soon as she got back.

36

It was the beginning of August before Belle was certain she was pregnant. She had tried to ignore her thickening waist and tender breasts, but now she was sure. What she was less sure about was, whose child it was – Jimmie's or Lachlan's. Not that this concerned her too much, for as far as Belle was concerned the child's father would be whoever she chose, and at the moment she favoured Lachlan. After all he loved her, didn't he?

Lachlan tapped on her window almost every night. Sarah's return made no difference, Belle just made sure the child was asleep before he arrived. They also met at other times whenever they had the opportunity, in the woods, on the moors and anywhere they thought they might get some privacy.

He waited for her and she unstrapped her creels so he could swing her up onto his horse. At first she had been scared but now she loved the feel of the horse's muscles beneath her and the way the wind ruffled through her hair. It made her feel wild and abandoned.

Their lovemaking consumed them. Sometimes it was gentle and loving, and at other times it was as violent and passionate as it had been on their first meeting. Belle had never before experienced the fulfilment she enjoyed with Lachlan and she did not want it to end.

She thought no one saw and was oblivious to any gossip. Lachlan, however, did not want his parents to know about her.

'They wouldn't approve,' he said, 'and I don't want them interfering with what we have.'

That did not matter at the moment and she was convinced the time would come when he would be proud to tell them about her.

Maybe that time was now.

Lachlan had avoided his parents for most of the summer, afraid they would, somehow or other, come between him and Belle. But now he had been summoned by his father.

Bates had been sent to fetch him. 'Your father wishes to see you in the library, Master Lachlan.'

Lachlan shrugged in annoyance. 'I was just going out. Can't it wait?'

'Your father said, immediately, Master Lachlan.'

Lachlan watched the receding back of the butler. It must be important if he'd sent Bates rather than one of the other servants.

Oh bother, what did his father want? Had someone informed him about Belle? But no one knew – they'd been so careful.

Sir Roderick stood, legs astride and hands clasped behind his back, staring out of the library window, while his mother sat in one of the leather chairs with her hands resting peacefully in the folds of her gown.

'You wanted to see me, Father?' Lachlan felt like running to his mother and resting his head in her lap, but instead he stood erect and proud, determined that this time his father should not dominate him.

Sir Roderick turned to look at him, his face as expressionless as a rough-hewn stone. Lachlan was taller than his father, but still could not rid himself of the feeling of intimidation the laird could generate in him. He felt his resolve crumble and the need to run to his mother for protection intensified.

'Your mother and I have been discussing your future, Lachlan. We have decided that it is time you and Clarinda were wed. We have already contacted Clarinda's parents about arranging the ceremony. In the meantime you will return to London and make all necessary preparations. That is all, you may go.' The laird rocked backwards on his heels as if the matter was closed.

Lachlan almost reeled under the impact of the words. London – he was being sent back to London, and to Clarinda. His shoulders slumped. His father's squat body seemed to tower over him and he grasped the back of a chair for support.

'I hadn't intended to leave so soon,' he mumbled, looking towards his mother for support.

Lady Catherine continued to study her hands and made no response. Lachlan remembered her saying to him all those years ago, 'There has always been an understanding and you must honour that understanding.' There would be no support from his mother because she wanted him to marry Clarinda.

'No doubt you hadn't,' his father rasped. 'But there has been enough dalliance already and you will be aboard the sailing packet that leaves Dundee harbour on Friday morning.'

Lachlan stumbled out of the library. He stifled a sob and dashed a tear from the corner of his eye. Men did not cry and if his father heard or saw, he would despise his son more than he already did.

Raven was waiting for him at the stables and Lachlan laid his cheek on the horse's back, savouring the strength of the stallion, before he saddled and mounted him. If only he had that kind of strength he would be able to stand up to his father.

The horse reared up in response to the reins and the bit, his hooves clattered down on the cobbles, and then he galloped unrestrainedly at the touch of Lachlan's whip. Lachlan leaned forward his head almost in Raven's mane. The wind whipped through his hair, and he rode the horse as he had never ridden him before.

The moor was desolate and Lachlan had never come this far before. He could see a town in the distance and thought it must be Forfar, but was not sure. He pulled on the reins and Raven slowed to a canter. Then, wheeling the horse round, he touched the whip to Raven's rump and galloped back in the direction they had come from.

When they reached the standing stones he slid from the horse's back and entered the circle. This was where he had first made love to Belle. At first he had thought it simply a romantic interlude before he returned to marry Clarinda, but he had not counted on falling in love with her. Now his father was sealing his fate. The wedding was being arranged and he would have to leave Belle. How could he live without her?

Lachlan lay within the circle of stones until darkness fell and then made his way to Craigden, and Belle.

37

Belle fidgeted. She had put on her best silk dress especially for tonight, smoothing it carefully over her swollen belly. Sarah was sleeping with Jeannie at Annie's house. 'The girls do like to be together,' she had told Annie, 'and Sarah wearies on her own.'

Where was Lachlan? He should have been here by now. She peered out of the window but there was only darkness.

When the tap on the window eventually came she flew to the door to unlock it.

'I thought you weren't coming,' she said, as he slipped inside.

'You know I can't stay away, Belle.' He pulled her into his arms and his lips sought hers with a bruising passion.

The silk dress lay in a crumpled heap on the floor as their two bodies intertwined, and Belle felt the fire in her mount until it almost consumed her. Nothing existed for her except the overwhelming need for Lachlan, unless perhaps, his ability to satisfy that need and quench her fire.

At last they lay in peace, his arm around her shoulder, his fingers playing with her hair, while her hand stroked his stomach. They lay for a moment, hip to hip, and body to body, savouring the warmth of each other.

Belle's hand stilled on Lachlan's stomach, 'I have something to tell you.'

'What would that be? That you love me. But I know that already.' She could almost feel Lachlan smile in the darkness.

'No, it's something else, something much more important.'

'What could be more important than telling me you love me?'

'I'm going to have a baby.'

His fingers stopped twining her hair. She held her breath. She had not meant to tell him so bluntly, but she had to tell him.

'Tell me you're pleased,' her voice was tiny with the hint of a sob in it.

'Of course I'm pleased.' He pulled her to him, 'I'm just surprised that's all.'

'What will we do?' She hoped he'd say, come away with me but he was silent. 'What will your father say?'

'My father mustn't know,' his voice held a harshness she had not heard before.

'Why not? It will be his grandchild.'

'My father would disown me, He mustn't know Belle. You must convince Jimmie the child is his. It won't make any difference to us.'

The warmth seemed to have seeped out of the bed. 'Hold me, Lachlan, I'm cold.' There was a lump in Belle's throat and the tears she wanted to shed would not come.

'Is it time?' Ian asked Ellen as they left her father's house.

She laughed, teasing him, 'Time for what?'

He smiled back at her. They got on surprisingly well considering their relationship was, in many ways, a business one. 'Time to decide whether we are to be wed or not. Time to . . . ' Ian could not finish, unsure how to put it into words.

'I do believe you're blushing,' Ellen grinned. 'I didn't think I'd ever see that.'

Ian grasped her hand. 'You know what I'm asking.'

Her face became serious. 'Of course I know what you're asking. And the answer's yes, but not till it's dark.'

They walked upriver towards the inland basin and then followed its banks until it narrowed down again into a river. A family of ducks floated in the water just offshore and geese screamed their way overhead. A pheasant fluttered in front of them but Ian paid it no heed. He would have caught it for his mother's pot if he had not been engrossed with

Ellen.

Retracing their steps in the gathering gloom they made their way to the wood outside the village. That would be as good a place as any to carry out their intentions.

Ian led Ellen to a thicket which was bordered by bushes and small trees. Leaves formed a canopy over their heads blotting out the sky and the stars. 'No one will see us in here,' he said.

The grass was soft and mossy and Ian pulled Ellen down onto it. He hesitated for a moment, uncertain how to approach Ellen for she was not like the girls he usually picked up in Invercraig when he was in the mood for some loving.

They lay in silence for a few moments and then Ellen leaned over and kissed him. He pulled her to him and she responded to his caresses enclosing him in her strong arms. Her legs were equally strong when he finally entered her and she clasped them round him as if to draw him even further in.

Ellen's fervour surprised Ian who had spent the summer courting her with no more than a kiss on her cheek or a swift peck on the lips for a reward. Both of them knew, however, that her fertility would have to be tested before they could wed. And the success of Ian's arrangement with her father had been the indicator of when that would have to be done. Ian hoped she would become pregnant quickly so he could earn his share of her father's boat.

The couple were lying in each other's arms when Lachlan tethered Raven just outside the perimeter of the thicket. Ian laid a finger on Ellen's lips and they watched as Lachlan made his way to Belle's cottage.

'We must keep this to ourselves,' Ian warned Ellen.

'Why should we? Jimmie should be told what Belle gets up to when he's not here.'

Ian hugged Ellen close to him. If Jimmie threw Belle out he might turn to Ellen, and Ian could not afford to lose his share in the Bruce boat. 'It would destroy Jimmie if he knew. Don't you see that, Ellen? It's better to hold our tongues.' He felt the indignation seep out of her, and her body relaxed against his.

'Aye, I suppose you're right and I wouldn't want to harm Jimmie.'

Ian walked Ellen home savouring what he had learned about Belle. There would come a time when he would be able to use that knowledge to his own advantage, and he was used to biding his time.

Lachlan spent the next two days trying to decide what to tell Belle. He lay in her arms each night but there was more despair in his lovemaking than joy. He tried to tell her he had to leave and that his father had decreed he was to marry Clarinda without delay. But he could not think of a way to say the words that should be said.

Each time he choked on the words Belle would soothe him. 'Hush, my love,' she'd say. 'You'll get used to it and I'll do what you want and let Jimmie think it's his baby.'

Lachlan buried his face in her hair and moaned, and still the words would not come. He lay with her as long as he dared and then dressed in silence, taking care not to wake her. The leather pouch he had prepared with the twenty guineas, he left on the pillow beside her head. There was a tear in his eye and an ache in his heart as he silently left the cottage. 'Farewell, Belle,' he whispered. 'If our circumstances had been different I would have stayed with you forever. But that cannot be.'

If he had delayed his departure from Belle any longer, his father would have caught him. As it was he was able to saunter down the stairs as if he had spent the night slumbering in his own room.

'The coach is waiting.' His father's voice sounded a bit gruffer than usual.

His mother kissed him on the cheek. 'We'll come for the wedding. Until that time, take care,' she murmured in his ear.

Her eyes glistened with unshed tears and on impulse

Lachlan hugged her. He could see his father turning away in embarrassment but Lachlan did not care. He would hug his mother if he wanted to.

When Lachlan arrived at Dundee harbour and boarded the packet for London, he wondered whether Belle would realise he had left. He should have told her and now it was too late, and she would think it was because of the baby. 'Oh, Belle,' he groaned. 'If only I could have stayed with you.'

He watched Dundee recede into the distance as the ship sailed out of the river mouth. And for a long time after that he stood and watched, although there was nothing to see except the waves.

38

Jimmie leaned on the rail enjoying the sting of the wind and the splash of spray on his cheeks as the *Eclipse* raced through the sea, sails billowing and cracking. The smell of dulse and the scream of the gulls as they swooped above the ship indicated they were nearing a landfall. The Lerwick men already had their boxes and bundles on deck and there was a steady buzz and hum of voices as they made their preparations so they would be ready to disembark as soon as the ship dropped anchor.

The men were happy for they were coming home with the blubber from seven fish. Jimmie reckoned this would earn him almost fifteen pounds once the oil money was added on to his wages. Another two to three whaling trips would buy him his boat, although he would probably have to sign on for another two voyages after that in order to buy nets and equipment. He could not wait to tell Belle and see the joy on her face because she wanted him to be free and independent just as much as he did.

He turned to Ben who leaned on the rail beside him. 'How long d'you think we'll anchor at Lerwick?' he asked the older man. He remembered the several days it had taken to provision the ship on the way out. The huge joints of beef and ham that were loaded and strung from the masts, and the job he'd had spraying them with salt water so they would freeze once they set sail.

'The captain'll not stay long at Lerwick. He'll want to get back with his cargo. Don't you worry, lad. We'll be home before the week's out.'

Home, Jimmie thought. Home to Belle. He had so much to tell her he wasn't sure where he would start. He'd tell her about the beauty of the frozen seas. Cliffs of ice rising out of a startling blue sea, and the whiteness of a landscape that seemed to stretch forever. The shadows that sometimes looked blue, sometimes purple and sometimes black. The eeriness of the land and sea where sound was muffled, and the silence was broken only by the cracking of ice and the movements of the ship.

He would not tell her about the whale chase. As an oarsman he always got a close up view of the kill. The chase was exciting enough but the first kill he'd seen had horrified him. The harpooneer had aimed well and the whale was speared. It had dragged the boat for miles before it submerged.

'Hang on tight, lads,' the harpooneer said, and everyone knew there was a risk of the whale taking the boat down with him, or coming up underneath it, or lashing it with one of his flukes. But the whale surfaced just in front of the boat and another harpoon was aimed and met its target. Then another and another.

Jimmie found the thrashing of the whale distressing because it was so obviously trying to escape. But when the final death throe came with the spout of blood and spray from the whale's blow hole, he felt sick. He wiped the whale's blood from his face and looked over at Ben, but the older man merely grinned at him.

'A dirty business,' he said. 'But you'll get used to it. After all, they're only fish.'

Since then Jimmie had been involved in another six whale kills. He did not feel any better about it, but he concentrated on the boat he would buy with his earnings and the pride Belle would feel for him.

It was daylight when Belle woke and Lachlan was long gone. The rough blanket rubbed against her skin with a sensual suggestiveness as she blinked and stretched. It brought back memories of their lovemaking the night before and she was reluctant to rise and dress. She stroked the outline of her breasts running her fingers down her waist and over the swell of her belly. Lachlan had caressed her in such a fashion. He liked to see her and hold her after she had removed all her clothing. No one but Lachlan had ever seen her completely naked and she revelled in his admiration.

Belle moved her hand to the hollow in the bed that had been Lachlan, as if by doing so she could bring him back. She lay for a moment and then sat up. She would have to dress before Sarah returned, because it would not do for the child to see her like this. The child probably guessed too much already.

As she swung her legs over the edge of the bed she saw the leather pouch. Frowning, she lifted it and opened the drawstring so she could peer inside. The coins made a soft, clinking noise. She upended the pouch so that the sovereigns spilled out in a glistening heap onto the pillow.

Belle had never seen so much money before. It was a fortune. She ran her fingers over the mound of coins, feeling the hard, coolness of them. Eventually she counted them back into the pouch and clasped it to her breast. Why had Lachlan left her this money? Although she asked herself the question she knew the answer. He wasn't coming back.

The desolation did not set in immediately, but she felt cold. So she dressed, turning from time to time to finger the pouch. She did not want the money, she wanted Lachlan, but he was probably gone and would not return. Why else would he have left her so many sovereigns.

She shrugged her shoulders, as much in despair as in defiance. If Lachlan did not want to come back, well to hell with him, she would survive. She always survived and she still had Jimmie.

Her fingers tightened on the pouch. She would keep Lachlan's money but she had better hide it so Jimmie did not ask awkward questions. And anyway, it might come in useful for the future if Jimmie ever left her and she had to seek her independence.

39

Lachlan stepped ashore at London docks. His face was ashen and he worried that his legs might not hold him up. The sea had been relatively smooth on the way down the coast but he had never been a good sailor and was happiest when his feet were on dry land.

London docks always stifled him with the smell of bodies and the toing and froing of sailors, dock labourers, merchants, and doxies. Not forgetting the dippers, of course. Many a purse had been lost here. He pushed his way through the crowds and hailed one of the new Chapman cabs in preference to a cabriolet and sank down in the seat.

The journey seemed to take forever as the cab battled its way through mobbed streets. He tried to close his ears to the interminable din as he held a handkerchief to his nose. There never seemed to be any fresh air in London and he missed the country already.

The Hope-Stanley mansion never failed to impress Lachlan and, although it was not as large as Craigallan House, it was nevertheless opulent, even by London standards. Aunt Beattie, her skirts swishing to keep up with her small, rotund frame, came hurrying to meet him in her usual dynamic fashion.

'Lachlan, my boy, you're back. Oh, how we've missed you. Clarinda has been distraught. But now this. The wedding. The preparations. The house has been a veritable hive of activity. But, I'm forgetting, you'll want to see Clarinda.' Aunt Beattie paused for breath before continuing in her non-stop fashion. 'She's in the small drawing room. She'll be so pleased you're back. She has been so distraught, my boy, so distraught. Now she will be happy again, as we all are.'

The drawing room had an air of peacefulness. Lachlan had expected Aunt Beattie to accompany him inside and was thankful when she did not.

Clarinda sat on a cream coloured, brocade chaise longue with her feet on a matching footstool. Her azure-blue dress billowed out around her making the perfect foil for her delicate, blonde beauty. She did not stand up, otherwise he might have remembered how intimidating her height was, but simply held her hand out to him as she gazed at him with calm blue eyes.

Lachlan caught his breath. He had forgotten how lovely she was, remembering only her coldness towards him.

'The time has come then,' she said. 'And you have made up your mind at last.' She hesitated a moment. 'Tell me one thing,' she said, 'and I'll never ask again. Was this your decision or your parents?'

Lachlan crossed the room and lifted her fingers to his lips. He could not admit to her it was his parents' decision. It would make him look less than a man in her eyes and he had to convince her he was a man.

'Of course it was my decision,' he said. 'I would not have returned otherwise.'

Clarinda smiled, a long slow smile that seemed to light up her face. She had never smiled at him before and Lachlan was amazed at the warm feeling it invoked in him. Maybe it wouldn't be so bad after all.

She patted the chaise longue, saying, 'Sit by me. We have a lot to discuss.'

Lachlan sat on the edge of the seat, unsure where to look or what to do with his hands. 'You realise we have never been alone before,' he mumbled. 'It feels strange.'

Clarinda's laughter sounded light and tinkling. He would hardly have heard it if he had not been sitting so close to her.

'But now the date has been set for our wedding we can be alone on occasion. Aunt Beattie is a very considerate chaperone. However, she won't leave us on our own for too long so we must make the most of the time we have.'

Lachlan thought fleetingly of the many hours he had

spent in the arms of Belle, and of her dark and fiery beauty that was so different from Clarinda's. He pushed the memory to the back of his mind, for his future was here and now with this woman who sat at his side. He wondered what Clarinda would be like between the sheets and knew instinctively she would disappoint him unless he could win her love. Lachlan was aware he held an attraction for women and Clarinda was a woman, wasn't she? He turned his full attention onto her and with a smile he started the task of wooing her.

Sarah's birthday had come and gone. She knew she was four now because Jeannie told her. Ma hadn't mentioned it at all, but then Ma had been in a funny mood for the last month or so, and Sarah was trying to stay out of her way. She wished her da would come home, maybe her ma would be happy then and she would not have to hide so much.

The day the *Eclipse* sailed into the river mouth Sarah was playing on the foreshore.

'Jeannie. Jeannie,' she shouted. 'Look, look. It's a big ship.'

Jeannie stopped in her task of spreading the nets out on the stones so that they could be cleaned of all the muck that gathered in them during a fishing trip. Shading her eyes with a hand she watched the progress of the ship as it neared Invercraig harbour.

'D'you think it might be my da's ship?' Sarah jumped up and down. 'He's been gone an awful long time.'

'It's a whaler, that's for sure. You can tell by the smell.' Jeannie studied the ship. 'I can't see the name though.'

'It must be my da's ship. It just has to be. Try to see the name, Jeannie, please.'

Jeannie put her other hand up to shade her eyes, squinting with her concentration. 'I can almost see the name,' she told Sarah. 'I think it's the *Eclipse* but I'm not sure.'

Sarah jumped up and down, tugging at Jeannie's skirts. 'It's my da's ship,' she squeaked. 'I knew it was my da's ship.'

'You must run and tell your ma then, and I'll go and tell my ma.'

Sarah climbed the bank and ran along the river path, not stopping to see whether Jeannie went to tell Annie. Her little feet skimmed along the path dislodging stones and gravel.

She burst into the small house. Belle was sitting on a stool in front of the dead fire, staring into its black embers.

'Ma, Ma,' she shouted. 'Da's ship's back. I saw it sailing up the river.'

Belle turned slowly to look at her, then rose clumsily to her feet. Sarah frowned. Ma had got fat and did not look as pretty as she used to, maybe that's why she was unhappy, but now Da was back Sarah was sure she would be happy again.

'Are you sure, Sarah,' Belle whispered.

For a fleeting moment Sarah thought she looked scared, but she must have imagined it. Maybe her ma was just unsure and needed to be convinced.

'Yes I'm sure, Ma. Da'll be home soon, and then you'll be happy again. Won't you?' Sarah stopped. Maybe she had gone too far. But Belle did not seem to notice so she let out her breath again.

Belle turned and started to pick up the clothes that were lying around the room. 'I'd better get things ready for him. You go watch, and run and tell me when you see him coming. There's a good wee lass.'

Sarah ran out of the house and back down the river path. She was pleased that Ma had started to tidy up because the house had been getting messier and messier. Now that Da was home, things would be different.

40

Belle waited all day for Jimmie to come home. She had tidied the house, lit the fire and put the soup pot on to simmer, and there was nothing left to do. She fidgeted and fretted, anxious to see him and yet dreading the moment when he would walk in the door.

The baby inside her jumped and kicked reminding her of his presence. She was sure it was a he because it did not feel anything like the first time when she was pregnant with Sarah, and she hoped Jimmie would be pleased. But why wouldn't he? They had tried so hard for another child since Sarah's birth. And now it had happened, and she was not sure if it was Lachlan's baby or Jimmie's. She pushed the thought of Lachlan out of her mind. He had not given her a thought when he left so why should she bother about him. The baby was Jimmie's and that was an end to it.

Unable to tolerate the house any longer, she walked down to the river bank and along the path until she had a good view of the ship berthed at Invercraig harbour.

Sarah came running up to her. 'I've looked and looked for Da but he's not coming yet. He will come home, won't he?' There was a catch in the child's voice and not for the first time Belle wondered how much she knew about Lachlan, although she had always waited until Sarah was asleep before she welcomed Lachlan into her house.

'Of course he'll come home but they have to see to the unloading first.' Belle's voice held more certainty than she felt. 'Listen, Sarah. You can hear the barrels thumping down on the dock as they take them off the ship.'

Mother and child listened to the distant thudding and thumping noises, and Belle hoped her guess was correct.

'Come on, Sarah.' Belle took the child's hand in her own.

It was small and warm. She felt a sudden affinity with her daughter who was as concerned as she was that Jimmie might not return. 'It's time you were home and bedded. You can have a wee plate of soup to warm your stomach and in the morning your da will be home. I'm sure of it.'

Darkness was falling when Sarah eventually went to sleep and still Jimmie had not come home. Belle had been staring into the fire for what seemed to her to be an eternity before she heard the welcome rattle of the latch being lifted and the door opening.

Jimmie looked different. The beard and the breadth of his shoulders made him look more of a man. It was as if a boy had left and a man had returned in his place.

Shyness swept over Belle. She had never been shy with Jimmie before, but now she was uncertain of this man who was her husband.

'Belle! Oh, Belle!' Jimmie dropped his bundle on the floor and held out his arms.

Belle stood up, hesitated a moment, and then ran into his arms. 'Oh Jimmie,' she sobbed on his shoulder. 'I thought you were never coming and I've waited so long.'

His arms felt strong and hard as they enclosed her in his embrace. She felt safe and protected and she resolved to herself that she would never look at another man again.

Jimmie held her close to him. He could feel her heart fluttering against him and the wetness of her tears on his face as he bent over to kiss her. He also felt the unmistakable movement of her stomach as she pressed closer to him. He ran his hands down her body and then looked at her with amazement.

'Belle, you're with child.' He ran his hands over her waist and round to her belly. 'I can feel it.'

Belle hung her head. 'You're not pleased? I thought you would be.'

'Of course I'm pleased.' He picked her up and swung her around. 'But what a time for it to happen, when I'm away and can't look after you.'

'It couldn't have happened when you were away,' Belle said, drily. 'It must have been that last night before you left. D'you remember?'

'How could I ever forget. It was just like it was when we were courting.' He kissed her gently. 'Well I'm here now and I won't go away again. Not until after it's born anyway.'

He led her to the bed. 'I've missed you, Belle. 'You'll never know how much I've missed you.'

Belle struggled out of his grasp. 'I've made you some soup. You'll be hungry.'

'The only hunger I have just now is for you, Belle. The soup can wait.' He pulled her down on the bed and fumbled with the fastenings of her dress.

'Don't be so impatient. I'll do it myself, you'll tear it.' Belle forced his fingers away and unfastened her dress. She removed her clothes until she stood before him in her shift which she did not take off. 'I'm ready,' she said, as she climbed into the bed beside him.

Jimmie's need for her was so great that his lovemaking had an urgency he could not control and it was over too soon. But there would be plenty of time for loving before he returned to the whaling. And soon there would be a child, a son to carry on his name. A son to inherit the boat he was going to buy with the money he made at the whaling.

Jimmie sank into a deeply satisfying and dreamless sleep with Belle resting in the crook of his arm.

Belle lay awake long after Jimmie fell asleep. She felt numb with an emptiness that was like an aching void consuming her, spreading and swelling until it encompassed her whole body. She had thought she could forget Lachlan, but Jimmie's lovemaking had instigated a bitter surge of memories, and now she lay, still full of raging needs that Jimmie had been unable to meet. The throb in her loins was like an itch she could not scratch, and filled her with longings that only Lachlan could satisfy.

Jimmie's arm around her felt oppressive, as if he was trying to imprison her. She was unable to shrug it off and be free. Just as she would never be able to be free of Jimmie and her life in Craigden.

All of a sudden she realised that her utmost wish was to have been born a man. If she had been a man she could have been free and led her own life. She could have made love with as many different partners as she wanted to, and no one would have thought any the worse of her. But because she was a woman she had to marry, had to be dependent on a man, and was expected to be faithful. Life was unfair.

Eventually she fell into a restless sleep, still imprisoned by Jimmie's arm.

41

The blanket twisted around Sarah's small body as she tossed and turned during the night. She dreamed of her da, lifting her up and whirling her around until her head spun. But then his image got all confused with the man who visited Ma during the night, until she wasn't sure what her da looked like.

She woke with a start. Daylight was just beginning to seep into the gloom of the house so she knew it was morning. Ma wasn't awake yet, but then Sarah often awoke first, although Ma did not know that. Sarah liked to lie in the warmth of her bed in the early morning keeping her eyes closed, and listening to the birds. They were always at their loudest and most musical at that time, and she would imagine she could fly with them and perch in the trees to sing. She liked to sing but Ma called it caterwauling and it seemed to annoy her, and Sarah did not like annoying her ma.

This morning she couldn't rest comfortably because the blanket was wrapped around her neck and shoulders, and her feet were cold. She sat up and tried to untangle the bedcovers and as she did so she glanced over at Ma's bed to see if she was awake.

Her ma lay at the back of the bed, almost hidden by the bulk of the man who had his arm thrown over her. Sarah squinted, trying to distinguish his features, but it was no use there wasn't enough light. Quietly, she got out of her truckle bed and padded over to where her ma and the man lay sleeping. He was awfully hairy and Sarah was not sure whether it was Da.

She leaned over for a closer look. He stirred and opened his eyes. Sarah jumped back in fright ready to run back to the safety of her bed however a huge hand shot out and grasped her arm. She whimpered with fright.

'Why my wee pet, d'you not know your da then?' He grinned at her. 'Is it the beard? Here, feel it.' He pulled her hand towards his face. 'Is it not nice then?'

Sarah fingered his beard. It was rough and wiry. Not soft like her ma's or her own hair. 'It feels funny,' she said, but she was not frightened anymore for this was her da.

Jimmie released Sarah's arm when Belle turned and murmured, before throwing her arm around him.

'It's all right, my love. I'm still here. Sarah can maybe run to her gran's so we can have time to talk.' Turning, he smiled at Sarah, 'I have a lot to tell your ma, so put your clothes on, my wee pet. Gran'll give you some breakfast.'

Sarah looked towards her ma to be sure she had her permission to go, but Belle's eyes had widened with the startled look of someone who does not quite know where they are. They reminded Sarah of the way rabbits looked just before Davie clubbed them. Sarah did not like hurting the rabbits, but Jeannie always followed Davie, and Sarah would put up with anything to be with Jeannie.

'Can I go, Ma?' Sarah was forced to ask because she was not even sure if Ma knew she was there.

'Yes, off you go, but don't make a nuisance of yourself.' Ma's voice was so low Sarah could hardly hear it.

It didn't take her long to pull her clothes on and to slip out the door of the cottage. Da had his hands on Ma's shoulders and was pulling her towards him even as she was closing the door. Sarah hoped he was not going to hurt her, but they had told her to go and she daren't disobey Ma.

Jimmie's hands were rough and his arms muscular. Belle's resistance made no difference as he pulled her towards him and into his embrace. His beard bristled against her face, rasping her skin.

'Not now, Jimmie,' she protested. Her mind and thoughts were full of Lachlan and she was afraid Jimmie had heard her murmur Lachlan's name as she wakened and turned to him. For it was Lachlan who had come to her in her dreams and it was Lachlan she had wanted so badly when she awoke.

Jimmie laughed. 'You've always been a tease, Belle. But you know you want me just as much as I want you.'

She lay still. It was useless to struggle, he was too strong for her, and he thought she was just teasing him as she had often done in the past.

The bed was hard and unresisting as he came down on top of her and despite herself, she was aroused. She enjoyed his strength and the hardness of his body but when she closed her eyes it was Lachlan's face she saw.

Tears slowly slipped down her face, moistening the pillow and Jimmie's arms. She blinked hard but could not stop the flow that was emptying the sorrow from her heart.

Jimmie rolled off her. 'Why, Belle, what's wrong?' He wiped the tears from her cheeks with sea-roughened fingers. 'I haven't hurt you, have I?'

'I don't know what's wrong, Jimmie. I just feel as if there's a well of tears inside me and I can't stop them from spilling over.'

'You're a strange lass, Belle. But then you always were. As long as you're sure I haven't hurt you? I couldn't bear to hurt you, Belle.'

'No, you haven't hurt me, Jimmie.' She smiled at him through her tears. 'I'll be all right, just give me a minute.'

Belle slid out of the bed and started to dress while Jimmie pulled himself higher up onto his pillow, to watch her. Belle felt the heat of a blush spread upwards from her neck to her face. Although she realised now that she did not love Jimmie, she was fond of him, and it wasn't fair to him that her mind was occupied with someone else. Lachlan did not deserve to be in her thoughts, for he had used her, and treated her badly. She would be better off loving Jimmie. She would love Jimmie, she'd force herself.

Belle fastened the last button and turned to kneel beside the bed. She stroked Jimmie's cheek and fingered his beard.

'I'll be a good wife to you, Jimmie,' she murmured and kissed his forehead.

'You're a good wife now, Belle.' He grasped her shoulders and kissed her.

The salty taste of his lips reminded her of the sea, as they pressed firmly on hers. She nestled up to him and responded, determined to prove her love. As he pulled her into the bed, she pushed her skirts up around her waist so she could straddle him. She paced herself and him, enjoying the feeling of power and control. Eventually, unable to contain herself any longer, she collapsed on top of him in an agony of delight.

42

As the day of Lachlan's wedding to Clarinda drew closer he became more and more nervous.

'A spring wedding would be nice,' he murmured to Clarinda as he sat with her in the small drawing room. But their families were insistent it should be sooner so the date was set for mid-November.

Lachlan felt obliged to spend more time with Clarinda and the couple sat most evenings in the small drawing room. Aunt Beattie no longer observed all the formalities expected during a courtship and, after a substantial amount of small talk, she eventually left them on their own. As soon as she withdrew, Lachlan eased himself off the uncomfortable straight-backed chair and joined Clarinda on the cream chaise longue. He enfolded her hand within his own, the feel of her fingers fluttering within his grasp reminding him of a butterfly he had once caught. Clarinda was like that butterfly, delicate and fragile.

He often felt like grabbing her and crushing her to him, but was afraid to. He compensated for this by lifting her fingers to his mouth and caressing them with his lips, laughing as the colour mounted in her cheeks. As the wedding day approached he wondered what it would feel like when he kissed her properly. Whether she would respond, and whether there was any passion at all beneath her cool exterior.

Lachlan occasionally thought of Belle, but a visit to the night-houses or supper rooms provided him with a choice of female companionship able to satisfy any of his needs, and Belle became simply a memory.

The house buzzed with activity. The servants cleaned and polished everything they could. The silver sparkled, the floors gleamed, new linen was purchased, curtains and hangings were made, and Clarinda started to spend a large part of her time with her dressmaker. There was a great deal of whispering and mystery surrounding her choice of material and the design of her wedding dress.

Lachlan's father had written to say he and Lady Catherine would arrive the week before the wedding. So Lachlan haunted the docks, meeting every sailing packet that arrived. He knew his parents would expect to be met and did not want to incur their wrath for, although he no longer lived in the family home, Lachlan was still wary of his father's anger.

Eventually Lachlan saw the familiar figure of the laird on the deck of the Dundee registered ship, *Mary Stewart*, as it positioned itself for mooring at the jetty. He hurried to meet it and was almost level with the ship as it ran out its gangplank.

Lachlan watched as his father handed his mother onto the gangplank and he hurried up it to take her hand.

'Thank you, Lachlan. I was feeling a bit under the weather.' Lady Catherine smiled at him.

Carefully, Lachlan guided her down onto the safety of the quay. 'You look marvellous,' he told her, although thinking she appeared somewhat peaked. He could not stop himself from adding, 'You will soon feel yourself again.'

His father's bull-like figure strutted down the plank. 'Well, my boy, it's good to see you,' his voice was as rough and gravelly as Lachlan remembered. 'You'll soon be a man and not before time too.'

The laird surveyed the crowded docks before turning to his wife. 'Come Catherine, we must get away from this mob.' Turning to Lachlan, he said, 'You have a carriage ready for us I hope?'

'Of course,' Lachlan answered, stiffly. 'It's just down here.' He led his parents through the crowds to where the carriage was waiting.

'I am so looking forward to this wedding, Lachlan,' his mother whispered to him as he helped her into the carriage.

'I've waited such a long time for it.'

Lachlan's heart was heavy. He had always adored his mother and he could not tell her he was only marrying because they wanted him to. So he smiled and said, 'Yes mother, it will be a fine wedding and Clarinda will be a beautiful bride,' because he knew that was what his mother wanted to hear.

Aunt Beattie was already in the hall waiting for them. She hugged his mother and offered her hand to his father. 'Roderick, it's been such a long time,' she murmured, turning an unattractive shade of pink as he pressed the hand to his lips.

Lachlan hid a smile. It was common knowledge in the family that Aunt Beattie had set her cap at his father and been disappointed when he had married her cousin Catherine.

Recovering her composure, Aunt Beattie said, 'Come Catherine I will show you to your room myself. I have arranged for you to have the services of Rachel while you are here. She has the makings of a good lady's maid, she's good with a needle and absolutely marvellous at dressing hair. I'm sure you'll like her.'

Lachlan watched with amusement as Aunt Beattie, still talking animatedly, slipped an arm around his mother's waist and led her towards the stairs.

The house suddenly seemed claustrophobic and Lachlan sighed as he turned towards the garden, for with the arrival of his parents it seemed as if another step had been taken towards his impending marriage. Perhaps a walk in the fresh air would improve his spirits.

43

Belle could feel Hamish's eyes on her as she plodded through the stable courtyard, but she ignored him. Let him think whatever he wanted to, she didn't care. He was only a groom after all and he would not dare gossip about his master.

The outer corridor was cool, so she was glad to reach the warmth of the kitchen. Thankfully she eased the creels onto the edge of the table so that it took the weight off her hips and stopped the straps cutting into her.

The clattering of pots and pans seemed to fade into the distance as the heat increased. She shivered and grasped the table to stop the room spinning around.

Strong arms grasped her. 'Sit down, lass, before you fall down.'

Belle felt the hardness of a chair pushed under her and sank back into it, closing her eyes until the room stopped revolving. She felt a hot cup thrust into her hands and closed her fingers around it.

'Drink up, lass. You'll feel the better of it.' The voice was not quite so far off now and was vaguely familiar.

Belle looked up ready to express her gratitude, but was unable to speak when she saw that it was Mrs Ross who was staring at her with concern on her face.

'Well, drink it up then. It's only hot tea, but it'll revive you.'

Belle took a sip and felt it burning all the way down to her stomach. Taking another sip, she rolled it over her tongue and round her mouth before swallowing. She liked the taste, although it was quite different from the ale she was used to drinking. Ordinary folks didn't drink tea, it was too expensive, so this was a rare treat. She took another sip and another, and could feel the coldness leave her and the warmth return to the room.

'That's better. Now you'll take your creels off and sit for a while. I'll not have you tramp down that road until you're rested. What's Annie thinking of sending you out on the road anyway? By the look of you, it's an easier job you'll need to do, not carting around those heavy creels. I'll have a word with her.'

Belle fumbled with her creel straps and was glad when one of the maids came to help her. 'What's wrong with Mrs Ross, she's never had a kind word for me before,' she whispered to the girl.

The girl giggled. 'Oh, she's all right. She shouts a lot but I've known worse.'

Belle watched Mrs Ross bustle about the kitchen. For someone so fat she was light on her feet and moved easily between the fire and the large table in the centre of the room. Two of the maids giggled over the sinks as they peeled vegetables, another had flour up to her elbows as she sank her hands into a bowl, while yet another sat in a corner polishing cutlery.

Belle turned her eyes away as Mrs Ross approached her. She could hear a chair being pulled over and then a strong hand closing over hers.

'Ah, you're feeling a wee bit warmer now, but I'm not letting you away yet. I'll not be having your death on my conscience.' Mrs Ross patted her hand. 'You'll have a bite of stew before I'll let you go, and I'll send Lizzie down the road with you, just to make sure you're safe.'

'Thank you, but there's no need,' Belle mumbled. 'I feel fine now. It's just that I'm so clumsy and heavy and I think the heat of the kitchen affected me. I'll be all right once I'm out on the road.'

'Nonsense, I'll hear no arguments. You'll eat your stew and Lizzie will take you down the road. That's an end to it.'

Mrs Ross bustled over to the girls at the sink. 'Will you stop your giggling and get on with the job, or do I have to warm your ears for you. Just because the master's away doesn't mean I'll have any slacking.'

She returned to sit beside Belle. 'It's a firm hand that's needed with this lot. They'd not do a hands turn if they got off with it.'

'You said the master's away?' Belle was curious, she hadn't realised the laird was not at home. She noticed Mrs Ross giving her a quizzical glance and did not want her to start wondering why she was interested. 'Does that mean you won't need so much fish?' she finished, lamely.

'Of course I'll take the fish, lass,' Mrs Ross patted her hand. 'I have all these idle skivvies to feed for a start, even before I start on the house staff. The master being away doesn't make that much difference. And speaking about eating, you haven't finished your stew yet, so sup up.' She turned and shouted at the girl in the corner, 'Hurry up with that silver, Lizzie, I could have polished the whole house, the time you're taking.'

The girl, hardly more than a child, answered with a frightened squeak, 'I'm near finished Mistress Ross.' She rubbed frantically on a knife, 'See this is the last one.'

'Good lass. Now get a shawl and walk down to the village with Mistress Watt. She's not feeling so well.'

Lizzie was silent as they walked through the empty stable courtyard. Buckets clattered and clanged from the depths of the stables and Belle guessed that Hamish was feeding the horses.

'Are you always this quiet, Lizzie?' Belle eased up one of the straps binding her creels round her hips. She never seemed to be able to find a comfortable position for them.

'Mistress Ross says I'm not to speak to or look at any of the men or boys who work here.' Lizzie glanced around, 'So I usually stay quiet until I'm past the yard.'

'But there's nobody here today. So you're safe.'

'Mistress Ross says they hides and spies on you.' Lizzie glanced over her shoulder. 'They're not to be trusted, she says, and if I gets into trouble, I'm out the door, she says.'

Belle looked at the child. She was small and scraggy. Not much bigger than Annie's Jeannie. Wisps of dull, brown hair escaped from her white mob cap and her eyes lacked sparkle. It was almost impossible for Belle to imagine her getting into trouble. 'How old are you, Lizzie?' she asked, noticing how the child's hands twisted together in front of her.

'I'm fourteen summers, Mistress Watt.'

'Well, Lizzie. I won't let anyone harm you while you're with me, and anyway getting into trouble isn't as bad as Mrs Ross thinks it is. Believe me, you won't always be so frightened of boys.'

'If you say so, Mistress Watt.' Lizzie hurried as they reached the end of the courtyard, obviously glad to leave it behind.

Belle plodded after the girl, her body now feeling as heavy as her spirits. 'Not so fast, Lizzie,' she panted.

'Oh, Mistress Watt, I'm sorry. I forgot you weren't well.'

Lizzie's eyes seemed to be boring into her belly and Belle wondered what she knew about having babies, or had Mrs Ross frightened her so much that the child was afraid to think about it.

'My name's Belle, Lizzie, don't call me Mistress Watt, it reminds me of my mother-in-law. And I'm not unwell. I'm just going to have a baby.'

Belle saw Lizzie's eyes widen as she looked away and was not sure if the look that had passed over the child's face was one of horror or if she was simply embarrassed.

'There's nothing to be frightened of, Lizzie. It's a natural thing for women.'

'My ma died having a baby.' Lizzie's voice was flat and emotionless.

'I'm not going to die, Lizzie. My baby's going to be born and he'll be a lovely baby, the most beautiful baby in the world.' A vision of Lachlan floated in Belle's mind and she could almost see him standing before her, tall, straight and handsome. Her son would look just like him.

The vision faded, leaving Belle sad and alone. Where was Lachlan now? What was he doing? And did he think of her?

'Lizzie?' Belle's voice was tentative. 'Have you worked at the big house for very long?'

'Since June, Mistress Belle. My da said I should go into service and maybe someday I could be a lady's maid.'

'What's it like to work for the laird? I've often wondered.'

'I don't see him much. I'm usually in the kitchen. But his lady's very nice and gentle. Sometimes she comes downstairs.'

'What about the young master. D'you ever see him?' Belle tried to keep her voice casual.

'He's not here now, but I stays out of his road anyways. Mrs Ross says he'd get a girl into trouble and best stay clear of him. Mrs Ross spoils him though, when he comes to the kitchen. And Meg's sweet on him, but the other girls say he never pays her no heed.'

'Mrs Ross said the family were away from home, so I suppose he's gone with them.' Belle did not want to admit to Lizzie that she knew Lachlan had left almost two months ago.

'Aye, they're all away now. The young master left a while back and now the laird and his lady have gone as well. Going to see the young master get wed, I'm told. I haven't seen the young master's lady but they say she's the most beautiful . . . '

Lizzie's voice faded as Belle felt the dizziness swamp her. Panting for breath her feet slowed and stopped. She leaned against the wall that bordered the road and rested her creels on top of it. Lachlan to be wed, it was unthinkable. No wonder he had left so suddenly. He wouldn't want the complication of a child, not when he was about to be wed.

'Are you feeling ill again?'

Lizzie's anxious voice penetrated the fog that engulfed Belle's mind. Shaking her head to clear it, she said, 'I'm all right now, Lizzie. I just came over a bit faint that's all.'

Belle hoisted her creels back onto her hips and started to walk towards Craigden. She had to get home, home to Jimmie and Sarah, home where she was safe.

44

Ian bent his head over the nets and shook them. He didn't want to make it obvious he was watching Belle. He had known it was her as soon as she'd come into sight, making her way towards the village. She did not walk like the other women. There was a swing to her hips and a swagger that seemed to come naturally to her, even when she was heavy with a pregnancy.

He often dreamed of her in the bright coloured silks she had worn when she first came to Craigden. Now she wore the familiar fishwives clothes, with the plain blue skirt, gathered up to show the striped petticoats underneath. The rough garments did not mar her beauty in any way, but the anticipated feel of the silk and the smoothness of her skin made Ian almost sick with desire.

Out of the corner of his eye he saw Ellen approach along the river bank. She must have seen Belle and he wasn't sure if she guessed about his longings for his sister-in-law.

Ian was tied to Ellen now and his future was secure. By the time Christmas came he would have a share in the Bruce boat and a brand new wife. He would have to put Belle out of his mind and his thoughts.

Ellen reached the boat and leaned on the bow. 'I've told Da the date's set. Have you told your ma yet?'

He could feel her eyes watching him as he spread the nets out onto the river bank. Looking up he met her clear gaze, and smiled at her. She was so open and honest and reliable. He almost felt as if she was his mother. 'I wanted to tell Ma when we were together. I thought it would be nicer.'

She leaned over and grasped his hands. 'You're one of the nicest persons a girl could have, d'you know that?'

'I couldn't do better myself,' he said, as Belle swished

past both of them.

They watched her as she headed towards Annie's house, the creels bumping off her hips in time to her steps.

'Belle's a strange one,' Ellen said. 'She doesn't speak much to the women but the men fairly have eyes for her.'

Ian was afraid to speak for fear Ellen guessed what he was thinking.

Ellen tightened her grip on his hands. 'Let's go and tell your ma now,' she said.

Belle slumped down at the table. 'I'm sorry Annie, but I came over all queer when I was at the big house. If it hadn't been for that maid, Lizzie, I'd never have made it down the road.'

Annie tapped her pipe out on the side of the fire. 'You are pretty big, are you sure you've got your dates right?'

'I think so, but I suppose I could have got them wrong. I just feel so heavy. It's not like it was with Sarah.'

'A second bairn's never like the first, and you're on the small side. You haven't the stamina of the fisher folk so I suppose you'd better rest until the birthing.'

Tears welled up in Belle's eyes, for Annie never resisted an opportunity to let her know she was not one of them. 'I'm as strong as any woman in the village even if I'm not so big.' Anyway, who would want to be as big and clumsy as the fisher women, she thought. None of them were as pretty as she was. She saw it every day reflected in the men's eyes. They didn't watch their own women the way they watched her.

'Ach, Belle, I didn't mean it like that. All I'm saying is you should rest now. I'll see to the selling of the fish, Jeannie'll help me. Sarah can stay here as well, until after the birthing. It'll give you a better chance, and after all, we don't want to lose you.'

Belle stared at her mother-in-law in amazement, for although the two women had learned to tolerate each other, she could not remember a time when Annie had shown any sympathy for her. She never seemed to be able to do anything to please Annie.

'All right, Annie. If that's what you think is best.' Despite her resentment Belle couldn't help but feel relief that she would not have to go out with the heavy creels.

The door groaned open and a whisper of wind rippled round the room. Belle shivered and pulled her shawl over her shoulders as she looked up. She thought for a moment it was Jimmie framed in the light and rose from her seat with a smile on her lips, but sank back down when she realised it was Ian.

Ellen, almost as tall as Ian, followed him into the house.

'We've something to tell you Ma.' Ian grasped Ellen's hand and pulled her further into the room. 'There's to be a wedding.'

A hiss of air escaped from Belle's lips. She could feel the room sliding away from her. How did he know, and why would he be the one to tell Annie? What difference did it make to them anyway?

Ian regarded Belle thoughtfully, as he said, 'It's me and Ellen, Ma. We're to be wed and we want your blessing.'

'Why, that's grand news lad, I'm fair pleased for you both. I hope it'll be a proper fisher wedding this time, not like the last one.'

'Aye, that it will, Ma. Ellen thought the week before Christmas would be a good time. The boats are usually laid up then.'

Belle sensed Ian watching her as he spoke to his mother. Ever since she'd come to Craigden his eyes had seemed to be watching her, and he always made her feel uncomfortable. She had this vague notion he knew what she was thinking, and she had suspected for a long time that he knew about Lachlan. Confused thoughts flitted through her mind. It was his own wedding Ian had been talking about, not Lachlan's. But she wasn't sure whether he had deliberately tried to mislead her and had been teasing. She turned her head away and stared into the fire convinced that Ian was a cruel man who took pleasure in hurting those around him.

'Are you not going to wish us good luck, Belle?' Ian had his arm around Ellen's waist and he pulled her closer to him, but Belle knew his eyes were on her.

'Aye, Ian. I'll wish you good luck and good fortune.' Belle twisted her lips into a smile. 'You'll be a man of wealth now that you've managed to get a share in the Bruce boat. It's always what you've wanted, isn't it?'

45

The gale continued to howl round the corners of the shack and Belle woke with a start after a night of disturbed sleep.

It was dark and the gloom was filled with odd noises. She thought for a moment Lachlan was knocking to be let in, and she stared into the darkness, trying to pierce the shadows, but it was only the wind rattling the windows and doors.

She turned over in the bed to face Jimmie who was snoring gently at her side and threw her arm over him, comforted by his nearness and warmth. He mumbled her name and held her close, although he did not wake.

Fragments of the dream clung to her mind. The fire, the stone circle, the fuzzy shapes of things larger than men, the chants, the pointing fingers, and everywhere, the Reverend Murdo screaming at her. His finger growing longer and longer, his voice more and more accusing, until she could no longer stand it.

She shuddered within the safety of Jimmie's encircling arm.

She mustn't ever let Jimmie go. He was her security and her safety. As long as she was with him nothing bad could ever happen to her.

And yet her mind, this morning, was filled with thoughts of Lachlan. They had come unbidden and unwanted, and she was unsure why his image had come so strongly to her when she had been so successful over the past few months in banishing him from her heart and mind.

At least Jimmie wouldn't have to leave her today, for the November storms had been raging for the past five days since the fifteenth day of the month, and the fishing boats had been unable to leave the village.

Resting her hand on Jimmie's chest where she could feel

the strong, steady beat of his heart, Belle gradually drifted back to sleep.

Lachlan lay beside Clarinda, unsatisfied and disappointed. He had been as gentle as he could be, but she had cried out in pain when he entered her and had then lain still and rigid.

'Are you all right,' he whispered into the darkness but there was no response. He was sure she was still awake, although her body lay, silent and still, far away from his on the edge of the four-poster bed.

Staring into the darkness he could only just make out vague shapes and, as his eyes tried to penetrate the shadows, memories of the nights he had spent with Belle crept unbidden into his mind. He remembered how he would lie, spent and sated, after tumbling her. Never once had he left Belle's bed unsatisfied or disappointed.

It was odd how after months of never giving any thought to Belle she had persisted in invading his thoughts. She had come to him during his dream the previous night and lain by his side. Her breath had sighed in his ears and he had felt her familiar fingers stroking him and her lips brushing his cheek. It was early morning and still dark when he'd wakened and felt the familiar excitement he had always felt when he was with her. He had reached out his arms but she wasn't there. And then he had remembered. This was his wedding day and Clarinda would be his. He had drifted back to sleep thinking that perhaps Clarinda would banish Belle from his mind.

It had been a vain thought and any hope he'd had of Clarinda being able to satisfy his needs and longings had dwindled with the passing of the day.

Lachlan sighed, and turning his back to Clarinda, he tried to sleep.

The storms of November passed and the boats returned to sea, although the fishing was sparse. The villagers were silent and an air of melancholy hovered over the huddle of houses nestling below the cliff. Even the river was muted, flowing softly to the sea and back again, the waves striking the rocks with a sibilant hiss and gasp so different from the thundering impact they'd had only a month ago.

Belle's stomach had become so swollen she could not bend or move about easily and she spent many hours staring into the fire, thinking of nothing except her misery. All she could think of was the birth to come. She gave little thought to Sarah, who was now staying at Annie's house.

Annie visited, bringing soup and oatcakes. 'You have to keep your strength up,' she'd say, or, 'Are you sure you're feeling all right? You look fair worn out.'

Belle could see the little worried frown on Annie's weather-beaten face, but nothing Annie did or said could alter her view that the older woman couldn't have cared less for her and was only concerned about the baby she was carrying, Jimmie's son. For Belle was convinced the baby would be a boy.

'I'm fine,' she told Annie. 'I'm just weary. I'll be glad when it's all over and I don't have to drag all this weight around with me.'

'You'll manage to Ian's wedding, I hope.' It was more of a demand than a request.

'Ian would be that disappointed if you weren't there.'

'Why would Ian bother? It's not me he's marrying, it's Ellen.'

Belle noticed Annie's face cloud over and felt a twinge of guilt for it wasn't often she managed to upset Annie.

Annie turned to leave, and Belle waited until she pulled the door open before adding, 'Of course I'll come. It's high time he was wed and I wouldn't miss it for anything.'

Annie's smile did not reach her eyes. 'I'll let him know. He'll be pleased.' The door clicked shut behind her and Belle was alone again.

Belle woke early on the morning of the wedding day and slid clumsily around Jimmie and out of the bed. Her toes curled with the cold when her bare feet hit the floor. She reached for her shawl and pulled it round her shoulders shivering as she did so.

The windows were frosted with the image of fern-like patterns, as if someone had traced them with fingers of ice. Her breath clouded in front of her when she opened the door and looked out. There was hardly a puff of wind, and the river caressed the stones on the river bank with little ripples and eddies, the early morning sun glinting off the wavelets as they lapped against the pebbles. Boats rocked gently, moored by silver ropes to a silver shore, for no fisherman would set sail today. Smoke seeped out of the chimneys of most of the cottages and Belle knew the womenfolk were up and preparing for the festivities.

She felt different this morning. It was as if a cloud had lifted and, despite her bulk, she felt light and energetic. Her stomach no longer seemed to be pressing on her lungs and her breathing was easier. Inhaling the morning air she gasped at its sharpness and shivered with the iciness of it, before closing the door and turning back into the room.

Lowering herself to her knees she started to clean the ash from the fire before laying sticks and twigs to rekindle it. Suddenly she was hungry and she was glad when the flames started to crackle and spark for now she would be able to make the oatmeal porridge.

Jimmie stirred in the bed. 'You're up early the day, Belle,' he muttered. 'Is anything the matter?'

Belle heaved herself onto her feet and approached the bed. Sitting on the edge of it she stroked Jimmie's face and smiled at him. 'I wasn't comfortable and felt like getting up.'

He grasped her hand and held it against his face. 'Och, Belle. You're so bonny. I wish we could . . . ' He buried his face in her stomach and groaned.

'It won't be long now, Jimmie. Just another month and then you'll have the son you want and I'll be bonny again.' She kissed the top of his head. 'There's porridge ready if you want it.'

46

Sarah was sure she hadn't slept any longer than usual, but Jeannie was not beside her and the fire was blazing, sending flickering red fingers of light into every corner of the room. The house resounded with voices and laughter and Annie bustled about among her menfolk, her cheeks almost as red as the fire.

Jeannie was clattering bowls onto the table but turned towards Sarah as she stirred in the truckle bed. 'You're wakened are you? I thought you were going to sleep for ever. D'you not know this is Ian's wedding day and there's lots to do.'

Sarah grinned. Jeannie was funny when she tried to be like Annie. But Sarah wasn't scared of Jeannie.

'Get up and put your clothes on then. We can't get the bed rolled away until you're out of it. Not unless you want rolled under the box bed for the rest of the day.'

Sarah swung her legs free of the scratchy blanket and jumped onto the floor. She didn't fancy being rolled away with the bed into the spider hole under the box bed in the alcove. Jeannie always laughed at her when she lifted the blanket to inspect the bedding before she got into it at bedtime. 'You're too pernickety, so you are,' she'd tease, but Sarah couldn't help it because she was scared of spiders.

Annie swung the swey hook round so that the porridge pot was no longer hanging over the fire, and taking both hands she heaved it off the hook and onto the wooden table.

'Eat up,' she commanded, ladling a dollop of porridge into each bowl, 'because there won't be anything else until after the wedding. And don't stop eating until that pot's empty.' She turned back to the fire and grasping a large flat griddle, hooked it on the swey hook and swung it over the fire to heat it up for the oatcakes to cook.

Sarah, balancing on a stool between Jeannie and Davie, supped her porridge while she watched the men and listened to the deep rumble of their voices. She could not quite understand what a wedding was and why it was so important, stopping Granda and her uncles from taking their boat out.

The pot was not so heavy when it was empty but it still needed both girls to carry it. Jeannie held the semi-circular handle with one hand but Sarah, who was smaller, grasped it with both hands and walked in crab-like fashion to the shore. The heavy pot bumped off her legs, but she liked to help Jeannie so she did not complain.

The river was gentle. Birds perched on the water rocking and bobbing on the wavelets as if resting on a liquid bed. Sarah liked to watch them but couldn't understand why they did not sink.

Jeannie dropped to her knees on the frosted pebbles. 'You can let go of the pot now, wee Sarah. We're here.'

Sarah loosened her grip and watched as Jeannie started to wash the pot out. It didn't seem very difficult. 'I could do that,' she said.

Jeannie's hair hung over her face as she concentrated on the pot. Without looking up, she said, 'It's too awkward for you to do but you can help with the porridge bowls.'

Pushing a pebble around with her toe, Sarah considered this. 'But the bowls aren't here so I can't do them.'

'Run back to the house and bring them, you daft gowk.' Jeannie's voice sounded exasperated but was not unkind.

Giving the stone one final push, and Jeannie one last glance, Sarah turned towards the house. She did not want to face Annie on her own but she wanted to please Jeannie.

Timidly she pushed the door open but no one seemed to see her. Annie bent over the griddle, her cheeks aflame. Granda peered down from the loft, shouting, 'Catch this lot then,' and a heap of ribbons, streamers and bunting came flying down to land in a heap on the floor. 'Can you not catch anything you useless lot,' he roared. But he was laughing as well.

Sarah carefully gathered up the bowls into her arms. Annie looked up from the fire. 'You're making yourself useful, are you?'

'Yes Granma,' Sarah mumbled, and quickly escaped through the door.

The water made Sarah's hands tingle as she washed the bowls. When she was finished she sucked her fingers trying to get them warm again.

Jeannie laughed at her. 'Come on, I'll race you up the shore and back again. That'll warm you up.'

The men were already decorating the boats when the two girls came racing back. Sarah collapsed onto the stony shore gasping for breath because, as always, she had tried to keep up with Jeannie, although the older girl had longer legs and could run faster.

At last she managed to gasp, 'Why are they putting ribbons on the boats, Jeannie? I've never seen them do that before.'

'It's because of the wedding. They always decorate the boats. It's a celebration, see.'

Sarah was not sure what a celebration was, but she liked the colourful effect of the beribboned boats. Maybe Granda would give her a ribbon for her hair if she asked him nicely. She fingered the thick bunch of dark hair that hung down her back and the knot of string that held it in place. A ribbon would make her look pretty. Maybe as pretty as her ma.

47

Jimmie slipped his arm around Belle's waist as they walked towards Annie's house. 'It'll soon be time for the parade to the kirk,' he told her. 'And if I'm to be best man I can't be late.'

Belle looked at him in dismay. 'What about me? I'll never manage to walk up the cliff path.'

'That's all right, Belle. I spoke to Ma and you can sit at the fire while we all go to the kirk.'

'Sit with me, Jimmie, I don't want to be alone.' Belle gripped his arm. 'You don't have to go to the church. Stay with me.'

'I can't, Belle. I'm to be Ian's best man. I have to stand up in the kirk beside him.'

'Angus or Davie could do that,' Belle pleaded. 'You have to stay with me.'

'No, Belle. This is one time I can't do what you ask. Ian asked me and I will do it.'

Jimmie's tone was final and Belle knew it was no use arguing with him, but she felt the melancholy creep over her and the brightness seemed to have gone out of the day.

By the time they reached Annie's house most of the village people had congregated on the strip of land that separated the houses from the shore. Ian came hurrying towards them looking strangely tidy in a new round-necked sweater Ellen had knitted for him, and his best navy trousers.

'I thought you weren't coming and I'd have to come and get you,' he said.

'No fear of that.' Jimmie gave Belle's waist a squeeze. 'It's just that we're not as fleet as we used to be, and we took longer to get here than usual.'

Annie appeared in front of them. 'It's time we were away

or the bride will get there first. And that will never do.' She grabbed Ian's arm. 'You and Jimmie will lead the procession and I'll see everyone follows in pairs. And as for you Belle, you'd better go in the house and sit at the fire, for it'll not do you any good to walk up that path. You can keep an eye on the pot if you want to be useful and see it doesn't dry up and burn.'

The huddle of houses was unusually quiet and deserted after the procession left and Belle walked down to the shore where the boats floated gently in the water, their ribbons wafting in the gentle breeze. A sense of peace swept over her for there was no sensation of watching eyes or prattling tongues.

She turned and walked among the tables that had been set out on the foreshore, ready for the feast to come. The whole village would have been cooking and baking, and she knew that as soon as everyone came back the pots of herring and potatoes would be brought out and the tables would be heaped with oatcakes.

Belle retained the sense of peace for the rest of the day. It seemed as if she was enclosed in a small private world of her own. She nodded and smiled in the right places but no one, not even Jimmie, could penetrate her cocoon.

Darkness came early and fire brands were lit to illuminate the shore. The wedding guests had eaten their fill and Joe, the landlord of the village inn, had donated several barrels of ale, so most people were quite merry.

Cadger Wullie was playing his fiddle and the long reel was about to start. The villagers lined up in two rows facing each other and with a lot of hooching and skirling the dance commenced.

Belle watched for a moment but the music and the skirling beat upon her brain. The flare of the fire brands hurt her eyes and the smoke wafted around and into her nostrils making her feel slightly queazy. She slipped out of the light and leaned against the back of a cottage wall where she drew in great gulps of air.

Feeling slightly better she turned to make her way back to

the shore, only to find Ian blocking her way.

'I saw you slip away,' he said. 'I thought I'd join you.'

Belle rested her hand on top of her stomach. 'Where's Ellen?'

'Dancing with Jimmie. The best man has to dance with the bride, d'you not know that? So as you can't dance I thought I'd keep you company.'

Belle could barely make out his face in the darkness, and she could not see his eyes. However she could almost smell and taste the menace that faced her.

'What d'you want with me?' She tried to keep her voice calm and controlled for she knew instinctively that Ian would like her to be afraid.

'I want you, Belle.' He leaned over her. 'I know what you are, you see. And I want some of it as well.'

Ian placed his hand flat on the wall behind her. Belle tried to pull herself away from the sour, whisky laden breath that sprayed over her, but could not move because her back was against the wall of the house.

He slipped his hand underneath her skirt and stroked her with a surprising gentleness. 'You've known for a long time that it's you I want.'

Belle placed both hands on his shoulders and tried to push him away, but he was immovable.

'You've made a mistake. I don't want you, Ian.' Belle's breathing came in gasps for, even though she found Ian's attentions unwelcome, her body still betrayed her.

Ian laughed, 'Oh yes, you do. You want me all right. You see I know you, Belle, and I know exactly what you are.'

'You don't know anything about me, Ian Watt. And what gives you the right to think you do.'

The rough stubble of Ian's chin scraped her skin as Ian brushed his face against her cheek. Anger rose within her quenching the needs of her body, and a nauseating revulsion swept over her.

She struggled but his grip was sure and strong. 'You can't,' she gasped. 'I'm pregnant. It's not decent.'

'What do you know about decency? It's never bothered

you before.' His breath engulfed her. 'You think I don't know what you were getting up to with the laird's son, the fancy Lachlan. Well I know more than you think and my time will come, Belle. Just wait and see if it doesn't.'

'I'm not afraid of you and if you don't let me go I'll scream rape, and then what will your bonny new wife think of you. And you the grand new boat owner too.' Belle's voice was scornful, masking her fear.

Ian let her skirts fall and heaved himself up off the wall. 'Just remember, Belle,' he said as he turned away, 'my time will come.'

Belle leaned for a moment against the cool, hard stone, panting as she struggled to regain some composure. As soon as her body stopped quivering and her breathing steadied, she emerged from the gloom at the back of the house into the brightness of the fire-brand lighted night.

'Good evening, Mistress Belle.' The Reverend Murdo's greeting gave no indication of whether he had seen or heard anything but Belle thought there was a knowing gleam in his eyes.

The long reel was almost finished when Belle returned to the table, and it wasn't long before a flushed and panting Jimmie joined her.

'I'm tired and not feeling too good, Jimmie. Will you take me home please?' Belle had been feeling well all day but since her encounter with Ian there had been an odd, churning sensation in her stomach.

Jimmie looked anxious but all he said was, 'It's been a busy day for you. I shouldn't have kept you out so late.'

He waited while she got into bed but Belle's thoughts were confused and she wanted to be alone, so she insisted he return to the wedding reception.

'I won't stay too long,' he promised her. But Belle knew that once he was with his brothers they would keep him with them until the whisky and the ale ran out.

The darkness closed around her like a comforting blanket and she snuggled into the warm spot in the middle of the bed. She lay there for what seemed like an eternity and gradually her mind quietened and her body relaxed.

She wasn't sure how long it was before the first pain struck her, and then the next one, and the next. She screamed for Jimmie but he wasn't there. And then she cursed Jimmie and she cursed Lachlan. Finally she cursed Ian, for if the baby was coming early it could only be his fault.

The labour wasn't long and finally a boy was born. But the pains continued and to Belle's amazement a second boy was born. She traced the wispy fair hair first on one head and then on the other and marvelled at how perfect they seemed.

Belle placed a baby at each side of her and settled down to wait for Jimmie to come home.

PART THREE

1838-1840

48

1838-1840

The inn was the only two storey building in Craigden. Like most of the fishermen's houses it was built with the gable end facing the river and the front facing into the village. At the rear, a rickety stair led up to the living quarters, while the public bar entry was at ground level at the front of the building. The slightly larger area of ground in front of it had the grandiose name of village square and this was where the men gathered to exchange news and information of where the best fishing grounds were. The younger fisher lads preferred to do their drinking across the water in Invercraig but on a Saturday night the inn was where the older men met.

Joe had been landlord of the inn for many years. He was a bluff good-natured man who was renowned for appreciating his own wares just a little too much. His wife, Peggy, who had been a fisher lass before she married him turned into a martinet who ruled her husband and the inn with a firm hand. Peggy, however, had died suddenly just last year, and Joe had amazed everyone by remarrying with unseemly haste. His new bride, Madge, was an Invercraig lass whose brother ran one of the more notable hostelries in the town.

Madge knew she had not been accepted in Craigden and was regarded with suspicion by the women. But she didn't care because she was not dependent on them for her living, for no Craigden woman would deign to set foot in a drinking establishment. As long as the men continued to drink at the inn, that was all that mattered.

The inn was not as busy as her brother's establishment in Invercraig, and Madge was dissatisfied. If she could attract the fisher lads as well as their fathers she knew the place could do better. But the village folk would not tolerate the doxies from Invercraig in their village, and Madge knew better than to bring strange women over to be barmaids. If she wanted to employ a barmaid it would have to be a village girl.

She had already approached Jeannie Watt with an offer of employment. Not that Jeannie was much to look at. She was a bit too thin and scrawny. It was a pity the girl who was always with her was too young for she was going to be a beauty.

'You could make a bit of money for yourself,' Madge said to Jeannie. 'It's only waiting at the tables and serving behind the bar, and it's not as if you don't know the men who come here. It would be better than paddling for mussels on the back sands. You can't be making any money doing that.'

'I don't think Ma would like it,' Jeannie said, but there had been a look of longing in her eyes.

'Go and ask her then.' But Madge knew what the outcome would be, for Annie Watt was renowned for being the head of her family and for always having the last word.

It was just as Madge expected, and Jeannie did not come to work for her.

Madge contemplated the problem as she swept the bar floor. Opening the door she whisked the rubbish over the doorstep and out into the square. The wind would do the rest when it funnelled its way up and down the streets and openings, and in between the houses.

It was late September and there was the suggestion of coolness in the air. The whaling ships had returned just last week and the thought of the extra money in the young men's pockets tormented Madge.

Her eyes narrowed as she watched the young woman approaching the square. She was different from the other fisher women. She was smaller and daintier and she would look marvellous in a silk dress instead of the rough woollen clothes she wore.

Madge had seen her before and knew she must be an incomer, just as Madge was. It was obvious in the way the women treated her that she was not really one of them. But Madge had also seen the way the men looked at her and how they turned their heads to watch her as she passed them.

Madge made it her business to find out who the woman was and knew that she was Annie Watt's daughter-in-law, Belle. She also knew there was no love lost between the two women.

Composing her face into a smile, Madge waited for Belle to get within hailing distance.

So far Belle had not spoken to the innkeeper's new wife, although she had seen her several times and, like the rest of the women in the village, she was curious.

She wondered how old the woman was and guessed she was maybe in her thirties which was quite a bit younger than Joe. Belle couldn't help wondering what she had seen in him, for Joe had neither the bearing nor the weather-beaten good looks of the older fishermen.

Each time Belle had seen Madge she had been wearing a different dress. Belle tried hard not to envy them, for her own silk dresses lay at the bottom of a sea-chest. No doubt they would have grown a harvest of green mould by this time for they had been in the chest for the past eight years.

Over that time Belle had grown accustomed to the scratch and scrape of rough wool against her skin. She now regarded it as a penance for her wrongdoing which she was reminded of every time she looked at the twins.

'It's a fine day.' Madge leaned on the shaft of her broom and smiled at Belle.

Belle smiled back at her, 'Yes, it is,' she said.

'Why don't you sit a while and give me your chat.' She laid the broom against the wall of the inn and gestured towards the wooden bench in front of the window.

Belle looked in the direction of the shore where the twins were happily engaged throwing stones in the river. Their whoops of delight when they occasionally managed to skim a stone over the surface of the water mingled with the screech of the gulls and the constant shushing noise of the waves. She could hear faint cries of, 'my one bounced more than yours,' and, 'no it didn't.'

'The bairns will be all right. You can see them fine from here.' Madge was already seated and she patted the bench in an invitation for Belle to join her.

The wood was hard and cool beneath Belle, although the sun was warm on her face. She leaned her head back onto the hard stone of the window sill and gave a contented sigh.

Madge turned to study her and Belle could hear the silk rustle of her dress. It had a sensuous sound to it. Belle had not forgotten what it felt like to wear silk next to her skin and she resisted an urge to reach out and stroke the shiny material.

'Your man was right. You are prettier than all the other women in the village.'

Belle looked at her with startled eyes. 'You've met my Jimmie?' The flash of jealousy was unexpected for she had never thought that Jimmie ever looked at other women. Surely he wouldn't have paid his attentions to Madge. Belle shook her head in disbelief. Madge was older than Jimmie, although she was handsome in a hard sort of way.

Madge laughed, 'You don't have to worry. He dotes on you. Says you're the best thing that ever happened to him.'

It was as if Madge guessed her thoughts, and was laughing at her. Annoyance pricked at Belle like a red-hot needle and she lowered her eyelids so Madge would not see it.

The older woman laughed again, a tinkling, bell-like laugh that was out of keeping with her appearance. 'He came in for a jug of ale with his da. We just chatted.'

'Oh,' Belle murmured, opening her eyes wide. She was not sure what to make of Madge. The woman wanted something, she was sure of it. But what?

'He told me he was just back from the whaling.' Madge looked at Belle with a studied gaze. 'You must miss him when he's away.'

'It's only temporary.' Belle picked at her dress. Jimmie had told her that after three whaling trips he would have enough money for his boat, but he had only recently returned from his fifth trip and still he hadn't bought a boat. It wasn't the first time the doubt had surfaced in Belle's mind, that maybe he liked the whaling and would never give it up.

'He's saving for a boat of his own. Right?' Madge had stopped looking at Belle and was watching the twins. 'You're so lucky, having children,' her voice was almost inaudible.

'It's because of them that it's taking so long to save.' It was funny how some people came over all sentimental about kids, Belle thought. It would not have bothered her in the slightest if she'd never had any, although she had to admit to herself that she did love the twins.

'Yes, he told me. But he said he didn't mind and that eventually he'd have enough money for his own boat.'

'He seems to have told you a lot,' Belle said drily.

Madge's laugh tinkled out. 'Men tell a barmaid a lot when they're in their cups. And that's one of the reasons I wanted to speak to you. I think I can help.'

'Help. How could you help?'

'I need someone to work in the inn. You know, some cleaning and tidying up, serving at tables and so on.'

'I suppose the so on means serving ale in the bar.' Belle was intrigued. The idea appealed to her. It would mean she would get out more and she would not have to work with smelly fish.

'Well, what if it does? It's only the village men you'd be serving, there's no harm in that surely. And I'd pay well.'

Belle could almost feel Madge's eyes boring into her. 'I don't know,' she said, 'I'd have to talk to Jimmie. He might not approve.'

'I had a feeling you could always get round Jimmie.'

Belle twisted the rough wool of her skirt round her fingers until they turned white with the pressure. 'Oh, I can get round Jimmie all right. But there's still Annie to contend with.'

'Ah yes, Annie. I'd forgotten that Annie was Jimmie's ma.' Madge's voice became soft and thoughtful, implying she knew how Annie would respond. 'But surely Jimmie's your man now. Why should he pay any attention to his ma?'

Why indeed, thought Belle. And why should I care what Annie thinks? She rose from the seat, 'I'll think about it,' she said, as she turned to leave.

49

The fishing had been good. Jimmie enjoyed being home and going out with Da and his brothers on the *Bonnie Annie*, and now as the boat skimmed back up the river he felt a deep sense of satisfaction. Some of these days, he promised himself, he would have his own boat. The thought dampened his pleasure and, not for the first time, he felt sadness grip his mind. His own boat seemed as far away as ever and by the time he had enough saved his own sons would probably be old enough to come out with him.

With the sure instinct of a seaman he turned the sail to catch the wind, and as they drew level with Craigden he pulled the ropes to furl it and allow the boat to drift inwards to the shore.

'I see you haven't lost your skill with the sail.' This was as high praise as he would ever get from his da.

'Aye, Da. Once you learn, you never forget. I just wish I could sail in the wee boats all the time. It's not quite the same in the whaler.'

'No, lad. I don't suppose it is.' His da looked at him with expressionless eyes. 'You don't have to go back, you know. You could stay here and help me.'

Jimmie smiled. He knew his da would like him to stay, but he also knew it would be difficult for the *Bonnie Annie* to support two families. 'It's good of you to offer, Da. But I'm determined to have my own boat, and I'll not give up the whaling until I've got it.'

James sighed. 'The whaling's a dangerous business. We worry about you.'

The boat scraped bottom and Jimmie jumped out to pull it further into the shore. 'You've no need to worry about me, Da. I'm careful,' but even as he said it a shiver swept over him and he remembered his last voyage where the massive ice sheets had threatened to squeeze the ship in their icy grasp.

Sarah scooped another mussel out of the pail and deftly split it open with the knife. The pale pink flesh trembled for a moment on the edge of its shell and then slid into the basin with a slight plop. She shivered. It wasn't a very nice job and she always wondered whether the mussel suffered, but she was helping Jeannie, so she did it without a grumble.

'You'll soon be as quick as me.' Jeannie looked up from her shelling.

Sarah beamed with pleasure, although she knew that Jeannie's fingers worked a lot faster than hers. Maybe she was getting quicker. She threw the mussel shell on the growing heap in front of them and picked up another one.

The two girls worked on in silence. Jeannie, tall and lanky at fifteen, had not grown any prettier, but Sarah didn't notice because she loved Jeannie more than anyone else, except maybe Da, of course.

Sarah held the knife in a firm grasp, although she was careful of the blade which was short and very sharp. She was sure of her movements and had the confidence of a child who felt quite grown up, although it was only six weeks ago she'd had her eighth birthday. She was a sturdy child, used to looking after herself, and as a result had become quite independent.

Mingled with the slap of the waves on the shore and the familiar scream of the gulls her keen ears now picked up the sound of voices. She looked towards the river, and giving a scream of delight, she sprang up sending the pail of mussels tumbling over. She ran towards the shore, leaving Jeannie to pick up the pail and replace the mussels.

Sarah reached the shore seconds after her ma and the twins. She slowed to a stop and stood watching as her da swung first one twin, then the other, into the air. Da never swung her into the air any more, but then Sarah had never chuckled with delight the way the twins did. Da bent over and rubbed his face against her ma's cheek, and she could hear Belle respond with her throaty laugh.

With slow steps she turned and made her way back to Jeannie and the mussel pail.

Belle waited until she was sure Sarah and the twins were asleep before she broached the subject of working at the inn.

'It's a good offer, Jimmie,' she said, as she knelt by his side and took his hand into hers.

'I'll not have you working in a public bar.' Jimmie glared at her. 'No Craigden woman would ever set foot over the doorstep of the inn. It would be a disgrace.'

'It's not as if I'd be the only woman. Madge would be there.' Belle's tone was soft. She had expected him to object and knew she would have to use all her persuasive powers.

'That makes no difference. No wife of mine will set foot in the inn.' He was still glaring at her and Belle was tempted to glare back, but instead, she dropped her eyes and made herself look confused and vulnerable.

'Think of the extra money, Jimmie,' she said, looking at him through half-closed eyelids. 'Think of the boat you want. It's taking a long time to get it and I fear for you at the whaling.'

Belle watched as he hesitated. She knew how badly he wanted his own boat and she had guessed that he had no love for whaling. She also knew that even though he hesitated he was not about to give in to her.

'Aye, it's right enough I want my own boat,' he said. 'But I'll not have you working in an inn so I can have it.'

'Where's the harm, Jimmie, if I only do it while you're at home. You could take me there and bring me back again. I'd come to no harm.' She reached up and stroked his face with the tips of her fingers. 'It's only Craigden men that drink there and we both know them all. Where's the harm?'

Jimmie grasped her hand. 'Don't you see, Belle. I'm only trying to protect you. Besides, Ma wouldn't approve.'

'It's nothing to do with your ma, Jimmie. You're a grown man and you make your own decisions, and I would rather have your support than your protection.'

'I still don't like it, Belle. I would prefer you didn't do it.'

Belle could feel him weakening but knew that he wasn't ready to give in, however she still had her trump card. The one he could never resist.

'Come to bed, Jimmie. Let's sleep on it and we can decide in the morning.'

50

'It's such a bore,' Clarinda's voice broke into his concentration.

'What is such a bore, my dear?' Lachlan was not really interested but felt it his duty to enquire. Four years of marriage had not made much impression on him. He still felt as far away from Clarinda as he had when he'd first met her, although she did not frighten him as much as she had then.

Her hand stilled over the petit point she was stitching. 'I think I am with child. Such a bore,' she sighed.

Lachlan looked at her in astonishment. It did not seem possible that their occasional, frigid sexual encounters could have had such a result. He lifted his handkerchief to his nose and sniffed delicately. 'You're sure, my dear.'

'According to Doctor Beagle, I am.' She smoothed her dress over her knees, although it was already sitting perfectly.

Lachlan looked at her, but she appeared no different from usual. 'My father will be pleased. He has wanted us to have an heir for some time.'

'What about you? Are you pleased?' Clarinda's normally smooth voice sounded a little harsh.

'Of course I'm pleased, my dear. However, you do realise we will have to return home.' Lachlan felt a surge of longing for Scotland, and realised it would be a relief to have an excuse to return there and so end the futile, useless life he had been living in London.

Clarinda stopped smoothing her dress. 'But this is our home.'

'This may be our home now, but my heir will also eventually be the heir to all the estates of Craigallan, and as such should be born at Craigallan House. That's where all the previous heirs have been born. It is a tradition of our family.'

'I won't go,' Clarinda's voice rose.

Lachlan looked at her with interest. He could almost swear there had been a hint of anger in her voice which was unusual, for Clarinda seldom expressed any emotion. This was what made her so uninteresting.

'You will go. You wanted the title that I will eventually have and this is what goes with it. I'll brook no argument. Our son will be born at Craigallan House.'

'Methinks you got a bargain, sir. For in return for your father's title you have gained my fortune.'

'It was a fair bargain, madam. I did not hear you complain at the time, and you would have lost your fortune to your husband no matter who you married. At least you will get some return from our bargain.'

Clarinda recommenced stitching her petit point, stabbing the needle in and out of the tapestry with a studied concentration. 'It seems I have no choice in the matter.' Her voice was muffled, and Lachlan could not see her face.

'That is right, madam. You have no choice in the matter. Our son will be born at Craigallan house as have all the Craigallans before him.' Lachlan stood up. 'Good day to you, madam. I will see you later, and I will expect you to make your arrangements to travel north for we must go before you become too unwell to travel.'

Lachlan left the room, quietly closing the door behind him. An evening at his club seemed to be in order, and afterwards an assignation at Madame Fleur's establishment would help to regenerate him, for he felt quite drained.

Clarinda dashed the tears from her eyes with the back of her hand and stared at the closed door. Lachlan was such an infuriating man. She had thought he was soft and pliable when she married him, but he seemed to have turned into a cold, sadistic brute. Always trying to goad and annoy her. It seemed as if he had never forgiven her for the pain and suffering she had felt that first night of their marriage.

No one had told her what to expect, and no one had told her it would be painful. Even now when he forced himself on her it was still painful. But she endured, didn't she? What more could he expect of her.

No doubt he would be away to his club again, and he would return drunk and demand his rights. Sometimes she preferred it when he did not return, even though she knew he was carousing in one of the brothels and indulging his desires with a common whore.

At least in Scotland he would not have his clubs and brothels, so it might not be too bad after all, although she was not looking forward to the cold and the isolation of Craigallan House.

Reaching out her hand she pulled the silken bell pull. 'Will you let my aunt know I wish to speak with her,' she demanded of the maid who answered it.

Aunt Beattie would know what to do. She would discuss it with her.

Belle rummaged in the foot of the sea-chest and pulled out her red silk dress. Giving it a shake she held it up to the light and was pleased to see it wasn't in too bad a condition. If she hung it outside in the air, the creases would blow away.

Jimmie leaned up on one elbow and peered over the edge of the bed. 'You're not going to wear that, are you?'

'Of course I am. Anyway you used to like this dress. You said it made me look like a romany gypsy.'

'I don't want my wife to look like a gypsy,' Jimmie protested.

'Don't worry. I won't wear it all the time, only when I'm working in the evenings.'

'That's what I'm worried about.'

Belle threw herself at the bed and, lying on top of him, she murmured, 'But you'll be there to protect me and just think how exciting it'll be when you get me home.' She wriggled provocatively until he groaned with longing.

'The bairns, Belle. You'll wake the bairns.'

'You mean you'll wake them with your moaning and groaning.' Belle rolled off him and slid to the floor. 'Come on, then. Tell me you like it, and tell me you want to see me wear it.' She wafted the dress before him, 'And maybe I'll let you help me put it on.'

51

Sarah led her brothers along the path. 'Come on,' she urged the two small boys whose eyes were still heavy with sleep. 'Ma says we've to go to Granma's. She says we've to tell Granma that she's busy and can we stay a while.'

'I'm hungry!'

'Me too!'

Sarah's own stomach was grumbling in protest, for Belle had not given them any breakfast.

'Granma'll have the porridge pot on the fire. I'm sure she'll give you some if you ask nicely.' Granma would probably grumble and call their ma lazy as well, but Sarah was used to that. Once upon a time she had been frightened of Granma, but she wasn't so bad, although Sarah knew she did not like their ma.

Half-dragging and half-cajoling the twins, Sarah eventually reached Annie's house. She put her hand on the door but it opened before she could lift the latch.

Davie started to emerge but stopped on the doorstep to answer Annie, 'Ach, Ma,' he said, 'I didn't mean it. But I was having such a good time and it was morning before I knew it.'

Annie's voice was indistinct but sounded angry.

'I'm not a bairn anymore, Ma. I'm twenty now and should surely be allowed to stay out without having to ask your permission.' He turned and slammed the door, almost falling over Sarah and the twins in his haste.

'Well, well, well. Look what we have here.' A smile lightened his face, dismissing the frown that creased his brow.

Wee Davy gave a squeal of delight and threw himself at his uncle.

'Uncle Davie,' he shouted, wrapping his arms round his namesake's knees.

Jamie held back, clutching Sarah's hand. He was less boisterous than his brother and more reserved.

Davie reached down and swung the child up by his armpits and then whirled him around. Setting the child back onto his feet, wee Davy shouted, 'More, Uncle Davie. Swing me some more.'

'No, no, Davy. I have to go now, but I'll see you later.' He smiled at Sarah, 'It's best I get out of Ma's way for a while.' Davie turned and strode towards the river.

'What's all the racket out there.' The door opened and Annie stood on the doorstep peering out. 'Oh, it's yourself then, is it? And what would you be wanting at this time in the morning.'

Sarah grabbed wee Davy by the shoulder to stop him from following his uncle. She met Annie's eyes with a long cool stare which masked her nervousness. 'Ma said we were to come,' she said. 'Her and Da will be along later.'

'Oh, they will, will they? I don't suppose that lazy, good-for-nothing ma of yours gave you any breakfast, did she?'

'We don't need breakfast.' Sarah ignored the grumbling noise her stomach was making.

'But I'm hungry,' Davy protested.

'Me too,' said Jamie.

Annie snorted. 'I thought so, she hasn't fed you. You'd better come in then. The porridge pot's on the fire.'

Belle dressed herself slowly, aware that Jimmie watched her every move. She stretched her arms upwards and pulled the dress over her head until it fell in folds from her shoulders. After wriggling her arms into the sleeves, she pulled the bodice around and over her breasts. She smoothed it down over her body and then twirled for Jimmie's benefit, enjoying the feel of the silk and the swishing sound of the skirt as it swirled around her legs.

'You like it, Jimmie, don't you?' She twirled again and

smiled at him.

'Aye, Belle. You're real bonnie in the dress. But d'you not think you should have waited until later to try it on. We have to go see Ma, d'you not remember?'

'I'm ready to go to your ma's now.'

'You can't go dressed like that Belle, Ma wouldn't like it. You know how she is.'

'I'll go like this, and if she doesn't like it that's too bad. Anyway what better way to let her know what we decided.'

'She'll not like the idea of you working at the inn.' Jimmie's voice was troubled.

'She'll come round, and after all if it lets you buy a boat sooner, surely she'll be pleased.'

'I'm not so sure . . . '

'Of course it'll be all right.' Belle leaned over him, stroking his cheek and fingering his beard. 'And anyway it's our lives, not Annie's, even if she is your ma.'

As they walked along the river path Belle could see that he was still troubled. She frowned. Annie had no right to have such a hold on her Jimmie. She might be his ma but Belle was his wife. And surely a wife was more important.

She slid her fingers into his hand, feeling the warmth as it closed around them. 'You've never regretted it, have you?' Her voice tailed off. He seemed far away from her at that moment.

'Regretted what?' Jimmie stopped and looked at her.

'Taking me . . . marrying me. You could have had anyone else. Someone your ma would have approved of and given her blessing to.'

'You're a silly wee besom.' Jimmie placed both hands on her shoulders and pulled her to him. 'You're the best thing that ever happened to me Belle, and I don't care what anyone else thinks.'

'You care what your ma thinks, you always have.' A tear glistened on her eyelash. 'I've always known that, and I sometimes think that Annie will win out in the long run. She'll have you back and I'll be pushed out.'

'You'll never be pushed out. I'll make sure of that. Ma

has to accept you or she loses me, it's as simple as that. Come on now, we've news to tell her and if she doesn't like it that's too bad.'

52

The air simmered with anger as Annie glared at Jimmie. 'What kind of man are you that would allow your wife to work in a public house and dress up like a common dockside whore.'

A vein pulsed in Jimmie's forehead and the colour rose in his cheeks as he shouted, 'I'll not have you speak of Belle in that way.'

Annie glared at him. She could feel the heat rushing to her head until it felt as if it would burst. 'You've taken leave of your senses. She's always been a bad omen for you, sending you away from your own folk to the whaling, and now this.' Annie spluttered, lost for words.

'It doesn't matter what you say, Ma. It won't make any difference.' Jimmie turned away from her. 'Come on, Belle, there's no point in staying here.'

'You're no son of mine,' Annie shouted as the door closed behind them.

Annie sank down onto her stool and looked at the closed door. She lifted her pipe from the ingle neuk of the fireplace and sucked on it, even though it was empty. What was happening to her and her family? She seemed to be losing them, one by one, first Jimmie, then Ian, and now Davie. She still had Angus and Jeannie but for how long she wondered. How long before they rebelled against her authority for she no longer seemed to be in control.

The changes had happened since Belle came into their lives. She had seen the way her sons looked at Belle, and sensed their envy of Jimmie. However, she had managed to get Ian safely married to Ellen, although she never seemed to see them anymore. Ian was too busy being the master of his boat, and of Ellen as well.

Davie was always in Invercraig. How long would it be before he brought another Belle into the family. Annie shuddered. And Jeannie had lost interest in working with the fish and wanted to work at the inn. Annie had put a stop to that though. Luckily for her Jeannie still did as her ma bid her.

She sucked harder on the pipe and stared at the closed door. She could still hear Jimmie's voice saying, 'That's the way of it Ma, and if you don't like it that's too bad.'

'Ah, Jimmie lad. If you'd married one of our own kind it would never have come to this,' Annie muttered to the dead fire. 'One of our own folk would never have considered working at the inn.' and yet, she thought, our Jeannie would have if I'd let her.

What a disgrace, she would never be able to look at the other women again. She could hear them now, 'Her good-daughter, you know the one, that Jimmie's wife, she's working at the inn. All fancied up in her silks and satins, and goodness only knows what she gets up to. I've told my man he's not to go there, but he goes anyway. There's nowt you can do with men once they make their minds up.'

A tear trickled down Annie's cheek and splashed on the parchment skin of her hand. She had sent Jimmie away, 'I don't want to know you if you do this,' she'd said. But it wasn't him she didn't want to know. It was Belle.

Jimmie lay listening to Belle's breathing. It was light and even and he wished he could sleep as well. She had come to his arms as usual but it had not been the same. He had kept on imagining her laughing into the men's faces as she served their jugs of ale, and their expressions of longing as they watched her hips swaying between the tables and benches.

He could hear his ma's angry voice, 'No self-respecting woman would work in an inn, and no fisher woman would set foot in one. It's a disgrace, that's what it is, and if you're going to go through with it you needn't bother coming back to me. I'll not share the disgrace with you.' He had never thought he would have to choose between Belle and his ma, he had always thought he could have both. And now he had chosen Belle and wasn't sure he'd done the right thing.

'We did the right thing,' he'd said to Belle as they lay in bed. 'Didn't we?'

'Of course we did, Jimmie love. Just think of that boat you're going to be able to buy. A bigger boat than even Ian has, or your da.'

'Aye,' he'd said, but his thoughts had been troubled.

53

The November fog muffled the sound of Lachlan's footsteps as he paced the deck. The damp, clammy white mist enveloped him with a chilly embrace but he did not feel it. He was on his way home.

Clarinda had taken to her cabin at the beginning of the voyage and had refused to come out, so Lachlan had left her in peace. In any case he was somewhat tired of her constant whinging. Doctor Beagle had assured him that Clarinda was perfectly healthy and Lachlan was certain she was only trying to attract his attention. It simply was not possible for anyone to be as sick as she said she was.

The foghorn droned with a lugubrious tone, but there was no answering blast.

Lachlan leaned on the rail listening to the splash of waves that he could not see. The taste of salt on his lips made him wonder what it would be like to live on the sea, and he recalled how he had often watched the fishermen leave in their boats, nets neatly coiled in the bottom, only to return later when they were swelled with fish. And he thought of the whalers leaving Invercraig harbour to venture into the arctic seas with their cargo of men off to seek fortunes. How he envied them, and yet he knew he could never emulate them. His fortunes lay in the land and helping his father to manage his many business interests.

Lachlan was uncertain how long he stood at the rail, feeling the heave of the ship under his feet as it rocked gently on the soft swell of the waves. The mist seemed to have penetrated to his bones and he shivered as he pulled his collar tighter around his neck. Shadows of men passed him their footsteps muffled by the fog. Everything seemed to have a surreal quality.

'T'would be better if ye went below, sir.' The man's voice seemed to have an eerie echo as it materialised out of the mist behind him. 'Tis not a night to be astanding on deck, and t'will be morning afore we reach Dundee.'

Lachlan had not heard the bosun approach, but he liked the man with his no-nonsense attitude that refused to defer to his aristocratic status.

He turned now with a smile on his lips. 'Yes, I suppose you're right, but I was just enjoying the silence and mystery of it all. There's something about a sea-mist that is fascinating.'

'Aye, I know what ye mean, sir. But it's also dangerous and a seaman needs all his wits about him without having to worry about the passengers.'

'Ah! I hadn't thought of that,' Lachlan frowned. 'In that case it might be better if I went below.'

He turned and made his reluctant way back to the cabin, bracing himself for the onslaught of Clarinda's complaints.

Sarah missed Jeannie. She missed the hand that was always there when she stumbled. She missed the cheerful voice that told her about the river and the sea, and about the different kinds of fish and what to do with them. She missed hunting crabs in the rock pools when Jeannie managed to escape from Granma Annie and the constant tasks the older woman meted out. Most of all she missed Jeannie's company, for the older girl had become like a mother to her.

It wasn't Jeannie's fault she couldn't speak to her anymore. It was all her ma's fault. If Belle had not gone to work at the inn, things could have remained the same.

Sarah could still hear Jeannie explain, 'Ma's that mad she won't let me speak to any of you any more.'

'Why not?' Sarah felt the tears prick the back of her eyes but she blinked them away. She was too old to cry now that she was past her eighth birthday.

'It's because of your ma. My ma says that none of us can have anything more to do with any of you now that your ma's working at the inn. She says no self-respecting fisher-woman would set foot past its door. She says the whole village is up in arms about it.'

Sarah did not dare look at Jeannie for fear the tears would spill over so she looked at the river instead. The river, ever changeable with all its moods, was never quiet. It might murmur or it might roar, but it would never withhold its voice simply because someone went to work at an inn.

'That's silly, not speaking because my ma's working at the inn. I never heard anything so daft.'

'Aye, I suppose you're right Sarah, but I can't go against Ma. No one ever goes against Ma.'

Sarah understood what Jeannie meant. Annie was a strong-willed woman and her family were all afraid to cross her. 'Is Granma mad with me too?'

'She says your da's not her son any more, so I suppose that means she's not your granma anymore.' Jeannie grasped Sarah's hands within her own. 'I'll never forget you, and I'll not stop caring about you. But you must see I can't speak to you now.' Jeannie let go the younger girl's hands and turning from her she strode away.

Sarah watched her go and, despite her desperate blinks, a tear rolled down her cheek. She dashed it away with the back of her hand, and muttered, 'If Granma says she's not my granma anymore, that's fine with me. I only ever thought of her as Annie anyway.'

Her insides felt bleak and empty and she was almost choking on the lump in her throat as she blindly made her way home.

'You're back at last,' Jimmie greeted her as she lifted the latch and pushed the door open. 'It's not before time. I'm needing to get away to see your ma's all right. It's her first night working at the inn.'

'I know that.' Of course she did, she thought, hadn't it brought enough grief to the family already.

'Well if you knew it you should have come back earlier. You'll need to see to the twinnies, give them their supper and then bed them.'

'Aye, Da,' she said to the door that slammed shut behind him. 'That's all you care about, isn't it. The twinnies and your Belle. Never mind about me.'

54

Madge leaned her arms on the bar counter as she watched Belle serving the men with their jugs of ale. She had been right in her instincts, the girl was a natural. She had a certain way of flicking her skirts as she moved about the room that accentuated the curve of her hips. Her smile seemed to embrace everyone it touched, and the way she had of looking at the men from under half-closed eyelids had a sensual quality. They could hardly keep their eyes off her. It wouldn't be long now before business started to improve.

'How's it going?' she asked, as Belle returned to the bar with some empty jugs. 'Are you getting the feel of the job?'

'It's going fine, Madge. I'm real grateful to you for giving me the work, and it's not too difficult. The only thing is . . . ' she hesitated.

Madge studied Belle's flushed face as she waited for her to continue.

'I'm not sure of Jimmie any more . . . at first I thought I had him convinced it was a good idea. Now I'm not so sure.'

'He'll come round, lass. The men always do. And if they don't there's ways and means of convincing them.' Madge winked at Belle. 'I'm sure you know all about that.'

Belle's laugh was always a surprise to those who heard it with its deep, throaty undertones, and Madge, listening to it thought Belle would be able to charm any man she set her mind to. Yes, the girl had definite possibilities, she just needed some direction and Madge was the one to give it to her.

Madge carefully stepped over the recumbent body of her husband to refill the jugs from the barrel of ale. She pushed them over the bar to Belle, 'Here you go, lass. There's some drouthy men over there.'

The door of the inn swung open and a swirl of fresh air eddied gently round the room making Madge look up. She filled two jugs with ale and approached the men who stood there. 'You'll be Belle's Jimmie, then' she said, looking up into his face.

He grinned down at her, his eyes crinkling at the side with amusement. 'And you'll be Madge, the temptress who's given my wife big ideas.' Madge felt a stirring of envy. This man was worth holding on to and she wondered if Belle knew how lucky she was.

'Aye, I'm Madge, and you're welcome to my inn. I've poured you a jug of ale. This un's on the house, but you'll have to buy the rest. There's a jug for your friend as well.' She looked up into Ian's face as she handed the ale to him. He looked so like Jimmie that he must be a brother, the only difference was this face left her feeling uncomfortable. She shivered, and then laughed. 'Close the door and keep the draught out, otherwise I'll think someone's walking over my grave. And I'm not nearly ready to go yet.'

'I could do with something a bit stronger than ale,' Ian grumbled, as he laid his jug on a table and sat down on the bench. 'You might've thought she'd give us a whisky. I'm sure she could afford it.'

'Ach, you're lucky to get the jug of ale. You wouldn't have got that for nothing in Invercraig.' Jimmie looked around. 'The place is not that busy for a Saturday night.'

'Nothing but old men, I told you this place was a dump. You should've come to Invercraig with me. I could've showed you some really lively places.'

'I expect you could, but I promised Belle I'd come so she doesn't have to walk home herself.'

Ian's laugh did not sound pleasant. 'Belle's well able to look after herself. She's never needed you to walk her home before.'

'That's different. She didn't work in the inn then.'

'You're just frightened she'll go off with someone else.

Admit it.'

Jimmie's face reddened. 'I trust Belle,' he said. He lifted the jug to his lips and turned his back on Ian so he could observe Belle as she moved deftly between the tables filling jugs here and there. His eyes narrowed as he watched her smiling and joking with the men she served, and a doubt niggled its way into his consciousness that maybe there was something in what Ian said, after all. However Jimmie knew he would die before he would admit that.

Belle returned some empty jugs to the bar and murmured something to Madge before walking towards Jimmie's table. 'Madge says I can take five minutes to sit with you,' she said as she subsided on to the bench.

'Are you sure you can spare five minutes for your husband?' Ian leaned over and gripped her hand. 'You seemed to be having a good enough time without him. But then you'd feel quite at home here, it's what you used to be accustomed to before you were lucky enough to marry my brother.'

'Jimmie, you don't think that, do you?' Belle's eyes had widened and darkened as she struggled to pull her hand away from Ian's grasp.

'Of course I don't, Belle.' Jimmie felt embarrassed because he was not quite sure what he believed. He looked into her eyes and felt ashamed. He had no reason to doubt her, for she had never been anything else but a good wife to him. 'Let go of her hand, Ian,' he demanded. 'You've no right to grab her. You've a wife of your own to manhandle if that's what you want. I'll not have you hurt Belle.' He put his arm around her shoulder and kissed her forehead. 'Never you mind him, Belle, he's just ill-tempered the night.'

'Is he ever anything else?' she asked, as she slid off the bench to return to the bar.

Sarah lay awake until she heard her ma and da lift the latch of the door, but she turned her face to the wall for she did not want to see them. She knew her da's arm would be round her ma's shoulders and that he would kiss her and rub his cheek against hers, and Sarah didn't want to see.

If it wasn't for Ma, then maybe her da would put his arm around her and kiss her. She knew her da loved her. He was not like her ma who couldn't stand the sight of her, but Da always said, 'You're a big girl now, Sarah, and it's not right that I should be akissing and acuddling you.' Although, for the life of her, Sarah couldn't think why he should feel like that for it did not stop him kissing her ma and she was even bigger.

'Shh,' Sarah heard her da say. 'The bairns are sleeping and we don't want to wake them.'

Her ma laughed. 'They'll not wake up now. Once they're asleep that's them until morning.'

Sarah pulled the blanket up over her ears. She didn't want to hear them, and more than anything she did not want to hear the rustlings and moanings that she knew would happen next. She screwed her eyes tight shut and willed herself to fall asleep, even though she knew that sleep would only come in its own good time.

55

It was mid-morning when the London packet docked at Dundee. The sun was trying hard to shine but only succeeded in producing a pale glimmer, nevertheless the harbour had a welcoming feel to Lachlan. He was almost home.

As soon as the ship tied up to the dock, he went below to fetch Clarinda. 'Come along, Clarinda. We've arrived.' He frowned at the still open cabin trunk. 'I'm sure I don't know why you needed so many dresses considering you've hardly left your cabin.'

Aunt Beattie tutted at him. 'A lady has to be at her best at all times. It doesn't matter who sees her or who doesn't. Now get out of my way and let me finish packing the trunk.'

Lachlan frowned, Aunt Beattie could be quite uppity when she liked. If she did not start remembering her place he would make sure she was shipped back to London.

He stifled his annoyance. It would not do to arrive home with Clarinda in one of her moods. 'Clarinda, my love,' he said, as affably as he could. 'Would you mind asking your Aunt Beattie to hurry, I saw my father's carriage waiting on the docks so we don't want to delay too long.'

Clarinda's voice was cool, 'I'm sure the carriage will wait. Another few moments will not make a great deal of difference.'

It seemed an eternity to Lachlan as he waited for the trunks to be unloaded and packed onto the back of his father's travelling coach. Hamish finished strapping the baggage on, tugging and pulling at the ropes to test their strength. 'You're sure that's the lot, are you?'

Lachlan nodded. It wouldn't have hurt Hamish to call me sir, he thought, however he said nothing.

'If you help the ladies into the carriage, young sir, we'll be on our way.'

Hamish would appear to be something of a mind-reader, thought Lachlan, as he handed Clarissa into the carriage and then Aunt Beattie. The two women spread their skirts over the seats so that Lachlan had difficulty in finding a comfortable corner to sit, and he envied Hamish his solitary seat on the box in front of the coach.

The road to Invercraig followed the coastline and rarely was the sea out of sight until they came to the moor, where the road curved inland. However, it was not long before the inland basin came into sight. The tide was out and all that could be seen were the mudflats where the fisher-women went to collect their mussels. Lachlan remembered them with their skirts kilted up to their waists and their sturdy legs striding into the mud, but there were no women on the mudflats today, and only a few circling gulls to welcome him home.

Lachlan leaned out of the coach window as they approached the entrance to the main drive. There was a choking sensation in his throat and he was not sure whether it was the dust thrown up by the carriage wheels, or whether it was the sight of the familiar black gates with the Craigallan crest picked out in gold paint. He could see the dumpy figure of old Mrs McKay swinging the gates open so that the carriage would not have to halt, and he removed his handkerchief from his mouth long enough to wave to her as she smiled and bobbed her welcome.

The coach slowed as it followed the long curving drive. The trees and rhododendron bushes seemed to have grown taller and thicker while he had been away, forming a green protective tunnel. At last the house came into view and the coach swung round the semi-circular drive to stop in front of one of the stone balustraded stairs that curved their way towards the front entrance to the house.

'We have arrived, my dear,' he said to Clarinda as he waited for Hamish to open the carriage door, however it was his father who swung the door wide and held out a welcoming hand.

His father's gruff greeting, 'You've come back then, lad.' And his mother's warm arms closing round him made him feel young and carefree. I'm home, he thought as he returned his mother's hug, and I'll never leave it again.

56

Annie turned her back on Jimmie as he waded ashore. It had been three weeks since they had quarrelled and she could not bring herself to look at him because of the shame Belle had brought to the family.

'Aye, you're still not speaking to Jimmie then.' Ellen had pulled the creels down to the shore in readiness for the unloading of the fish.

'Jimmie's no son of mine.' Annie refused to meet her eyes. 'I'll have nothing to do with anyone who allows his wife to work at the inn.'

'I can understand how you feel, but surely you can't deny your eldest son.'

'Ian's my eldest son now.'

Annie held her head down as Jimmie passed them, but she looked up and watched him climb the bank to the path along the river's edge.

'He'll be looking for Belle no doubt,' Ellen said.

'She'll not have the gall to show her face here. She knows what we think of her.' Annie busied herself with the creels.

'You're a hard woman, Annie. To deny your first born.' James dumped one of the crans of fish at her feet.

'And you're a foolish man to keep on taking him out in the boat. You know what I think and you should tell him there's no work for him.'

'That would be cutting off my nose to spite my face, woman,' James roared. 'I need the lad's help, and I'll not be having you tell me how to run my boat.' James stumped off.

'Aye, you've fair annoyed your James.' Ellen put her arm around her mother-in-law's shoulder, but Annie shook it off.

'That's as it may be but he's a silly old fool and he's just as besotted with Belle as the rest of the men. I'll not forgive her for what she's done to all the men of this village and that includes your Ian.'

'What do you mean?' Ellen's voice was sharp. 'My Ian can't stand the sight of Belle. He's always saying what a trollop she is.'

'I suppose that's why he's always watching her, and why he's never away from the inn.'

Annie enjoyed taunting her daughter-in-law, because Ellen was so self-righteous. 'Just look at him now and have a look at who's coming.'

Annie smiled to herself as she watched the younger woman's head swivelling between Ian and Belle as if not knowing who to look at first.

An ugly flush stained Ellen's neck and crept upwards to her face, her hands clenched into fists and she kicked the creels at her feet before glowering at Annie. 'She needn't think she's getting my man,' she hissed. 'I'll not stand for it.'

'Trollop,' Ellen shouted, as she ran to a group of women busy packing their creels further along the shore. 'D'you see her flaunting herself there, she's nothing but a trollop and she'll not be satisfied until she's bewitched all our men.'

'Aye, that's so,' replied Meg Forbes, 'I can't keep my man away from the inn and it's all her fault.'

'That Madge is just as bad. I don't know what Joe was thinking of taking her for a wife.'

'Joe's never sober long enough to know what he's doing.'

'Aye, and he's never sober enough to know what his wife's doing.'

'Madge and Belle, they're a fine pair. Just wait until Jimmie's back at the whaling, then there'll be no stopping them and none of our men will be safe.'

Listening to the women Annie felt a twinge of remorse for taunting Ellen, however, although she found the tone of their voices disturbing she said nothing.

It was as well that Jimmie was at home just now, she thought, because he would be able to protect his wife. She feared what the women would do if Belle had no one to look out for her.

Belle strolled along the river path, enjoying the breeze that ruffled her hair. She felt light-hearted and free, even though Sarah and the twins dogged her steps. She had never thought she would appreciate Sarah but the girl had her uses. If it were not for Sarah she would have been tied down looking after wee Davy and Jamie for, although Belle doted on the two boys, they needed a lot of looking after.

The boats were already anchored by the shore and her heart soared when she saw Jimmie striding to meet her. He was a fine man and he was hers.

She frowned as she saw Annie turn her back on him for she knew how vexed he was that his mother refused to acknowledge him. However, Belle was pleased he had supported her, though she knew he wasn't happy about her decision to work at the inn. Belle was convinced Annie would get over it eventually and things would go back to what they were.

'Why the frown?' Jimmie picked her up and hugged her. 'A bonny lass should never frown. It's not becoming.'

'I was just thinking that if it wasn't for me your ma wouldn't have turned her back on you.'

Jimmie put her down and stroked the frown from her face. 'Don't you worry about that. It doesn't matter to me what anyone else does or thinks, as long as I have you.'

'You are sure of that, are you, Jimmie? After all, I've come between you and your own folk.'

'My folk are here. You, Sarah and the twins are all the folk I need.'

Belle looked towards the shore where Annie stood with her hands on her hips and her legs astride, watching them.

The fisher women had stopped their work and gathered together, which was unusual, and from the frequent glances in their direction, Belle guessed they were talking about her.

She shivered and, grasping Jimmie's hand, said, 'I feel

cold Jimmie, let's go home.'

She did not want to face up to the women today and hear their sniggers and sly comments.

57

It was Lachlan's first day out of bed since he had arrived home and he stood at the dresser in the breakfast room thinking how good it was to be up and about and how hungry he was. Later he would have a walk in the grounds or maybe take Raven for a canter. Surely that would not tax him too much.

'I see the invalid has recovered.' Lachlan hadn't heard Clarinda enter the room but he turned at the sound of her voice.

'Thank you for your concern, my dear. I had been wondering when you would visit me in my sick bed, and decided I would have to arise if I wished your company again.'

'Your mother advised me to wait until you were better as I am unused to the coldness of your Scottish climate. I did tell her of your foolishness in staying on the deck of the ship during the worst of the weather, and she said it was no wonder you contracted such a horrendous cold. She also said it would be most unwise if I were to be infected, particularly in my delicate condition.'

She selected a sausage, a sliver of mushroom, a slice of bacon and a generous portion of kidneys, and then stood considering her plate. 'Do you think I should have some eggs as well,' she murmured.

There was nothing wrong with Clarinda's appetite, Lachlan thought, as he said, 'Ah yes. I'd forgotten about your delicate condition. Tell me, my dear Clarinda, are you settling down in your new home?'

'As well as can be expected, although this could never take the place of our London house.' Her voice developed a hint of anxiety, 'It will only be temporary, won't it,

Lachlan?'

'That remains to be seen, Clarinda my dear.' Lachlan was in no mood to commit himself, or to relieve her of her anxieties.

He frowned as he studied the salvers on the dresser. 'This isn't good enough,' he said, as he tugged on the bell pull.

'Yes, sir.'

'Damn, you gave me a start, Bates. Do you always creep up on people?'

'I'm sure I'm sorry, sir. Is there something you wanted me for?'

'Yes, Bates. We don't seem to have any fish and I have a fancy for some.'

'Yes sir. Mrs Ross informs me that there will be fish later today, when the fishwife calls.'

'Very well, Bates. I suppose this will have to do then. You may go now.'

Lachlan was thoughtful as he piled scrambled eggs and some kidneys onto his plate. Now that he felt well again, maybe an encounter with the fishwife was just what he needed.

'Bon appetit, my dear,' he murmured to Clarinda as he sat down.

'Best we get back to what we're supposed to be doing instead of standing gossiping.' Annie glared at the women defying them to contradict her.

'You're not saying you approve of that one's goings on,' Meg Forbes nodded her head in the direction of Belle.

'No I don't approve, but that's no reason to be spiteful.'

'Spiteful, is it?' Meg Forbes spat on the ground. 'You'll not be saying that when your James is taking his place in the queue. Will you now?'

'My James has more sense. And so should your men. If you can't hold them then you should be looking to yourselves and not to anyone else.'

Annie bent over her creel. 'Jeannie!' she shouted. 'It's

time you were starting on your fish round. The chat around here is not very healthy.'

Lachlan walked slowly in the direction of the back drive. 'I feel the need of some fresh air,' he'd told Clarinda who had shuddered at the thought of it.

It was a typical crisp December day and he inhaled until he felt the air tingle his lungs with its coldness.

The trees rustled and whispered as he passed by, seeming to welcome him home with beckoning branches, brown and bare while they waited patiently for another spring.

He followed the path until he was sure he was out of sight of the house, for he knew that Clarinda could not understand his preference for wild and open spaces. The grass crunched under his feet when he stepped off the path and headed for the trees. Now he was really at home.

His rhododendron hideaway was still there, a bit more overgrown but still as friendly. He crept into the centre and long forgotten memories flooded back. Elsie, who had been gone from his life for a long time, he remembered with regret, although her features escaped him and all he could remember now were trusting brown eyes that seemed to brim with love for him. And then there was Belle. How could he ever have forgotten Belle with her strange green eyes, her tumble of russet brown curls, and her tantalising ways.

He felt a sense of the past returning as he heard footsteps on the path at the other side of the bush. Belle, it must be Belle on her way to the farm with her baskets of fish. Pushing out of the shrubbery he was in time to see the familiar figure of the fishwife with her blue skirt and striped petticoats walking up the path away from him.

'Belle!' he shouted to her retreating back. 'Wait for me, Belle.'

It was as if she hadn't heard him for she kept on walking at a steady pace. Lachlan's legs quivered and his eyes blurred as he ran after her, and he had almost exhausted himself by the time he was near enough to grasp her arm.

Bewilderment clouded Lachlan's mind as he stared at the strange face that looked at him with an expression that was almost as confused as his own.

'Did you want something, sir?'

Lachlan's legs wobbled and he tried to control his breathing. 'I'm sorry I startled you,' he gasped.

'You don't look well, sir. Maybe you should sit down, although there's only the grass and that might not be fitting for the likes of yourself.'

'The grass will be fine provided you help me as I don't particularly wish to fall.'

Her hand was strong and firm, although the girl looked quite slight. 'Don't leave me, will you. I might need you to help me up after I've caught my breath.' He stretched his legs and leaned against the dry-stone dyke. The grass was cold beneath him and the stones of the wall dug into his ribs, but he was glad of the rest.

The girl traced the toe of her shoe in the path, pushing a pebble round and round. He remembered Belle doing that when she was unsure of herself.

'I'm sorry if I startled you but I thought you were someone else. We used to have a fishwife come to the house and I thought . . . well the dress looked the same from the back . . . it wasn't an unnatural mistake to make . . . ' Lachlan was breathing easier now but how could he explain to her he was waiting for Belle. 'You're new and I had no fish for my breakfast,' he ended lamely.

The girl's eyes were a smoky blue and seemed to look right through him. 'You probably thought I was Belle,' she said.

'Was that the last fishwife's name, Belle?' Lachlan had never felt so awkward in his life. There was something about this girl that made him uneasy.

'Aye, but she's not a fishwife any longer, so you'll not be seeing her again.'

Was it his imagination, or was there a note of irony in her voice? Lachlan wasn't sure. She looked so naïve and innocent, yet at the same time knowledgeable beyond her years.

'Ah, that's a shame because she always made sure we got plenty of fish.'

'You'll not have anything to worry about there, sir. For if it's fish you want I'll easy manage to keep you supplied. If it's anything else you want, I doubt you'll have to look elsewhere.' She had stopped pushing the stone around with her toe and she leaned over to extend her hand to him. 'If you want a help up again you'd better rise now, for I have the rest of my round to finish.'

Lachlan grasped her hand and she pulled him to his feet. 'I can only thank you for your kindness, miss . . . I'm afraid I don't know your name.'

'It's Jeannie, sir. Jeannie Watt. No doubt you know my da James.'

She turned and walked on up the lane, the fish baskets bobbing up and down on her narrow hips, while Lachlan watched her until she was out of sight.

58

‘Just like the men. Nowhere to be seen when there’s work to be done.’

Belle laughed as she gave a final sweep to the floor. ‘Well what do you expect, Madge, when it’s Hogmanay. They’ll be making ready for the Old Yule celebrations tonight.’

‘Aye, and they’ll not be looking inside the inn when all the celebrations are taking place on the shore, that’s for sure. Help me get this table pulled out to the square, Belle, or we’ll not be making any money the night.’

Belle laid her sweeping brush down so that she could grab the end of the table and, between Madge pushing and Belle pulling, the two women manoeuvred it into the square in front of the inn.

Madge stood back and surveyed the table. ‘Aye, it’ll do fine there. Better bring out some benches as well though, just in case some of them want to sit down.’

‘More likely it’ll be fall down tonight instead of sit down.’ Belle had past memories of how drunk the men could get during the Old Yule celebrations.

‘Aye, well at least my Joe won’t have any further to fall. He’s flat out all the time.’

‘I’ve often wondered how he managed to run the inn before he wed you?’ Belle was not sure if she had gone too far because normally Madge never mentioned Joe’s habitual drunken state.

‘It wasn’t much of an inn before he wed me, that’s for sure. But it’s a damn good inn now, and a lot of it’s due to you Belle. The men like you, and even the younger ones are regular customers now.’

‘The women don’t have much time for me though. Have

you noticed?'

'Well, they don't like me either but as long as I'm pulling in their men's money, I don't much care. And it's the men that are in charge in this village. Their wives just have to get on with it.'

'I'm not so sure of that,' Belle frowned. 'I think if the women really get angry the men will step back.'

'Don't you go worrying your pretty little head about that. The women know fine that if it's not us selling the drink, it'll be somebody else, or their men will never be away from Invercraig. Come on in and have a jug of ale now, before we pretty ourselves up for tonight.'

Lachlan made his way to the kitchen. It was his favourite place since he had regained his strength and the faint smell of roasting meat wafting through the house had been tantalising him for quite a while.

The kitchen bustled with bodies and noise, and Lachlan hesitated on the doorstep before crossing the room to where a skiffy was turning a spit, which held an extremely large haunch of beef, over the fire.

Mrs Ross reached the girl moments before he did, and he saw the skiffy cringe as the cook shouted at her, 'If I've told you once, I've told you a dozen times. Keep that spit turning.' Mrs Ross covered the girl's hand with her own and turned the spit faster. 'Keep turning it like that or it'll be the worse for you.'

'You'd think the beef was for the laird,' muttered the girl as soon as the cook left her side.

'Who's it for if it's not for the laird?' Lachlan asked her.

'It's for the village, for those dirty fisher folk.' The girl gave the spit a vicious turn.

'Will you stop hindering my kitchen skivvies, or I'll be letting your da know that you're dallying your time down here.' Mrs Ross had crept up behind him.

'Now, now, Mrs Ross. You know full well I was only curious. I'd forgotten about the custom of supplying roast beef to the villagers for their new year celebrations. The smell is absolutely gorgeous.'

'Well keep your eyes off. It's not for you.'

'I'm sure you wouldn't miss just the tiniest bit, now. The smell has fairly titillated me and I'd do almost anything for a slice.' Lachlan slid his arm round the cook's ample waist, 'Just the tiniest smidgin of a piece, that's all.'

Mrs Ross laughed, 'I tell you, Master Lachlan, I'd swear you've lost your appetite and found a horse's. I've never known you to be as fond of your vittles as you are the now. Just a sliver then, and if you want more you'll have to go to the village the night and join in their Old Yule celebrations.'

'That's not a bad idea,' Lachlan said, as he chewed the meat.

59

Wee Davy wriggled his hand free from Sarah's grasp and ran towards the trees. 'I can find more wood than you,' he taunted his brother, Jamie.

'No you can't,' Jamie shouted back.

Sarah watched them go. 'Don't get lost.' Her words followed the two small bodies as they vanished into the wooded copse. She didn't know if they heard her and did not suppose it would make much difference anyway.

It was Da who had sent them to gather sticks for the bonfires. The twins had been following him since early morning and he had been getting more and more annoyed with them. 'Keep them out of the way,' he had told Sarah, and finally he'd told them to go and gather wood and sticks for the bonfires.

Sarah would have liked to remain with Da, but the twins were her responsibility so she grabbed their hands and hustled them along the river path.

'Want to stay and build the fires.' Wee Davy's voice had a familiar defiant ring to it.

Sarah felt a stab of annoyance. Why couldn't he be like Jamie? Jamie always did as he was told, and never caused any trouble. She wanted to snap at him and tell him he just had to come because Da said so, but she knew this would only make him even more belligerent.

'I'm big now,' he said. 'I'm four. I'm big enough to build fires.'

'Of course you are, Davy. But we've got something better to do. We've got to go and find sticks so you can build the bonfire. A bonfire's no use without it, you know.' Sarah tightened her grip on his hand.

'Can I look for sticks too, Sarah?'

Jamie looked up at her and she smiled down into his serious eyes. 'Of course you can, Jamie. You're just as big as Davy, and if he can do it, so can you.'

Davy tugged her hand. 'I know where there's lots of trees. It's past the houses, there's a road up to a big house and there's lots and lots of trees. Can we go there?'

'That depends. We'll go to the wood at the end of the village and see what we can find.'

Sarah did not want to go to the wood that bordered the path to the big house. She did not like going anywhere near the big house, for that was where the man came from, the man who came like a shadow in the night, the man who hurt her ma. He hadn't come for a long time but Sarah could still remember her ma's groans and screams as they wrestled in her bed in the middle of the night. Then when he had stopped visiting, Ma had cried, and she'd stopped smiling, and then after the twins came she had never smiled at Sarah again.

Sarah gathered some sticks and branches as she listened to the twins chasing one another through the trees, whooping and screeching as they went. There was plenty of wood here they wouldn't have to go any further.

Surveying the mound of sticks she had piled up at the edge of the copse engendered a sense of satisfaction in Sarah. Surely that should be enough to add to the bonfire and keep Da happy.

Time to gather up the twins, she thought, as she followed the sounds of their laughter. 'Come on, lads. We've got enough sticks for the bonfire but I can't carry them all myself. Now that you're both four and such big strong lads, you'll have no trouble carrying them.'

It was dark by the time Sarah and the twins arrived back at the shore and, although Sarah looked for her da, she couldn't see him. 'Which bonfire will we put the sticks on?' Sarah asked one of the fishermen.

'Here'll do fine,' he said, squinting at them in the gloom. 'What are you young uns doing roaming about in the dark, anyway?' he asked. 'Does your ma and da know you're still about?'

'My ma's working at the inn and it was my da that sent us for the sticks.' Sarah regretted speaking to the fisherman, she should have continued to look for her da.

'Ach, I know you. You're Belle's brats, aren't you? It's no wonder you're still roaming about, but you should be home you know. This is not a night for bairns to be about.'

Sarah grabbed Jamie's hand and looked around for wee Davy. 'Come on, Davy. We'd better go and see Ma.'

The village square bustled with bodies. Lanterns slung from the windows of the inn cast eerie, flickering lights over everyone, and Sarah hesitated before she pushed her way towards the wooden table where her ma was laughing with one of the men.

'Ma,' she said, tugging at Belle's dress.

Belle grasped Sarah's hand. 'Watch you don't tear my dress. The material's getting quite fragile, and I can't afford another one,' she said, turning to look at Sarah. 'What are you doing here anyway? You should be at home and getting Davy and Jamie to their beds.'

'I couldn't find Da.' Sarah felt the tears prick the back of her eyes but she refused to let them spill over. She was too old to cry. She was eight, after all.

'Just get them home, and get them into bed. I'll tell your da where you are. Off you go now.'

Sarah climbed into her own truckle bed once she got the twins settled. She closed her eyes but sleep wouldn't come, so she opened them again. The room was dark with shadows even the small square window was barely visible. She didn't like that window for it faced away from the village, and she was always afraid he would come tapping again, and if he did, would he hurt her ma again or would he hurt her instead.

Pulling the covers over her head she squeezed her eyes closed and willed the sleep to come.

60

It was dark when Lachlan crept out of the kitchen door. The house and its occupants slumbered quietly, oblivious to his movements. A cat moved in the darkness just in front of him, its eyes reflecting an eerie green glow that seemed faintly menacing. Lachlan held his breath and stepped warily round it, but it squalled anyway and slunk off into the darkness.

He passed through the stable yard, keeping as far away from the stables as he could get. He did not want to wake the household, although he felt justified in joining the villagers in their Old Yule celebrations. After all, a laird and his family should mix with the workers who lived on their land.

The drive was dark and the trees rustled with strange whispers, so he stayed on the path. The walk seemed interminable and he was glad when he could see the glint of water from the inland basin that ebbed and flowed with the tide as it fed the river.

He followed the water's edge listening to the gentle sough of the waves, knowing that when the sound became a trickle the water was being routed around the central island. The narrower part of the river now flowed towards the village, divorced from the main channel until it met up with its other half just before the village square. Equally well he knew that the main part of the river flowing past Invercraig would roar and tumble as it made its way to the sea.

The flames from the bonfires welcomed him and it seemed as if every village member was on the shore. Fiddle music squealed out in the darkness while men and women screeched and danced, their shadows, weird and elongated in the flickering light, leaping alongside them.

It had been a long time since Lachlan had visited the village or associated with the fishermen, and he suddenly felt out of place.

He stood for a moment and then made his way to the table in the village square. Helping himself to a jug of ale, a slice of roast beef, and an oatcake, he looked around for somewhere to sit, and spying the bench in front of the inn, he sat down with his back against the wall.

Lachlan was not sure how long he sat there, but he felt comfortable and he was loath to move.

He watched the dancers and his foot tapped in time to the fiddle. There seemed to be a wildness and an abandonment about the gyrating bodies, and he could almost imagine himself at a heathen gathering. He had an urge to join them but didn't dare. It wouldn't do for the laird's son to be involved.

Belle saw Lachlan approach and drew back into the shadows at the rear of the square. She leaned her forehead against the cool stone of the inn wall trying to stop her stomach from churning and quell the nausea that threatened to overtake her.

Why had he returned now? She had known he was home at the big house, but he had not sought her out. Neither had she attempted to see him. She had realized a long time ago that he had only used her, probably because his wretched Clarinda wouldn't bed with him.

The minister had blessed them in his church. 'We now offer our blessings to Lachlan and Clarinda,' he had said, 'on the occasion of their marriage.'

Belle hadn't blessed them. She'd cursed them, and hoped they'd rot in hell. They hadn't rotted in hell though, but continued to live in London. Long may they remain there, Belle had thought. And now here he was again.

She held her breath and watched as he sat on the bench beside the door of the inn. The stone wall bit into her forehead as she pressed against it. Why, why, why had he returned?

When she looked up again Madge was sitting beside him.

Please, please don't tell him I'm here, she thought. He brought me enough grief the last time.

Slipping round the end wall of the inn she made her way through the narrow space to the rear of the building and sat down on the stairs that led up to the inn's living quarters.

From where she sat she could hear the music and laughter and see the dancers on the shore. She wanted to join them, wanted to look for Jimmie, but she daren't move from the back of the building for fear of meeting Lachlan. She did not want the vague aches and longings that stirred within her to surface. She had to protect her life with Jimmie for that was where safety lay and where she wanted to be. Her body must not let her down.

She sat for such a long time she did not hear Lachlan come round the building.

'Belle! It is you, Belle. Oh, how I've missed you.' Lachlan grasped her hand and pulled her to him. 'Madge told me you might be here.'

Belle stiffened. She could not let him see the effect he had on her. 'Missed me, is it?' she said harshly. 'You didn't think of that when you left me four years ago, when you went running off to marry your precious Clarinda.'

'You don't understand Belle. It was a family arrangement. It was expected.'

'You always do what's expected, do you?'

Belle could feel her insides turning to fire despite herself. She must not let him know she still cared. It had not done her any good the last time. He had bought and paid for her, leaving her feeling no better than a bar-room doxy.

'I had to, Belle.' There was a note of pleading in Lachlan's voice. 'You will forgive me, won't you? We could have what we had before. We were good together. You know we were, Belle.'

'Oh, yes. We could have what we had before all right. You got a good twenty guineas worth, didn't you, Lachlan? Well if you want it again you're going to have to pay for it because there is no way I'm going to be dispensing favours to you out of the goodness of my heart.' Belle pulled her arm out of Lachlan's grasp, and with a flounce of her skirts made her way towards the beach to look for Jimmie.

Lachlan watched her leave. This was not the Belle he remembered, the passionate, compliant Belle who opened her door and her heart to him. That Belle could never have turned him down, and could never have resisted his advances. What a fool he had been to leave her. Still it could never have been. He would never have lived in a bothy with her, with no money and no future.

He sighed, such a pity for they had been good together and he had loved her as much as he was able to love anyone.

Turning his back on the village and the festivities he made his way home. Home to Clarinda.

61

The one-roomed shack Belle and Jimmie had called home for over eight years looked bare and neglected. It was not large enough for their voices to echo when they spoke, but there seemed to be a hollow sound that emphasized the emptiness of the room.

'We've had some good times here.' Jimmie's voice was pensive.

'I suppose we have. But that wasn't due to the house, Jimmie, that was because of what we had together, and we can still have that at Madge's place.'

'Aye, I expect you're right, but it won't be the same as our own place.'

'It was good of Madge to offer us the rooms.' Belle leaned against Jimmie as she looked around the room. She would be glad to leave for there were too many memories here, and she did not feel safe when Jimmie wasn't with her. 'You'll soon be away again and when I'm on my own Madge will be company for me.'

The Old Yule celebrations had marked a turning point in both Belle and Madge's lives. Belle had finally broken her attachment to Lachlan and sent him away, while Madge's Joe had slipped quietly into the river in the middle of the festivities. It was two weeks before his body was found on the back-sands where it had been carried by the incoming tide.

Madge started to rely on Belle more and more, and had finally offered her and Jimmie two rooms above the inn.

'You could have a share in the business as well, if you'd a mind to,' she said. But Jimmie was having nothing to do with that.

'The money we've saved is for the boat,' he told Belle, in

a voice that brooked no argument.

'Whatever you say, Jimmie,' Belle said, although she had been disappointed.

Belle knew Jimmie's heart was not in the move. 'We've plenty of time,' he told Belle. 'There's no hurry.'

January passed and then February, but by the end of March Belle was getting restless. 'You'll soon be away.' she said. 'Another few weeks and you'll be off chasing the whales again. I can't stay here while you're gone.'

'But it's only one more voyage, Belle my love,' he said, as he pulled her to him. 'And then we'll have enough for a boat. Aye, and all the nets and lines as well. Can you not stay here until I get back?'

Belle sighed in exasperation. 'It's not like the other times, Jimmie. Then I had your ma behind me, but now she's washed her hands of me and I know the women don't like me.'

'You know they wouldn't harm you, Belle. You're my wife after all.'

'The point is you won't be here. Don't you see, Jimmie, I'd feel safer living at the inn.'

So now they stood surveying the empty shell of the shack, while Cadger Wullie's cart trundled their belongings to the inn.

Cadger Wullie's horse had been pulling carts for many years and he was not inclined to move faster than a walking pace, so Sarah had no trouble keeping up.

Wee Davy and Jamie sat at the rear of the wagon their legs dangling over the end, while the family's furniture and belongings were stacked behind them. They thought it was a great adventure, however Sarah worried in case they'd fall off and she continually touched their knees and bodies as if this would ensure their safety.

Uncle Ian gave them a wave as they passed his cottage, but Ellen came out and stood behind him, arms folded and legs apart. She glared at them and Sarah turned her head away. She did not like Aunt Ellen. She often thought Ellen would hurt them if she could, and she was glad once the cart rolled past them.

The village women were not much better. They stood, in silence, on their doorsteps and watched the small procession pass. Sarah knew perfectly well they would gather together and whisper among themselves as soon as they were out of sight because this was what they always did. She spotted Annie on her doorstep, but her granma turned her back and went into the house, and Sarah wondered if Jeannie was there. She was sure that her aunt loved her just as much as ever, but Jeannie was afraid to defy Annie.

Sarah held her head erect and walked as tall as her small body would allow her to, for there was no way she would let these people see that she cared. But inside she cringed and wished that things were different.

Madge was waiting on the doorstep of the inn as the cart pulled into the square. 'Take it round the back,' she shouted, and Cadger Wullie nodded as he guided the horse around the end of the building.

Holding out her arms to Sarah, Madge said, 'My, would you just look at you. You're all out of puff. Come on to your Auntie Madge and let me give you a hug.'

Sarah buried her face in Madge's skirt, smelling the familiar scent of flowers mixed with ale. It was a comfortable smell, and Madge's arms were warm and welcoming as they hugged her. She was going to enjoy living here.

'Come on, my wee pet. While we're waiting for your ma and da to get here I'll show you the rooms you're to have.' Madge detached herself from Sarah's grasp and led the way to the rear of the inn.

Cadger Wullie had tied his horse to the wooden rail of the stairs, while the twins were pulling clumps of grass from the embankment at the base of the cliff. 'I've told them not to feed the horse but they don't listen,' he complained.

'I don't think they listen to anyone.' Madge laughed as she watched them. 'I can see I'm not going to have a dull life.' She squeezed Sarah's hand, 'Let's leave them to it and you and I will have a look at the rooms.'

Sarah had never been upstairs in a house before. The only houses she had ever known were the cottages in the village. She imagined the rooms above the inn might be like the net loft that her uncles slept in at Annie's house, but the loft was reached by a ladder. She listened to her footsteps clattering on the wooden steps and felt the vibration in the stairs as she climbed them. The breeze ruffled her hair when they reached the top and she waited patiently for Madge to open the door.

The lobby was lit by the window at the end of the passage that overlooked the entrance to the inn. There were two doors facing each other, one in each wall. Madge opened the door set in the left hand wall. 'These are your rooms. That other door leads to my part of the house.' She pushed Sarah inside. 'Well what do you think? D'you think this'll do? D'you think your ma and da will like it?'

Sarah couldn't answer. The room was like nothing she had ever seen before. It was large, with a window at one end facing into the square and a window in the opposite wall looking down river towards the sea. The door in the other wall led into a room almost the same as the one she was in.

Sarah ran from one room to the other, and from window to window.

'Well?' Madge asked.

'It's awful grand. I've never seen such a big house.' Sarah pressed her nose to the front window. 'I can see the square and I can see all the way over the roofs to the back-sands. And I can see Ma and Da coming along the river path. Oh Madge it's the best house there's ever been.'

Madge laughed at her, 'Well I can see you're going to settle here all right. Let's just hope that your da does as well.'

62

Ellen disliked Belle's kids as much as she disliked Belle herself. If her child had lived it would have been a nicer and better kid than those brats. And Ian had the cheek to wave at them. She prodded him in the shoulder, 'You shouldn't be waving to the likes of them, your ma wouldn't like it.'

'Ach, they're only bairns, Ellen.'

'Aye, but they're her bairns.' Ellen's voice was bitter. She had seen the way Ian gazed at Belle when he thought she wasn't looking. It was the same way all the men looked at her.

'That doesn't make any difference. Maybe if you'd had bairns yourself you wouldn't think the way you do.'

'Aye, blame it on me that the bairn was born dead. Just like you blame it on me that I've never caught again,' Ellen turned away from him. 'I'm going to see your ma. At least she thinks the same way I do. She's not besotted with Belle and her bairns.'

'Ach, leave it be,' Ian shouted after her, but Ellen was already striding down the river path.

The anger simmered and bubbled within her. If she had married Jimmie and not Ian she was sure she would have had bairns. Ian was just useless, he had married her for her da's boat and now he couldn't even give her a bairn because he was smitten with Belle. Well she would gladly have given him to Belle if she could have had Jimmie in return.

Ellen gave Annie's door a vicious push. It opened with a thud, banging off the cottage wall and jiggling the ornaments on the mantelshelf.

'Don't you bother to knock nowadays?' Annie looked up from her pipe. 'My you've a face like thunder. What ails you?'

'I've just seen the flitting. D'you know your Jimmie's going to live at the inn.'

'Aye, I'd heard, but it's nothing to do with me.'

'Well it should be. We should have run that Madge out of the village when her man drowned.' Ellen paced up and down.

'You know you can't do things like that. It's not charitable.'

'Is it charitable to watch that hussy making up to all our men. And Belle's no better. You mark my words, as soon as Jimmie's off to the whaling she'll be just as bad.'

Annie took the pipe out of her mouth and exhaled the smoke. 'I don't approve of what Belle is doing no more than you do, but as far as I can see her and Jimmie are doing all right together.'

'You're no better than my Ian. You're taking her side even if you're not speaking to her.' Ellen grabbed the door handle, 'But I'm right in what I say. She's a bad one, and time will prove it. Just you wait and see.'

The door slammed as Ellen left.

Belle rested her cheek on Jimmie's shoulder as he slid his arm around her waist. 'You'll like the new house, just wait and see if you don't.'

'Aye, maybe I will. It's just that I don't like to be beholden to anyone, particularly a woman.'

'You won't be beholden to Madge. Don't you see it's because she needs us. She'll be beholden to us.' Belle slipped her arm around Jimmie and hooked her thumb into the waistband of his trousers. 'We'd better make our way. The furniture will have arrived at the inn by this time.'

They turned away from the little house for the last time and strolled along the river path as if reluctant to let the past go.

The river was quiet and placid as it meandered along beside them until it widened out and joined the main flow that poured past Invercraig. Belle looked towards the sea, to where the waves crested in white peaks and troughs.

She shivered, 'Don't go back to the sea, Jimmie. Stay with me. We could have a nice living from the inn if we invested the money we have.' She hesitated, 'It would be safer.'

'The sea's my life, Belle. You know that. I could no sooner give up the sea than I could stop breathing, or loving you for that matter.'

'I know, Jimmie. It's just that I have this feeling . . . ' she was near to tears and she did not know why, 'I want to keep you safe, that's all.'

They had reached the village, and Belle was conscious of the gathering of women in front of one of the houses. The women stared and then turned their backs, but not before Belle had seen Ellen within their midst.

'See what I mean, Jimmie. The women don't like me.'

'Nonsense, you're just imagining it.' Jimmie gave a laugh, but Belle could see the worried frown on his face, and his steps quickened.

Belle was glad when they reached the inn and were out of sight of the women. It wouldn't matter any more. The women could gather and talk all they liked for she would not have to pass them every day, now that they had rooms at the inn.

Sarah came running down the stairs to greet them. 'Ma, Da,' she shouted. 'You should see the house. It's awfy grand.'

'My, but it is grand,' Jimmie murmured, as he looked at it. 'I can see why you wanted to move here.' He turned, 'I'd better get the furniture upstairs before Cadger Wullie gets fed up waiting.'

'I knew you'd like the house once you'd seen it,' Belle smiled at him. He was pleased, she could sense it.

'Aye, well, maybe I do. Mind, I'll miss the wee house though.' Jimmie ran down the stairs before Belle could answer.

63

It was May that year before the *Eclipse* sailed for the whaling grounds. The ship had been delayed waiting for a new sail from the sailmakers. Ben, Jimmie's shipmate, had left on the *Perseverance* in April, but Jimmie preferred to wait for the *Eclipse* to be made ready.

'I wish you wouldn't go, Jimmie,' Belle pleaded on the morning of his departure. She had not been able to shake off the feeling of unease that had settled on her.

'I must. You know I must. But this is the last time, I promise,' Jimmie said as he took her into his arms.

Belle clung to him as if by doing so she could prevent him from leaving, however Jimmie gently unfastened her arms and gathered up his kit. 'It won't be for long,' he murmured, as he kissed the top of her head and then left.

The early morning sun pierced the water where it trembled with a brilliance that made the ripples and wavelets gleam diamond-like, and then shafted itself upwards again to strike off the window-pane where Belle stood watching. Her gaze followed Jimmie as he strode along the river path with a strong, purposeful walk. Now and again he would look back and Belle would wave her hand, although she was uncertain whether he could still see her.

'Has Da left?' Belle had not heard Sarah join her but the child now stood at her side, her hand shading her eyes as she peered out of the window.

'Yes, he's gone.' A tear trickled down Belle's cheek.

'Don't cry Ma. He'll come back. I know he will,' Sarah's voice lacked conviction and Belle wondered if the child shared her feeling of presentiment. She felt a sudden affinity with Sarah, who posed no competition to her for Jimmie's affections when he wasn't there.

Belle wiped the tear from her cheek. 'I'm not crying. It's only the sun in my eyes.'

Lachlan had been glad to get away from the house and Clarinda's never-ending screams of agony. Other women seemed able to give birth without all this fuss, but then Clarinda was delicate, or so Aunt Beattie kept reminding him.

He had galloped Raven to Invercraig and was successful in getting rid of the tightness round his temples. Now he stood with Wullie McPhee, his father's factor, at the top of the *Eclipse*'s gangplank. He felt a lot more knowledgeable than he had the previous time he'd stood here four years ago, and Wullie McPhee knew it. Together they watched the supplies being loaded and checked each item off on the bill of lading.

Lachlan frowned as he studied it. 'There doesn't seem to be as many stores as usual,' he said, mentally comparing it with the supplies that had been loaded on to the *Perseverance* only a month ago.

'That's because we're late leaving,' Wullie explained. 'The ship'll only be in the arctic seas for about five months instead of the usual six or seven months, and your da's anxious to cut down on any wastage.'

'I suppose you're right but a few extra supplies might mean they wouldn't have to return so soon.'

'You should know as well as I do that it's dangerous to stay in the arctic seas too long. A ship could get ice-bound.'

'When I was in London I heard tell that American ships sailed to southern waters and stayed away for three or four years at a time. Maybe we should try that sometime.'

Wullie McPhee laughed, 'Aye, and pigs might fly. I can just see your da putting money into more ships when these are still able to sail to the Arctic and back again with a full load of blubber.'

'But the loads of blubber haven't been so big these last few years,' Lachlan reminded him, 'maybe it's time to think of something new.'

'That's because the whales are moving further north. All we have to do is out-think them, so the *Eclipse* is going to try further up the Davis Straits this time.'

'Isn't that more risky? As I recall the *Grenville* and the *Norfolk* were both trapped behind the ice barrier only two years ago.'

'Aye, that's so, greed got the better of them and they stayed too long. But what else can you expect from the English, they don't know when to give up. Us Scots are a bit longer in the tooth, you know. We wouldn't be so daft.'

Lachlan laughed, 'You're right of course. My father's never lost a ship yet, but I still think some extra supplies wouldn't go amiss.'

'Whatever you say, young sir, but it's you who'll have to answer to your da about the extra expense.'

'Don't you worry about that, just go and arrange the supplies with the ships chandler over there. I'll stay here and check what's coming aboard.'

'Aye, aye sir.' Wullie handed him the list and pencil and made his way down the gangplank.

Lachlan watched him as he pushed through the crowds. There was the usual crush of doxies, wives and sweethearts, along with well-wishers and the idly curious. The whalers were gathered in a group near the signing on table and he could hear their raucous voices as they shouted and laughed together. They would soon board ship to experience adventures that Lachlan could not even imagine. He envied them.

He was not aware he was looking for anyone in particular. But still he scanned the group for a familiar face, for the man who always reminded him of a green-eyed girl with a tumble of dark curls framing her face. And suddenly, there he was striding up the jetty looking fitter and healthier than he remembered.

The excitement building upwards in his chest threatened to choke him, and he had to grasp the deck rail so he did not sway. He thought of all the evenings he had spent sitting on the hard benches in the Craigden Inn, and Belle had not even glanced his way. Maybe if he went to the inn now that her man was away, then maybe, just maybe she might speak to him again.

'Are you all right, man? You look a bit under the weather.' Lachlan had not noticed Wullie McPhee climb the gangplank, he'd been so busy watching Jimmie.

He took a deep breath before loosening his grasp on the deck rail. 'I'm fine,' he said. 'Did you manage to arrange the extra supplies?'

'Aye, they're coming aboard now. Although what your da'll say, I hate to think.' Wullie took the pencil and the bill of lading from Lachlan and started to write on it.

The weather was fine and calm when the *Eclipse* sailed with the tide. From his perch on the yardarm Jimmie could see the village and the two-storey building that was the inn. He knew Belle would be at the window so he raised his arm in a wave, although he doubted she would be able to see it.

His feet swayed in the rope loops but this no longer worried him and he busied himself untying the ropes that held the sail furled to the yardarm. It was a pleasing sight when they dropped and then filled with the wind that would carry them to the fishing grounds.

He remained leaning over the yardarm until Craigden was out of sight. There was hardly any wind but he could feel a slight breeze pluck at his hair and stroke his cheeks. He closed his eyes for a moment savouring it and thinking of how Belle's fingers had stroked him last night. He would miss her. Just as well this would be his last voyage.

'Are you staying up here until Lerwick? Or have you frozen to the yard?' The seaman on his right had moved along the yardarm until he was standing almost next to him.

Jimmie laughed, 'I was just thinking of my Belle.'

'Well you'll have a long time to think on her. Now what about moving along and letting us keen lads get on with the work.'

'Aye, you're right. This is not the place for thinking of wives.' Jimmie's feet picked their way along the footropes as he slid his body along the yard. Reaching the ratlines he gripped the ropes in a sure grasp and slid down to the deck.

Five days later the *Eclipse* reached Lerwick and, after provisioning themselves and taking on extra hands, they sailed for the whaling grounds. The weather stayed calm and clear until they reached the Greenland seas, where the sea surged and throbbed with the force of the gales, and rain slatted down until the sails were heavy and sodden. Jimmie pulled on extra jerseys and oilskins when he took his turn as lookout in the crows nest. However, no whales were sighted.

The ship heaved its way onwards to the Davis Straits where they sailed through dark channels of water that led the way between glistening fields of drift ice. The sails stiffened and icicles hung from the rigging, while the shiprails and masts frosted and silvered in the arctic sun which never seemed to set. It was only six weeks since they'd left Invercraig but it felt like an eternity.

'Will you look at those ice floes,' Jimmie's breath misted before him as he spoke to the man next to him.

'You'd think you'd never seen ice before,' Andy replied.

'Oh, I've seen plenty of ice floes, but these are bigger than anything I've seen in the Greenland seas, and they seem to go on for ever. D'you not think it's a bit early in the season for so much ice?'

'They say there's always more ice in the Straits but that ships are safe until September. I wouldn't worry about it. The Cap'n knows what he's about.'

'Aye, I suppose so.' Jimmie slapped his arms against his sides to warm himself up and turned away from the rail. Soon they would find whales and be able to return home.

64

The inn was always busy on Saturday nights. Many of the young fisher lads now preferred to be served their ale by Belle and Madge rather than trek into Invercraig. Cadger Wullie was a regular and often brought his fiddle with him.

'What about a reel, Wullie?' Madge rested her hand on the man's shoulder. 'Let's liven the place up a bit, shall we?'

Wullie placed the fiddle beneath his chin and drew the bow across the strings. 'Whatever you say Madge. You know I'd do anything for you.' His fingers danced on the end of the instrument and the bow plucked music from its depths.

'Wullie fancies you, Madge.' Belle picked up a pint jug from the bar.

'He's not bad himself,' Madge grinned at her. 'I could do worse.'

'You'd better not let his wife hear you. She might have other ideas.'

'Oh, go on with you. There's thirsty men out there waiting to be served, and one or two of them, I'm thinking, wouldn't need a lot of encouragement from yourself.' Madge winked.

Belle wiped the bottom of the jug with a cloth and looked over to where Lachlan sat at the back of the room. He always seemed to be at the inn nowadays, touching her hand and placing his arm around her whenever he had the chance. There had been a time when she would not have been able to resist him, but he no longer had any effect on her and now she wished he would go away and leave her alone.

'What about a refill, Belle.' Ian sidled up to her at the bar. He was so like Jimmie in looks that Belle caught herself giving him a more welcoming smile than she meant to.

However, she knew that Ian would not need much encouragement to climb the stairs behind the inn and she did not want that.

'It's just as well you're my brother-in-law,' she said, 'or I'd throw you out of the door for being a nuisance.'

'You don't mean that, Belle. After all it's only a wee drink I'm asking for, where's the harm in that.'

'Well just make sure it's only a drink you want from me, for I have nothing else to offer you.' She filled his jug from the pitcher behind the bar.

The men's laughter after Ian returned to his seat seemed to be aimed at Belle and she frowned as she wondered what he had muttered to them on his return.

Madge patted her arm. 'Don't worry about them,' she said. 'The lads always have to have their fun, and when they can't have it, sometimes they make it up.'

'That's what I'm worried about,' Belle said. 'The fisherwomen already think the worst of me and I don't want to give them something to talk about.' She wiped the bar top with a cloth, although it was already clean. 'I wouldn't want Jimmie to get the wrong impression when he comes home.'

'He'd be a fool if he listened to them and your Jimmie's no fool.'

'Aye, I suppose you're right,' Belle sighed. 'I can't help but worry though.'

Lachlan was stiff and sore sitting on the hard bench. The fishermen were starting to drift away and he knew that soon Madge would be telling him to leave. He liked Madge, although he was not attracted to her, and he was aware that if he wanted to climb the stairs at the rear of the inn she would make him welcome.

It was no use though, because he couldn't get Belle out of his mind. Even the girls at Invercraig no longer held an attraction for him.

Sometimes he regretted coming back to Scotland. Life in London had been so uncomplicated, Clarinda had grudgingly bestowed her favours and he could always visit the doxies in the night houses for something more exciting. Belle had only been a distant memory then, but here she was too close and it had spoiled everything else for him.

Madge approached him. Strange how it was always Madge who provided his ale and saw to his needs. 'Time to go then, young sir.'

'Very well,' Lachlan said, rising to his feet. He watched Madge as she picked up the empty jug to carry it to the bar, and taking his chance he quickly crossed the room to where Belle was mopping up the ale puddles on a table. He grasped her wrist, 'Belle. Please Belle, will you not give me a kind word.'

'I have no kind words for you, sir,' Belle continued mopping with her free hand.

'You cannot be so cruel Belle. Please speak to me.'

'I have nothing to say, sir, and I'll thank you to return home to your wife.'

'We had something good between us, Belle. You know that.'

'I know nothing of the sort, sir,' she glared at him. 'It may have been good for you but it certainly wasn't for me.'

Lachlan groaned. 'You can't mean it, Belle.' He thought back to all those nights of passion. Surely she could not have changed so much.

'You took advantage of my good nature, sir, and I have no wish to repeat the experience.' Belle prised his hand from her wrist. 'Go home to your wife and bairn, sir, there's nothing for you here.'

The spirit seeped out of Lachlan and his shoulders sagged. 'If that's what you want Belle, I'll not bother you again.'

The cold night air made him shiver as he made his way home to the big house and Clarinda. There would be no welcome for him there for her door had been barred to him since their daughter was born.

65

The weather stayed fresh and crisp and, although land ice could be seen in the distance, the water remained ice-free. The *Perseverance* had arrived in the bay a month before the *Eclipse* and found the whales to be plentiful.

'Aye, man we've had a good fishing season,' Ben told Jimmie when the crews got together. 'Mind though, when we were sailing up the strait the ice fields were mighty awesome. I thought for a time it was a mistake and we'd get iced up, but I never expected this sea at the end of it.'

The *Perseverance* left Pond Bay in late August with its hold full of blubber. 'We'll stay on another couple of weeks,' Jimmie heard Captain Cargill say to Captain Jamieson of the *Perseverance*.'

'Don't stay too long,' Captain Jamieson replied, 'or the ice will cut you off.'

Captain Cargill surveyed the clear water of Pond Bay. 'Two weeks won't make any difference,' he said. 'The ice fields are still far off.'

'If you say so,' Captain Jamieson frowned, 'but mind the straits are more iced up than the bay. Don't underestimate it.' He raised his hand in a salute and stamped off to the bridge as the deck hands got the ship ready to sail.

Jimmie caught sight of Ben on the deck of the *Perseverance*. 'We'll have a jug of ale together when I get back,' he shouted across to the other ship.

'Aye man, I'll look forward to that,' Ben shouted back, 'and I'll let that bonny wife of yours know that you'll not be long behind me.'

Jimmie stayed at the ship's rail until the sails of the *Perseverance* vanished into the horizon. He wished he was returning with it, but their captain had decided they were to stay on. So stay on they would.

The month dragged on but no more whales were sighted, and it seemed to the men their luck had left with the *Perseverance*. 'We'll be going home soon,' the bosun said, however it was nearly the end of September before the *Eclipse* hoisted her sails for the homeward journey. The sea in Pond Bay was still clear, although the land ice seemed to be nearer and the occasional ice floe was sighted.

The ship headed south-eastwards, 'We'll follow the Greenland coast through Baffin Bay and then down the Davis Strait until we reach the Greenland Sea,' the bosun said, however it was not long before they reached an ice field that seemed to stretch forever.

'It's all right lads,' the bosun assured the men. 'If we sail north now we'll be able to get round the end of the ice, and when we reach Cape York we should find the channels down the coast. The current keeps them open most of the year.'

'Seems to know what he's talking about,' Jimmie's voice was doubtful.

Hamish McPhee, a man of little words, just nodded and said, 'Aye, he's sailed these seas before.'

The channel was open as the bosun had foretold and Jimmie's spirits lifted, for they were on their way home. Nosing her way southwards, the ship followed the black thread of water that wove a path through the ice. Jimmie could hear the crunch as it scraped the sides of the ship, but still they sailed on.

The water channels narrowed, and sometimes they had to break through a thin layer of ice where it had formed and created a barrier, but the bosun laughed at their fears and said this was normal for these waters. However, it seemed as if the ice was trying to grab and hold them, and it came as no surprise to Jimmie when the ship was seized in a frozen grasp.

'No need to worry lads,' the bosun said. 'The ice is quite thin so we can sally her free. Start from this side lads.'

The men lined up and on the bosun's command rushed to the other side of the ship and then back again, until the ship started to rock with their motion. 'That'll do for now lads,' the bosun shouted, 'the ship's free again.'

'At least this keeps us warm.' Jimmie's breath puffed out before him in hazy streams.

'Aye,' Hamish said.

The next time the ice gripped the ship, sallying did not work and they remained held fast, although they could see a clear channel just in front of them. They tried dropping one of the older whale boats onto the ice directly in front of the ship, but still the ice kept its tight hold on them.

'Nothing else for it lads, we'll have to mill-doll it through. It'll be hard work but the channels only just in front of us. We can do it.'

'It's all right for him,' Hamish grumbled, as he lowered himself to the ice. 'He just gives the orders. It's us what does the work.'

Jimmie slapped him on the back. 'Och, come on. The sooner we pull, the sooner we'll be free,' and grabbing a rope he slung it over his shoulder and started to pull.

The men on the ice pulled and strained on their ropes at the sides of the ship, while those left on board heaved the ice anchors onto the ice in front before pulling back on their anchor ropes, in an attempt to crack it. Gradually the ship inched its way forward.

'Watch as you get near the channel,' Hamish warned. 'You don't want to fall in else you'll never get out again.'

'We've nothing to worry about now lads,' the bosun said, once the men were on board again and they were sailing down the channel. 'That's us out of Melville Bay, the breaker's yard, that's what they call it. If a ship gets clear of that, the problems are over.'

'I thought he said we didn't have any problems,' Jimmie said drily.

'Aye,' Hamish said, 'the bosun always looks on the bright side.'

The ice creaked and groaned around them and sometimes the channel narrowed so much Jimmie thought it might disappear completely. However the ship sailed on, and for a time it seemed as if the bosun was right.

'We'll soon be home,' he told Hamish as the two of them perched on the yardarm. He leaned over to finish sawing the clump of ice that had formed on the mast. 'Ice away,' he shouted just moments before it crashed to the deck. 'I'll be glad when this watch is over,' he muttered. 'Someone else can have a turn at sawing off the ice for a change.'

'It's a job needs doing, else the ship'd get top heavy and overturn.' The older man was as taciturn as usual, but Jimmie preferred his company to that of some of the others. At least he was reliable and you knew exactly where you were with him.

The days, although much shorter now, seemed endless to Jimmie. Rations had been cut and he was always tired and cold. He seemed to spend all his time sawing ice off various parts of the ship, but as fast as he sawed it off it gathered again. Even when he went to the focsle to lie in his bunk the stiff blanket he lay under and the ice-hard pillow his head rested on reminded him that the ice was gathering inside the ship as well as outside on deck. At these times Jimmie felt he would never be warm again.

Jimmie wasn't sure how many days they'd been sailing when the ship became icebound once more. He wasn't sure where they were or how far away from the open water of the Greenland Sea they were. Even the bosun did not seem to know. 'We could be at the Devil's Thumb, or near the Frow Islands, or even as far south as Disko Island,' he said, 'it's difficult to judge now the ice has covered everything.'

The landscape stretched white as far as Jimmie could see. Massive mountains of ice loomed here and there, and there were no more black channels of water.

66

Belle hummed in time to Cadger Wullie's fiddling as she moved between the tables filling up the men's jugs from the pitcher of ale she carried. She enjoyed the attention the men gave her, the obvious admiration in their eyes, and being able to laugh and joke with them without having to give them any favours. Lachlan no longer visited the inn and she was glad. She did not want the complication of being tempted to lie with him again. Life was easier without that.

Ian was always there of course. Looking at her and wanting her, but she had learned how to handle him, and he always went home to Ellen. Jimmie was just a memory now. It was strange how when he was with her she was sure she loved him, but when he was gone she enjoyed the freedom of being her own person. Not for the first time she wished she had been born a man, with a man's freedom, instead of a woman who had to rely on a man to survive.

The door opened and a gust of October wind rustled round the room. She looked up and frowned to herself as she tried to figure out who the stranger was. He seemed oddly familiar.

'Belle,' he said. 'D'you remember me? Ben Stimson.'

She was thankful for the reminder and smiled her welcome. 'Sit down Ben and I'll get you a jug of ale.' She looked at the closed door, 'Is Jimmie not with you?'

'Nay lass, I didn't sail with Jimmie this time, but I promised to come in and tell you it'll only be another couple of weeks until he's back.'

Belle sat down beside him, the jug of ale forgotten. 'He's all right, isn't he? I mean you usually sail together and come home at the same time.' She had forgotten her earlier concerns about this last voyage, but now the tug of unease pulled at her thoughts and settled over her like a sea mist.

'Och, there's no need to worry lass. He was looking fine when I last saw him, they're just staying on an extra while so they can catch more whales, else their whale money won't be worth getting.'

Belle smiled again, 'I'd best be getting you that ale.' She stood up and walked to the bar to get a clean jug.

'Who's your friend?' Madge looked up from the barrel and placed a freshly filled pitcher of ale on the bar.

'Oh that's just Ben back from the whaling. He came in to bring me news of Jimmie.'

'He's a fine figure of a man,' Madge took hold of the jug and filled it from the pitcher. 'You tend to the bar Belle and I'll take Ben's drink over to him.'

'Be careful Madge, he's a married man. We don't need any irate wives knocking on our door.'

'Aye, but he's not a villager and what his wife doesn't see won't vex her.'

A frown creased Belle's brow as she watched Madge approach the table and sit down on the bench beside Ben. She knew perfectly well that Madge had been itching for a man for some time and was probably only flirting with Ben because he did not live in Craigden. It was bound to bring grief to them and they had enough trouble with the village women without this.

Jimmie would know what to do when he came back and it wouldn't be long now.

The *Eclipse* had been held fast for what seemed to be an eternity, and the explosive cracking and grinding noises of the ice as it moved, pressing against itself and the ship, merged with the creaking of the *Eclipse*.

It seemed as if each crunch and scrape might be the last, and the cry, 'Move out, move out,' was heard more often. The men were now spending more time on the ice than they were in the ship.

The men constructed tents from the spare sailcloth, while

whaleboats were up-ended to form a sheltering roof against the whirling arctic winds and frequent snow storms.

'If we can winter it out until the thaw comes in the spring, we'll be all right,' the bosun told them before he cut the rations yet again.

Hunting parties scouted the ice for bears or white arctic foxes, to provide fresh meat and top up their provisions. But there were also times when they were forced to eat the whale blubber they had stored in the hold.

Jimmie always forced himself to eat the blubber even though it made him feel sick, for he had seen too many of the crew succumb to scurvy and frostbite when their condition weakened too much.

Eventually nature won and the ship seemed to splinter before their eyes as the ice relentlessly crushed it.

'Well lads, it looks like the ship's finished,' the bosun said, unable to keep the sadness out of his voice. 'It'll never sail again, but we can use the wood.' He looked around, 'Where's the carpenter?'

Big Jock stepped forward, 'I'm here sir,' he said in a soft voice that belied his size.

'I want you to select a squad of men and build some sledges out of the wood.'

'Sledges, sir?'

'Aye, sledges. There's no point staying here now the ship's finished, but if we move out we'll need to take supplies with us. That's what the sledges are for.'

Jimmie and Hamish offered to help. 'It'll keep us warm and our bodies moving. Less chance of frostbite,' Hamish said in his usual taciturn way.

Jimmie had never worked with wood before but he followed the carpenter's orders and before long there were five sledges made. The bosun ordered them to load the supplies and the men set out pulling the sledges after them.

'Where d'you think we're going?' Jimmie asked after a time. 'There doesn't seem to be anything here but snow and ice.'

'Bosun says there's an all year round whaling station at

Kekerton on Baffin Island. There's also some strange folks called Inuit who travel around. Anyways, it's better than staying put.'

'Aye, I suppose you're right,' said Jimmie, but his voice lacked conviction.

The first man with their sledge died after two days, quickly followed by another and another, until only Jimmie and Hamish were left. On the fourth day a snowstorm blew up, blinding them with its ferocity. They struggled on for a time but had to stop and cling to each other until it abated. However, when it did so there were no other sledges within sight.

Jimmie looked all round the blinding white landscape. 'What d'you think's happened to them?' he asked.

'We'll have fallen behind, that's all.' Hamish's expression was troubled. 'If we keep going we're bound to catch up.'

Onwards they trudged but no further sledges were sighted, and it was only a day later when Hamish collapsed in the snow.

'Don't worry,' Jimmie told the older man. 'There's room on the sledge for you,' and he continued to walk onwards even when Hamish's body stiffened in death.

'It's a bonny landscape,' he told the corpse, 'even though there's something fearful about it at the same time.' His steps slowed, 'If you don't mind I think I'll take a wee rest now, Hamish. See the bonny lights in the sky there. Reminds me of my Belle, so it does. She's the bonniest thing you ever saw and she's got the queerest eyes, they're as green as the sea.'

Jimmie sighed and closed his eyes. 'Just a wee sleep Hamish, and then we'll be on our way.'

Sighing gently, Jimmie slept and dreamed of Belle. She held out her arms to him and wrapped them around his body. She kissed his cheek and stroked his hair, and as she did so the coldness subsided and he felt warm again.

67

Old Yule came and went and still Jimmie did not return home. 'Don't worry,' Ben told Belle. 'They'll winter on the ice and be home by spring.' However Belle could hear the doubt in his voice.

Ben stayed with Madge for all of October, before returning to his wife, and still visited most weekends. 'He would leave her, but she needs him,' Madge said, 'and anyway I don't particularly want him here all the time.'

'Folks are talking, you know,' Belle told her.

'I don't care,' Madge said, shrugging her shoulders in a nonchalant manner. 'They can talk all they like.'

Belle shook her head, surely Madge wasn't blind. Couldn't she see how this affair with Ben was affecting them. 'That's all very well for you, but I was spat on today. I don't like the mood of the women just now.'

'You're too sensitive, ignore them. The women don't count, it's the men who are in charge.'

'Aye, but it's the women who have the last word and they'll not put up with much more. They're afraid you'll start looking at their men.'

Belle had felt the tension for some time. She was conscious that when she walked through the village the women turned their backs on her, and today was not the first time someone had spat at her, although today the aim had been quite deliberate and she had spent some time scrubbing at the hem of her dress.

She never saw Annie or Jeannie in the groups of women who gathered to gossip about her, but she often saw Ellen. There was a feeling of menace that seemed to exude from her sister-in-law which spread to the other women, and Belle often thought that if she reached out she could touch the hatred in the air, it was so tangible.

Belle gave the table a final scrub. 'We should have cleaned up last night instead of leaving it for today.' She picked up the pail of dirty water and sluiced it out of the door into the square. 'I've had enough. I'm going for some fresh air.'

'You'll not see the ship coming yet. It's only February and Ben said they wouldn't return until spring.'

Belle paused with her hand on the door. 'Jimmie'll not be coming home,' she said quietly. 'The ship can't survive the ice. Besides, they didn't have enough provisions for the winter.'

'How can you be so sure?' Madge said.

'I'm sure.' Belle did not bother to explain that she had sought out Wullie McPhee, the laird's factor, to ask about the *Eclipse*.

'I'm sorry, lass,' he had said, 'but there's no hope. Even if the ship doesn't break up in the ice they've not enough supplies to keep them going.' He squeezed her hand in sympathy. 'I know what you're going through. I've a brother on board the *Eclipse* as well.'

The biting wind whistled round Belle as she made her way to the river mouth. When she got there the rocks were cold and wet but she sat on them anyway and watched the waves batter the shore. This was her thinking place, this was where she was able to be herself and not worry about what the women thought of her. This was where she could be alone and free. She listened to the scream of the seagulls and felt the pull of the sea. It seemed to call her, 'Belle, Belle.' The waves soughed in and out and she was tempted to go forward to meet them.

'Belle, Belle,' the waves splashed on her feet. She wiped her cheeks with the backs of her hands. 'I'm sorry Jimmie,' she said, 'I know you're sleeping down there and I'd like to join you, but I'm not ready yet. I've too much life to live and too much to do. But you lie safe in your cradle and when the time comes I'll join you.'

She stood up and turned round to clamber back onto the

path and came face to face with the Reverend Murdo McAllan. For a moment they stared at each other. 'You've been spying on me again. You're always spying on me, creeping up on your silent feet. Why don't you go and bother someone else.' She was so angry she wanted to hit him, but he was the minister after all.

The minister gasped and his mouth opened and shut several times. Finally he found his voice, 'Jezebel,' he hissed. 'You're not wanted in this village. You and your fornicating friend should leave. Leave now before you have to leave, for leave you must.'

'Why should we leave Craigden. This is our home and there's nothing you can do or say that could make us go.' Belle turned and hurried down the path towards the village.

'We'll see about that,' the Reverend Murdo screamed into the wind.

The minister's sermon the following Sunday was confused and incoherent. He ranted about Eve's temptation of man, the destruction of Sodom and Gomorrah, and the word Jezebel kept on recurring.

Ellen's stomach churned and she could feel the bile rising in her throat until she was forced to hurry out of the church. She leaned against the wall gulping air into her lungs as she tried to cleanse herself of the thoughts that pushed into her mind. It wasn't right to think such things on the sabbath.

The next day her anger still simmered. 'Get out of my way, Ian,' she snapped as she left the house. 'I have things to discuss with the women.'

Ellen tapped at door after door. 'We'll meet on the shore,' she told first one woman then another, although she did not knock on Annie's door.

'You heard the minister yesterday,' she said to the assembled women. 'There's Jezebels in our midst and we should cleanse ourselves of them. We should drive them from the village before they tempt our men away.'

'They're not doing any harm.' A voice spoke up over the

buzz of the women talking.

'Are you sure about that, Maggie Paton.' Ellen's voice was quiet but rose over the women's voices with no effort. 'Are you going to wait until your man doesn't come home because he's bedding one, or both of them, like that Ben Stimson. I wonder when his wife sees him and what she's thinking about it.'

Several voices said, 'Aye, you're right there.'

'What can we do?'

'We can drive them out.' Ellen's feet slipped on the stones almost throwing her off balance as she moved further up the bank so that she could see everyone.

'The men'll not stand for it. They need their ale of a night.'

'The men don't need to know,' Ellen said. 'We can do it after dark, after the inn closes. By that time the men'll be so merry they won't know what we're doing, and by morning when they sober up it'll be too late.'

'How can we drive them out?'

'We'll burn them out.' Ellen gave a grim smile of satisfaction as she imagined the inn in flames.

'I'll not stop you, but I'm having nothing to do with a burning,' Maggie Paton started to walk away from the group. 'Anyone else of a like mind had better come with me,' however no one else followed her.

'That's it settled then,' Ellen said. 'We'll meet at my house after the inn closes, and remember, not a word to the menfolk.'

68

Ian was the last one to leave the inn that night because he had stayed behind to help gather up the jugs and wipe down the tables.

'You'll have to leave now,' Belle said as they went out the door, and Ian knew she was suspicious of his intentions.

'Aye,' he said. 'Ellen'll be waiting for me,' but Ellen had been in a queer frame of mind all day and he wished he could stay with Belle instead. However, after all these years he knew that would never be a possibility.

The night was black and the moon was obscured by low-lying clouds, but his feet were sure on the path that led from the inn and meandered between the fisher cottages and the shore.

He heard the creak of the door before the voice whispered his name. He stopped to listen, and the whisper came again. 'Ian, over here.'

He turned in the direction of the cottage until the dark shape that stood at the door took form. 'What is it you want, Ma?'

Her hand reached out and closed over his. 'There's trouble afoot lad, and someone has to see no harm's done.'

'What d'you mean?' Ian could not make out her features in the dark but he could hear the rasp of her breathing, as if she'd been running.

'It's the women lad, and your Ellen's at the bottom of it. They're planning to burn the inn.'

'But they can't do that. Madge, Belle and the bairns are upstairs.'

'Aye lad, that's what worries me.' Annie hesitated for a moment. 'I know I've no time for Belle because she didn't do right by my Jimmie. But I'll have no truck with harming her, nor with harming the bairns.' Annie's grip tightened on his arm. 'They're not safe in Craigden any more. You've got to get them out, lad . . . before the women get there.'

Ian was having trouble taking in what his ma was saying so he patted the hand that grasped his arm in what he hoped was a reassuring fashion. 'That can't be right,' he said. 'The women of Craigden are not like that, and I know Ellen's been a wee bit strange lately, but I can't believe she would go that far.'

'You've got to believe it.' His ma's voice sounded desperate. 'It was Maggie Paton as told me. She was at the meeting. She didn't want to take part, although she'll not do anything to stop it. I can't be involved either, you do see that, don't you? Get them out, lad, or I'll never be able to live with myself.'

'Aye, all right Ma. I just hope you're right in what you say.' Ian turned back to the path as his ma's hand loosened its grip on his arm.

This is daft, he thought, as he retraced his steps. Belle's never going to let me through the door for a start. The inn loomed up out of the darkness and he could see the flicker of light at the upper windows. He stopped for a moment to watch and turned to leave again. Ma's imagining things, he thought, but as he turned he caught sight of the far off flicker of flaring torches moving along the river path.

'Oh, my God,' he muttered, as he ran round the corner of the inn and clattered up the rear stairs.

'Belle! Madge!' he shouted as he banged on both doors. 'Open up, for God's sake, open up!'

Madge eased her door open, and Ian pushed it wider. 'You've got to get out Madge, and you've got to get Belle to open her door. The women are coming to fire the inn. If you stay you'll be in mortal danger.'

'It's just the ale speaking, Ian. Go home and sleep it off.' Madge attempted to shut her door, but Ian was leaning on it.

'You've got to believe me Madge.' Ian glanced at the window at the end of the lobby. 'Look out there. See for yourself.' He watched her as her eyes widened in disbelief.

'Now will you get Belle to open up.'

Madge put her mouth close to Belle's door. 'Open up, Belle. You were right about the womenfolk. We've got to get out now, or we'll go up in flames with the inn.'

As Belle's door opened, Ian forced his way inside. 'Get the bairns up, Belle. We've got to get them out.' He could see the confusion on her face as she hesitated, so he pushed her to the window. 'Look out there. We don't have much time.'

'I knew those women were up to something,' Belle muttered as she headed for the bedroom. 'Sarah, wake up,' she shouted as she roughly shook the girl. 'There's going to be a fire so move yourself.'

Ian was already shaking the twins awake. 'Up you get lads. We're going for a midnight adventure.'

The two boys sat up, rubbing their eyes. 'What kind of adventure, Uncle Ian?' asked wee Davy as he reached for his breeches.

'You don't have time to dress,' Ian said, 'but take your clothes in a bundle and we'll stop later to let you put them on. That goes for you as well, Sarah, we don't have time to wait.' He looked round for Belle but she had returned to the front room.

'What in God's name are you doing rummaging in that sea-chest,' he roared, as he steered the children towards the door. 'You don't have time to take belongings. Get out now or you'll never see another day.'

He glanced towards the windows and knew by the flicker of light that was filtering into the room, that the women must have entered the square. He hoisted the twins up under each arm and headed for the back stair.

'Follow me Sarah, and if you know what's good for you Belle, you'll come too.'

The small group gathered at the foot of the stairs just as the first window broke.

'We can't go round the front of the building,' Ian said, as he turned in the direction of the river mouth. 'But there's a cliff path not too far away. It's a bit steep, but if we can get onto the top road they'll not know you're there.'

The two women climbed the path first, followed by Sarah and the twins.

Ian climbed behind them, ready to catch anyone who slipped, but apart from a few loose stones slithering down, they all made it safely to the top.

They sprawled, panting and gasping, on the damp grass.

'You can pull your clothes on now,' Ian said, 'while I go a bit along the path and check that it's safe.'

When he came level with the inn he lay down and peered over the edge of the cliff. The inn was well alight with flames rising through the roof, exploding with great crackles and sparks into the night air.

He shuddered to think that if it had not been for Annie's warning, Belle, Madge and the bairns would have been roasting inside.

Returning to the group, he said, 'If you're ready we'll go.'

The path was illuminated by the light from the fire so there was no danger of anyone sliding over the edge, nevertheless Ian breathed more easily once they had passed the vicinity of the fire and the path was darkening again.

'I'll stay with you until we reach the bridge to Invercraig and then I'll have to leave you.'

He looked at Belle knowing that if she just said the word he would stay with her forever. However, she looked away and he knew that, as always, it was a forlorn hope.

They reached the bridge safely, 'Well, this is where I have to leave you,' Ian said reluctantly. He looked at Belle, 'Have you somewhere to go? Will you be all right?'

Belle moved to his side and grasped his hand. She looked into his eyes and said, 'I'll never forget what you did for us tonight, Ian. But now you have to go back where you belong. Back to Ellen. You do understand, don't you?'

Ian bent and kissed her forehead. 'I understand Belle. You and I were never meant to be. Jimmie was always between us and I just wish I'd seen you first.'

He turned away so she would not see the rush of tears to

his eyes and, lifting his hand in a farewell wave, he strode off in the direction of Craigden.

Belle watched him go. She felt sad, although she was not sure why for she had no feelings for Ian. In fact she had always considered him an unpleasant person, and never trusted him. Tonight, however, he had behaved nobly and they owed their lives to him.

Madge had already moved off. 'Come on, Belle,' she shouted. 'The further away we get from Craigden the better it'll be for all of us.'

'Where will we go?' Sarah asked her.

'Well now. That's a good question. But I have the inn takings here so we have some money, and I'm sure my brother will be glad of an extra two barmaids.'

Belle stood for a moment watching the glow from the flames that outlined the village of Craigden, and then she turned to look towards Invercraig and the new life she must build there. Her life in Craigden was over now, and the past was the past. There was no Jimmie to hold her to the village any more. So now she only had the future to look forward to.

She patted the leather pouch that hung from her waist beneath her skirt. It was heavy with Lachlan's twenty guineas, and the money Jimmie had saved. This was her security. This would open her way to a new life where she would never have to rely on a man again.

Her pace quickened as she walked towards the future, the new life, and freedom.

Also by Chris Longmuir

DUNDEE CRIME SERIES

Night Watcher
Dead Wood

HISTORICAL SAGAS

A Salt Splashed Cradle

SHORT STORIES

Ghost Train & Other Stories
Obsession & Other Stories

CHRIS LONGMUIR

Chris Longmuir was born in Wiltshire and now lives in Angus. Her family moved to Scotland when she was two. After leaving school at fifteen, Chris worked in shops, offices, mills and factories, and was a bus conductor for a spell, before working as a social worker for Angus Council (latterly serving as Assistant Principal Officer for Adoption and Fostering).

Chris is a member of the Society of Authors, the Crime Writers Association and the Scottish Association of Writers. She writes short stories, articles and crime novels, and has won numerous awards. Her first published book, Dead Wood, won the Dundee International Book Prize and was published by Polygon. She designed her own website and confesses to being a techno-geek who builds computers in her spare time.

http://www.chrislongmuir.co.uk